ICE STATION WOLFENSTEIN

PRESTON CHILD

D1520132

Heiken Marketing

PROLOGUE

Detective Chief Inspector Patrick Smith could not tell which was annoying him more, the treacherous icy slush on the dark, ungritted path or the irritatingly cheerful neon Santa ringing his bell in the window. He half-walked, half-skated toward the door, occasionally making a lunge for the handrail to stop himself from slipping.

"It's all right for you," he scowled at the garish Santa as he reached the main door. "You've only got to get around to everyone's house one night of the year." He pushed the buzzer.

"Forth Valley Assisted Living, may I help you?" a tinny voice inquired.

"Lothian and Borders Police," Smith replied. "I'm responding to a call."

"Hang on a second." The intercom went dead. A few moments later, a short, middle-aged woman in a nurse's uniform and a thick cardigan appeared. "Thanks for coming out," she said, as she opened the door to let Smith in. "It's probably nothing, but I'm here on my own tonight and I just wanted to be sure . . ." She led him into a little room, scarcely bigger than a cupboard, crammed with paperwork. On one wall there was a board with a floor plan of the facility, with a little red bulb in each room. One of these, G21, was flashing urgently.

"It's Mr. Kruger's room," the woman explained. "He's got a door that leads out to the garden and it's been opened. I've looked on the security cameras but I can't see anything, and I've been into the garden to see if he'd got confused and gone out. He wasn't responding when I called out to him, and I haven't been into his room. I was about to go in, but then . . . I thought I heard people in the room. Not him—they were moving faster than Mr. Kruger can. It's probably just my imagination . . . I just thought I should call you, in case."

"You did the right thing," Smith reassured her. "Can you show me where his room is?"

They set off along the corridor. The door to G21 was firmly shut. The nurse tapped on it and called to Mr. Kruger.

There was no response. At the end of the corridor there was a door leading out to the garden, so they went out into the freezing night. Sure enough, the external door to G21 was open, the long curtains fluttering in the breeze.

Smith listened hard. He could hear nothing from the room. "Mr. Kruger?" he called. "Are you all right in there?" There was no answer. "This is DCI Smith from Lothian and Borders Police. I'm going to come into your room and check that you're ok." He reached for his baton and proceeded cautiously into the room. There was no movement, no sound. The security light in the garden provided a little illumination, just enough for him to make out a light switch on the wall. Smith pressed the switch.

The room appeared to be empty at first. DCI Smith took in the sight of the pale green walls, the narrow single bed, and the little electric fire with the armchair next to it. The chair was turned so that its back was to the door. There was no sound, no movement.

Then, suddenly, a dark figure broke cover and sprinted across the garden. Smith lunged toward the open doors yelling, "Stop! Police!" but the figure was moving fast. Indeed, the turn of speed was surprising considering the killer's size—he appeared to be tall and stocky, with a large head covered by a black balaclava. Long before Smith could reach him, he had vaulted the fence and vanished into the little wooded area behind the home. Cursing softly under his breath, Smith turned and stepped back into Mr. Kruger's room.

Mr. Kruger, dressed in his pajamas and dressing gown, was in his armchair. It took Smith a moment to notice that the old man had been tied into the seat with garden twine, that he had had a rag stuffed into his mouth to silence him, and that some of his fingers and toes were missing. His attention was entirely taken up with the ugly mess of red, sliced flesh where the newly dead old man's throat had been.

CHAPTER 1

YOUR MOVE, BRUICH. Get out of that one, if you can." Sam Cleave leaned back triumphantly, pushing the hair back out of his eyes. He reached for his cereal bowl and shoved a spoonful of cornflakes into his mouth, wrinkling his nose at the blandness of them.

Next to the chessboard was a tumbler of whisky left over from last night. He picked it up and carefully poured it over the cornflakes, distributing it evenly.

"That's better," he said, taking another spoonful. "Bruich, I saw you touch that knight. You've got to move it now."

Bruichladdich lifted his ginger head and meowed at Sam.

"Don't talk to me like that," Sam said. "That's the rules, you wee cheat. Now hurry up and move so I can checkmate you."

The cat reached out a tentative paw and kicked the knight, Sam's queen, and a couple of pawns off the board. He stepped onto the board, turned around a couple of times, then curled up and stared accusingly at Sam.

"What?" Sam demanded. "What is it? What are you looking at me like that for? You've had your breakfast. Don't you try and tell me you haven't." He spun his chair around to face his desk. An untidy pile of papers lay on top of his laptop. He picked up the bundle and transferred it to the floor, then opened the laptop and stared at the open document.

BRUNTFIELD RESIDENTS' FURY OVER PLANNED TESCO METRO

He had got no further than that. His digital voice recorder was full of sound bites from concerned citizens who objected to the presence of another urban supermarket near their expensive homes. He had not yet transcribed them. He was not sure that he would bother. They had all said pretty much the same thing, and Sam was struggling to care.

He closed the document. With nothing else open on the screen, all he could see was the desktop wallpaper—a smiling man and a woman with their arms around each other. The woman was tall and slim with long, ash-blonde hair and blue eyes. Her head was slightly tilted and her face turned toward the man, so Sam could just make out the little bump in her nose where it had once been broken.

The man was a little taller than she was, with brown hair and eyes and a five o'clock shadow. He was a little too thin, perhaps, and his dress sense left much to be desired, but with the woman in his arms he looked like the happiest man alive. Sam could hardly believe that just eighteen months ago, that man had been him. Sometimes, when he closed his eyes, he could still convince himself that he could hear Patricia's sweet voice and filthy laugh. He reached for the whisky bottle, again.

The buzzer sounded. Sam froze. Bruichladdich shot under the couch. "Let's just wait this one out, Bruich," Sam whispered. He had had too many mornings ruined by debt collectors banging on his door recently. It made it very difficult to ignore the growing pile of unopened mail accumulating behind the front door. Gingerly, as if they might hear him from the street outside, he picked up the bottle and took a swig. He counted out one minute, then two, then five. At last he reasoned that the coast must be clear and breathed a sigh of relief.

That was when the pounding at the door began. Damn it, Sam thought, They must have buzzed one of the neighbors and now they're in the stairwell. Ah well. Just lay low for a—

"Samuel Fergusson Cleave!" an authoritative voice called from the other side of the door. "Open up! Police!"

At once, Sam relaxed. He strode over to the door and flung it open. "Come on in, you old bastard," he said, welcoming DCI Patrick Smith into the flat.

Smith grinned. "I thought you'd never ask," he said. "I think I scared the students upstairs when I buzzed them. Told them it was the police; I think they thought I was coming to take their stereo away. Now they just think I'm here to arrest you." As Smith made his way into the living room and cleared himself a space on the messy couch, Bruichladdich emerged from his hiding place and jumped onto his lap. Smith scratched the cat behind the ears. "Hello Bruich. You never miss a chance to cover me in ginger fur, do you?"

"You should think yourself lucky," Sam remarked. "Some of us never get to see this side of Bruich. Some of us just provide him with Whiskas and get hissed at for telling him to get out of the sink."

"Well, it's not like you use it for washing up or anything."

"Touché." Sam gathered up some scattered pieces of crockery as nonchalantly as he could. "Want a cup of tea?"

"Please."

Sam disappeared into his tiny kitchen and put the kettle on. It was a stereotypical single man's kitchen, with chipped, mismatched mugs that had to be washed before use, well-hidden tea spoons, and milk that had gone past its use-by date over a month ago. In a moment of optimism, Sam opened the carton to see how it smelled. He took a sniff and recoiled, screwing the lid back on as fast and as tightly as he could, then dropped the whole thing into the bin.

However, even if he could not be trusted to have fresh milk, the one thing Sam could be relied on to have a ready supply of was tea bags. He put two in each mug, added the hot water and stirred until it resembled tar. He dumped a heaped spoonful of sugar into each, then added another for good measure and to make up for the lack of milk.

"There you go," he said, handing one of the mugs to Smith. "Now what brings you here?"

Smith, settled on the couch with Bruichladdich curled up on his lap, looked doubtfully at the tea. "Something I thought you'd want to know about. I got called out to an old folk's home last night. Some old boy was murdered. Pretty gory, to tell you the truth. We haven't let the media know yet, but we'll have to soon and I thought you might want to get in there first."

"Might be a bit too exciting for me these days, Paddy," Sam replied, taking a large gulp of scalding hot tea. "Covering anything more dramatic than whatever's upsetting the Bruntsfield mums might set me off on a downward spiral again."

"Sam, have you looked at yourself lately?" Smith asked. "Frankly, the only way is up. Ugh, what's this supposed to be? I thought you said it was tea?"

"Spoken like a true friend, Paddy." Sam said. "It is tea; it's just not the kind of puny tea you're used to. I know you boys on the force all think that you know about caffeine and tannins, but I wouldn't feed the stuff you drink to a baby."

"This is why no one would leave you in charge of a baby," said Smith. "You'd just put whisky in its bottle. Anyway, I need you to cover this. It's a bit weird and I'd like to know that there's someone out there who'll cover it sensibly. I have a feeling that the local papers are going to go nuts with this and blow it out of all proportion, which means that when the nationals get hold of it—and they will, because it's an old folk's home—it'll be a giant mess. If you cover it, the national papers will look to you because they know you. That way I'll know that they're getting something resembling the actual facts, not some nonsense dreamed up by some twelve year old waiting for her big break."

Sam shook his head. "Gory murders aren't my thing anymore," he sighed. "No murders, no drug deals, no international crime rings, nothing. How gory can it possibly be, anyway? Your beat is South Queensferry, for Christ's sake. Nothing interesting happens out there."

"Not usually, I'll grant you." Smith conceded. He took

another sip of his tea, as if trying very hard not to taste it. "But this . . . I've never seen anything like it. I mean, you don't expect this kind of thing to actually happen except on the telly. I got called out to check out a possible intruder at the assisted living facility—Forth Valley, do you know the one? No, of course you don't. Anyway, I got there and found this old boy tied to his chair, mouth stuffed with cloth, and he'd had his throat cut."

"Sounds to me like someone broke in, tied the old guy up while they robbed the place, then got spooked and killed him in case he identified them," Sam speculated. "What's so weird about that?"

Smith took a deep breath, staring intently into his tea as he spoke. "His fingers and toes had been cut off. Not all of them. Two fingers, both on the left hand, and the little toe on the right foot. But they hadn't been taken off in one go. When we found the digits, they'd been cut off bit by bit. Really nasty. And his throat wasn't just cut. It was slit. Neatly. Like whoever was holding the knife really knew what they were doing. If it was just an interrupted burglary you'd expect it to be messy, just someone slashing away because they were angry. But this . . . it looked like a professional job."

He looked up at Sam. "Now can you see why I'm worried about it getting sensationalized? It's bad enough already, and the last thing my department needs right now is some huge story about how South Queensferry's the kind of place where elderly people in secure housing facilities get hits taken out on them and get tortured to death on a regular basis. I really need someone who can handle this sensitively, Sam . . . Please?"

Sam leaned back in his seat and pressed his fists into his eyes. He was still a little hung over from the previous night, when he had made his first attempt at the Tesco Metro article and accidentally drunk himself to sleep instead. Listening to Smith was causing the slight ache behind his eyeballs to grow into a full-blown pounding headache.

"Paddy," he groaned. "I appreciate what you're trying to do, ok? I know you think you're being really subtle with all this stuff about your department, but it's bullshit and we both know it. Look, I know the state I'm in. I know you're trying to get me out of it and you think that if I get my teeth into a story that's more like what I used to do, it'll bring me back to my old self, right? Well, forget it. It doesn't work that way. You can only do what I used to do if you really care about it, and I don't any more. My days of valiantly pursuing a story to the bitter end, come what may, risking life and limb like some stupid bloody superhero? They're over. Sorry."

Smith grimaced. "Sam . . . you're right. I'm not subtle. But honestly, seeing you like this is painful. I know things have been tough. What happened to Patricia . . . it shouldn't have happened to anyone. You shouldn't have had to see it. I can understand that it's done a number on you. But this . . . Sam, you know damn fine that if you don't get your act together you're going to get fired. You're already on your final warning. I was hoping that this might, I don't know, fire your interest again." He looked Sam straight in the eye. "She wouldn't want to see you like this, Sam."

Sam's mug went flying, spilling tea all over the floor as he leaped to his feet. Bruichladdich was awake in a split second and dived back under the couch.

"Don't you dare tell me what she would have wanted!" he yelled. "You don't know what Trish would want. No one does. She's dead, all right? Patricia is dead and no one—not you, not me, not anyone—knows what she'd want." Smith put up his hands in a conciliatory gesture, hoping to calm things down, but Sam plunged on. "Maybe the only thing she'd really want is not to have been killed, did you ever think of that? Maybe that's the only thing that actually matters. Who gives a damn what happens to me? I don't." He collapsed back into his desk chair and glared at his laptop. "All I need is for the Post to keep me on long enough to let me drink myself into a stupor."

"Sam, I'm sorry—"

Sam shushed his friend and waved an aimless hand. "It's

fine," he said, "doesn't matter. Look, could you leave me on my own for a bit? I need to be on my own."

Smith was just about to leave when he saw Sam's hand close around the whisky bottle. "Isn't it a wee bit early for that, Sam?" he asked as gently as he could.

"Nope," said Sam, taking a prolonged swig.

DCI Patrick Smith decided it would be best to beat a tactical retreat. He showed himself out.

He did not even make it to the end of the street before his phone beeped. He took it out and read the text.

Sorry. I'm a grumpy bastard. When are we going to this old folk's home, then? Sam.

Forty-five minutes later, Sam and DCI Smith were in the car, approaching South Queensferry. At Smith's insistence they stopped at a café on the way out of town and he bought them both breakfast. Sam's preference for rolls containing black pudding, haggis, and fried egg topped with brown sauce turned Smith's stomach, but he was happy to know that Sam had eaten something that morning—and that it wasn't just whisky-soaked cornflakes. He had also persuaded Sam to have a quick shower before leaving the flat, but as far as he could tell it had not made much of a difference.

"So what else do we know about this guy?" Sam asked, as they got back in the car. He drew a cigarette from the packet, lit it, and took a deep drag. "Apart from the fact that he's dead."

With a pointed but unnoticed glance at Sam's lit cigarette, Smith rolled down his window. "He's German," he said. "Born in Potsdam in 1916. His full name's Harald Josef Kruger. No relatives, as far as anyone knows. The nurse at the home said nobody ever came to see him and he paid all his bills himself. No next of kin listed. Very neat, though. Organized. He didn't have much stuff, but his papers were all in order. Every bank statement for the past ten years, all his receipts, all his personal documents neatly filed. Not that it made for very exciting reading, as he's been in the home since 1998. There certainly wasn't anything to suggest that anyone would want to chop him into wee bits."

They turned off the main road, toward Hopetoun House, then turned again into a rather dismal housing estate. "Look, Sam," Smith said. "I know that you know the ropes, but just . . . be prepared for a bit of hostility here. The nurses are fine, but the facility managers aren't too chuffed to have us crawling all over the place. And if you find being in the room too much, just say, ok?"

"What, you think I'm going to lose it at the sight of blood, Paddy?" Sam chuckled.

"Just trying to be sensitive," Smith muttered. "It's your first crime scene since—"

"I know, I know. Since that crime scene." He sucked down another lungful of smoke. "But you know, Paddy, it's actually not my first since then. You have no idea how many crime scenes I see. There's the place on St Andrew Square where cyclists keep going onto the pavement when they're not allowed, and there's the newsagent on Easter Road that got cleared out of cigarettes twice in one year."

"Ha. Funny." Smith grimaced. "But you know what I mean. Just . . . watch yourself, ok?"

"Ok."

Despite DCI Smith's assurances that the nurses were comparatively friendly, Sam found himself on the receiving end of an icy reception. The staff nurse at the desk looked him up and down with frank disapproval.

"Do you have any press identification, Mr. Cleave?" she asked. The expression on her face made it clear that she did not believe that anyone so unkempt could work for a reputable paper.

"Nope," said Sam. "Sorry, but the days when we all stuck press badges in our fedoras are long gone. You can google me if you like, but I promise you, my byline picture looks even worse than the real thing."

"I can vouch for him," Smith said, flashing his ID. "He's here because he's the one journalist I trust to handle this sensitively, ok? Everyone else, you just keep telling them to contact the station."

The nurse looked deeply suspicious, but she let them pass. Smith led the way to G21 with Sam trailing in his wake. He watched carefully as Sam entered the room. The body had been removed, but the forensic team was still swarming all over the place and the bloodstains stood out starkly against the magnolia paint on the walls.

The dark stench of blood hit Sam like an uppercut. It took all his concentration not to recoil, or to run out of the room, or to throw up. He fixed his eyes on an unsullied patch of burgundy carpet and focused on breathing through his mouth. There was no way he would give anyone the satisfaction of seeing that he couldn't handle a little blood. Least of all himself.

Once he was sure that he wouldn't vomit, Sam raised his eyes and took in the scene. It was a completely anonymous room. Pale walls, standard issue bedding, a few small, banal pictures, the kind of default decoration that no one actually chooses. There was nothing to indicate the tastes or personality of the occupant.

Having got a grip on himself by checking out the mundane objects, Sam forced himself to look at the wing chair. He was standing behind it, so all he could see was the spattered blood on the wall and a little on the carpet. The worst, he knew, would be around the other side, where the old man's blood had soaked the fabric of the chair. He dug his fingernails into the palms of his hands. Come on Sam, he thought. You've seen worse. Get on with it.

"Are youse the police?"

Sam whirled around, grateful for the interruption. An elderly man in a pale blue dressing gown was standing in the doorway, supporting himself on a Zimmer frame.

"I said, are youse the police?"

A nurse came up behind the old man and began flapping and shushing him, trying to lead him away, but the man was having none of it. DCI Smith crossed the room in a couple of steps and positioned himself in the doorway, blocking as much of the view into the room as possible. In his best calm, professional voice, he began to reassure the old man that they were the police, and they were doing everything they could to find out what had happened.

Sam decided that he had taken a liking to the old man. Perhaps it was something about the unkempt hair, perhaps it was the belligerent refusal to listen to the nurse, but for a moment Sam felt as if he was staring his own future in the face. He walked over to the door and stood at Smith's shoulder.

"Who's this?" the old man asked, pointing to Sam. "He's no police, is he? Look at the state of him."

Yes, Sam thought, as the nurse led the old man away toward the bathroom. I definitely like this guy. He turned to Smith. "Have you lot got statements from everyone?" he asked. "Am I ok to talk to people?"

"Statements are done," Smith confirmed. "But honestly, I doubt you'll get much out of Mr. McKenna. DI Andrews was with him for the best part of an hour this morning and said that he hadn't seen or heard anything much, he just wanted to ramble on about how Mr. Kruger was a Nazi."

"Great!" Sam smiled. "I'll go and talk to him once he's out of the bathroom. If the Post doesn't like the Nazi angle, I can maybe try selling the story to News of the World."

"Hilarious," Smith remarked, deadpan. "Now come and I'll show you around the crime scene while you wait for him to do his business."

"But how come the police have to be here?" Mr. McKenna protested, as he and Sam sat down for a chat in the facility's lounge. It was a chilly room with plastic-covered seats. At

Smith's insistence, DI Andrews had been sent in to accompany them.

"He's here to protect you," said Sam, nodding amiably at the young DI. "I've not had a criminal record check, so I'm not allowed to be in here on my own in case I'm dangerous."

Mr. McKenna harrumphed a bit, muttering about health and safety gone mad and suggesting that these rules had not done Mr. Kruger any good. Sam did not mind. It was good to be out of the crime scene. DCI Smith's account of finding the body had brought up too many memories that now needed to be submerged again, and a good chat with an elderly xenophobe would do the trick, he thought. Besides, in this room there was a pot of tea and a pile of cheap, prepackaged biscuits, and Sam always preferred to be where the tea was.

"I've already spoken to the police," Mr. McKenna grumbled. "I'm not doing it again. Get one of the nurses if you've got to have someone in here."

Sam looked over at DI Andrews. "Would that be ok?"

"Fine with me," the DI replied, looking relieved. Sam wondered how their earlier interview had gone. "I'll send someone in."

A moment later, a young male nurse was in the room and Mr. McKenna was directing him to sit at the far end and not listen in. DI Andrews made a swift exit, before the nurse could insist he stayed, and as he left Sam was sure he heard Mr. McKenna muttering "Fuck the filth!" under his breath. He stifled a laugh and tried to maintain his professional composure, such as it was.

"No recordings," Mr. McKenna said, seeing Sam setting up his Dictaphone between them. "Just you write things down. And don't you put my name in your paper. I don't want any of this linked to me, right?"

"No problem," said Sam. "You'll be 'sources close to Mr. Kruger,' is that ok?"

Mr. McKenna laughed. "No one was 'close' to Kruger. Not really. But we chatted a bit. We're both fond of whisky, and you've got to talk about something when you're drinking."

"So what did you chat about?" Sam asked.

"Him being a Nazi, mostly," said Mr. McKenna. Sam spluttered on his tea. He had known that the Nazi accusation was coming, but he hadn't expected it to be so matter of fact. "It's true!" Mr. McKenna insisted. "I'm not just saying that because he was German. He told me about it. We'd both been engineers—me in the RAF, him in one of the big Nazi research centers. Peenemünde."

"Peenemünde?"

"Aye. It was a research station on an island in the Baltic, up near the Polish border. Luftwaffe base. It's where Wernher von Braun developed buzzbombs and V2 rockets.

Aeroballistics. That's what Kruger worked in. I nearly got killed by a buzzbomb when I was stationed in London. We used to laugh about how he probably built it."

Sam looked at the old man with interest. It was easy to forget that the residents of the facility had once been young people with active, complicated lives. Is this what's in store for me? Sam wondered. Anonymous old age, surrounded by staff who don't know or care that I used to be a real person? I wonder what this guy's life was like before he got dumped in here. "So how does someone get from working with Wernher von Braun to a retirement home in South Queensferry?" Sam asked.

"By getting old," Mr. McKenna replied. "You go where the kids are, if you've got any."

"I thought Mr. Kruger had no family?"

"Not now," said McKenna, "but he used to have a daughter. Elisabeth, her name was. Nice lass. I remember she used to come here sometimes to see him. You'd never have guessed them for father and daughter, what with her accent. She was American. Looked and sounded like a film star. That was because they were in California, you know. Or it might have been New Mexico. After Paperclip." He saw Sam's bemused expression. "Operation Paperclip? When the Russians came and the Yanks got all the Nazi scientists out?"

Sam nodded. "Heard of it. So what happened to

Elisabeth?"

"She married a Scotsman. That's why she moved here. But they died, her and her husband both. Car crash. In 2000, I think it was. Maybe 2001? No, 2000, because Mary Williams was still living in the room to the other side of mine and she died just before my 80th birthday. Anyway, after Elisabeth died, Kruger didn't have anyone else. I think that's why he left his box with me."

"His box?"

Mr. McKenna slowly leaned forward in his seat and called out to the nurse. "I need my box," he said. "There are things in it that I need to show to Sam here. I need you to go and get it for me. The wooden box. In my room."

The nurse, clearly accustomed to humoring Mr. McKenna's whims, was only gone for a moment. When he returned, he was carrying a battered wooden strongbox with a sturdy handle on the top. He set it on the table while Mr. McKenna fished out the key that hung on a string around his neck. As the nurse retreated to his chair at the other end of the room, McKenna handed the key to Sam.

"You get it, son," he said. "It's too fiddly for me these days."

Sam took the chunky brass key from him and fitted it into the lock. Despite the box's obvious age, it had been well maintained. It opened easily to reveal a neatly arranged selection of highly polished brass mechanical parts, folded papers, and a couple of small leather-bound notebooks. "Anything in particular I should be looking at?" Sam asked. "I'm not sure what most of this stuff is."

"Neither am I," said Mr. McKenna. "Most of the parts are things I don't recognize."

"He never told you what they were?"

"No. And I never asked. If he'd wanted to say, he would have." Mr. McKenna took out some papers and unfolded them. "You don't speak German, do you?"

Sam shook his head. "Not since school. If those papers aren't about how many brothers and sisters Kruger had, I won't be much use to you." He leaned forward to look at the papers. Some were neatly typed, some handwritten. He selected a notebook at random and opened it to see the same flowing script. These notes were brief, with lots of abbreviations, crossed-out sections, further notes added in the margins, hastily-scribbled equations. At the back, Sam caught a glimpse of a sketch. He smiled. Who ever thought about Nazi scientists stopping to doodle? "So why did he give you the box?"

"In case he died," Mr. McKenna said with a shrug. "They're not always that careful here when they clear out the rooms. If you don't have family to come in and do it for you. They just dump everything in a skip. They don't check for things that shouldn't be thrown away. If you've got something that's important to you, you pass it on to someone else so it won't go in the bin. I've got things from a few people. My son's got a list of the bits that he's to save when I go. Don't know what he'll do with them, mind. Probably just sell them. But at least they'll still be out there. I don't suppose I'll care, being dead."

"That's tea time, Mr. McKenna." The nurse stood up and moved toward Mr. McKenna, ready to help him back onto his feet.

"Can we have just a few minutes longer?" Sam asked.

"Sorry," said the nurse. "We serve dinner at five."

Sam bit back a sharp response. "Want me to take the box back to your room?" he asked Mr. McKenna.

"I don't want it," the old man whispered. "Can you take it?"

"Errr, sure." Sam was surprised. "Do you want me to pass it on to the police?"

Mr. McKenna scowled. "What would they do with it? They'd probably say I stole it or something. No, just you keep it. Or find someone who'd want it. I don't care. I just don't want it here."

Sam packed the papers and notebooks back into the box with great care while the nurse got Mr. McKenna to his feet, straightened his dressing gown and helped him balance. "Are you sure?" Sam called, as the nurse and Mr. McKenna made their way out of the room. "You could probably sell these. Could be worth a fair bit of money."

Slowly and painfully, Mr. McKenna took the handful of steps back toward Sam and clapped him on the shoulder. "Maybe I could," he muttered, leaning in close. "But do you think I want to end up like Kruger?"

Fair point, Sam thought. So you gave it to someone who doesn't care. Good choice. He locked the strongbox again, picked it up by the cold brass handle and made his way back to join DCI Smith in Mr. Kruger's room.

"Were you carrying that box when we got here?" Smith asked as they got back in the car.

"What, this?" Sam glanced at the box as if it had only just appeared. "Nah. The old boy I was talking to earlier, Mr. McKenna, he gave it to me. Apparently it's a super secret Nazi box and I might want to write about it or something. He wasn't taking no for an answer, so I said I'd take it. I'll keep it for a bit. He's bound to want it back eventually."

"Poor old guy." Smith shook his head. "I hope I don't end up like that."

CHAPTER 2

AND OF COURSE, we are all extremely grateful to the Knox family, without whom we could not have completed this amazing new building. It's a great example of how important our alumni network is, and how it continues to play an important role in the life of the university long after students have graduated."

Sam examined the end of his pen. The blue plastic cap was squashed and mangled where he had been chewing it, desperate for a cigarette. He had been stuck in this room for an hour and a half, being invited to admire shiny plastic chairs and partitioned "pods" that would serve in place of tutors' offices. The smell of fresh paint was giving him a headache, and he was surrounded by people with iPads and other technology that Sam refused to embrace.

He glared at the smooth young journalist to his left, who had no notepad in sight but was glibly recording the whole of the chancellor's speech on his tablet. The young man felt Sam's gaze and glanced over at him, shooting a pitying look at the disheveled figure with the cheap notepad and chewed Biro. He smirked. Laugh it up, teenager, Sam thought. Let's see how funny it is when print media dies and I'm ready to retire and you've got decades left in you. Then Sam realized that he had not been listening to a word the chancellor was saying, so he began scribbling furiously again.

". . . So please join me now in welcoming this local treasure to the stage!"

For a moment Sam worried that he had not caught the name of the "local treasure," but his fears were quickly assuaged. In such a small city, there were only so many nationally famous local authors to go around. This one got trotted out at every major function in the city and, to judge from the half-hearted applause, his appeal was starting to wear thin. Sam scanned the audience, checking out the reactions. At the end of the row a petite, pissed-off brunette caught his eye. She was fidgeting slightly, and Sam suspected that she was a fellow smoker who would much rather be outside looking for a place to shelter from the drizzling rain than in here watching a writer test one of the humanities department's new seats.

As soon as the writer had satisfied everyone that the seat worked and was fit for such activities as spinning around and rolling across the floor, the chancellor announced that the new humanities department was now open and invited everyone to the champagne reception. Sam, the dark-haired woman, and the rest of the smokers marched straight toward the nearest door. Just as he got his hand on the door handle, a waiter appeared next to Sam with a tray laden with glasses. He stopped to claim two of them, then slipped out before anyone could stop him to point out that taking the alcohol outside was strictly forbidden.

The brunette was clearly familiar with the new building already. She turned right and headed straight for a corner behind the reception area, sheltered from the wind that was sweeping down from Salisbury Crags. Sam followed her. It was a trick he had learned early on, after the smoking ban had driven him outdoors. Find the person who knows the layout; follow them to find the place where the wind won't stop you lighting up.

There were five smokers in the little group, all eyeing Sam's champagne glasses enviously, wishing they had thought to swipe some on their way out too. Sam held one of the glasses up. "I'll give my spare to anyone who fancies giving me a cigarette," he offered. There was a collective lurch forward as the other four rushed to offer him a smoke, but it was the brunette who got there first. She held out her cigarette packet and let Sam take one while she accepted the champagne and took a grateful gulp.

"Thanks," Sam said, dipping his head toward his lighter.

"No, thank you," the woman replied. "After a couple of hours of that, cigarettes alone aren't enough. Alcohol is definitely required."

"Yeah," Sam took a long drag. "Too early in the day for this kind of thing." He held out a hand. "Sam Cleave. Edinburgh Post."

"Nina Gould. I'm in the history department."

Sam quickly began to revise his assumptions about the brunette. He had guessed that she was an academic, because the audience was comprised of nothing but academics and journalists, but considering her stylish trouser suit and with her glossy bobbed hair, he had supposed that she was in one of the more glamorous departments—informatics, perhaps, economics, political science. Something up to date. He had trouble imagining Nina Gould spending hours poring over dusty tomes in dingy libraries.

"Cool," he said unconvincingly. "Look, I'm supposed to get a couple of vox pops from people about this new building. Mind if I ask you a couple of questions on tape?"

"Sure." Nina blew out a long stream of smoke. "Oh, wow, an actual tape recorder? I don't think I've seen one of these for about ten years! I thought 'tape' was something people still said out of habit."

Sam slotted a cassette into his Dictaphone. "I would have thought you'd appreciate it," he said. "What with you being a historian and all."

"Yes, but I specialize in the pre-war era, not the prehistoric."

"Funny." Sam pointed the microphone toward her. "Now, could you tell me what difference this new building is going to make to you as a . . . sorry, what was your job title?"

"I'm a research fellow specializing in 20th century European history. I'm sure we're all looking forward to making use of the wonderful resources the Braxfield Tower can offer. I have no doubt that the open plan pods for one-to-one teaching will make for a stimulating and challenging learning environment, and—"

"Hold on, hold on," Sam flapped at her, examining the Dictaphone. "I don't think that worked, the red light didn't come on. Can we try that again? Sorry."

As the last of their fellow smokers departed, Nina repeated herself word for word. Sam wondered if this was a prepared speech. The red light on the Dictaphone came on, then faded and died.

"I think it's knackered," Sam said. "Sorry about that."

Nina's face brightened. "Oh. Does that mean I can say what I really think?"

"Be my guest."

"Then let me tell you, off the record, that this place is a fucking stupid idea. It cost millions, it's barely fit for purpose, and I guarantee you that they'll end up building yet another new place and shifting everything there in about ten years. It doesn't even have decent desks—you can't spread out your books and stationery and settle in to do some research, you've got to sit in one of these study pods where there's only space for an iPad or a Kindle or some such thing.

"I mean, I don't mind if people want to use that kind of technology. I do it myself sometimes. But there are other times when I need proper books. And how am I supposed to give my students feedback out here? They cry at me, you know. I tell them why they get lousy marks and they spill out their little hearts and tell me how much pressure they're under, and I make soothing noises and tell them how to improve. How am I supposed to do that in the middle of an atrium—don't even get me started on calling it an 'atrium'—where everything's open and no conversation can be private? God! Whoever designed this place might have won a whole lot of awards, but they've never actually set foot in a university."

She took another lengthy drag on her cigarette, gripping it as if it had personally offended her. Then she downed the rest of her champagne.

"Sorry," she sighed, shooting Sam a rueful smile. "I'm just

not used to talking to human beings, you know? Most of the time I just see other academics, and saying all that to them could be professional suicide. Everyone hates the new building. You can see it written on their faces. But no one's going to say a word, at least not publicly."

"I suppose not."

"Look, I should go back in," Nina said, stubbing out her cigarette. "Nice talking to you. Sorry the vox pop thing didn't work out."

"Yeah, me too."

"If you want I can say it again and you can just take notes?" she offered.

Sam waved a dismissive hand. "It's fine. I can live without the vox pops. Anyway, now that I've heard the unedited version, I'm not sure I could use the official one."

Nina laughed, then set off back toward the main doors. As Sam watched her go, he felt a flicker of appreciation. It had been a long time since he had had even a few minutes' chat with a beautiful woman. Then the pleasant feeling gave way to a wave of guilt as Patricia's face surfaced in his memory. You've nothing to worry about, Trish, he thought. You never will. And I wish that I really believed that you could somehow hear this.

At 4:00 am, having already missed his deadline by four hours, Sam sat in his dark living room, lit only by the pale blue glow of his laptop screen. The cold remains of a fish supper lay on the table beside him, the sauce starting to congeal on the chips. Bruichladdich was tucking into the last of the fish, purring contentedly.

"It's no use, Bruich," Sam muttered. "There's just no way to make this interesting. It's just going to have to go in as it is."

He saved the article on the opening of the Braxfield Tower, attached it to an email and hit Send. His editors would either like it or they wouldn't. Much to his surprise, they had loved the piece about the Tesco Metro protests. His report on Harald Kruger's murder had made the front page, of course, but it had passed without any comment from the subs. None of the editorial staff seemed to feel that they had the right to amend the work of a prize-winning investigative journalist when he was clearly on his home territory. Reprimanding him over his manner of reporting on verbal abuse against traffic wardens was another matter.

"Done. Cheers, Bruich." Sam poured himself a whisky, downed it, and refilled the glass. He glanced at the clock. "Time for bed. Can't leave this lying around though, can I? I'm not waking up to find a drunken cat trashing the place." He knocked back the drink, then dragged himself through to the bedroom. Too cold to undress, he collapsed onto the bed fully clothed and rolled over, pulling the duvet around him like a cocoon. Within five minutes, Sam had plunged into a deep sleep. Within ten, the cat was curled up on Sam's head, also fast asleep.

Sam woke up screaming. It happened occasionally. He could never remember the exact events of his nightmares. All he could recall was the feeling of being helpless, in danger, and completely unable to do anything about it. Several people had suggested that he seek counseling—Patrick Smith, Sam's editors at the Clarion, then his editors at the Post, Sam's sister on the rare occasions when they spoke. Sam had refused every time. He did not need counseling to tell him that he was reliving Patricia's death night after night. He knew why he could not remember his dreams. His brain was having mercy on him by erasing the images every time he woke up. The feelings, however, were inescapable.

He checked the clock—7:00 am. Far too early for him to be up, but he knew he was unlikely to get back to sleep. Instead, he stumbled through to the kitchen and made himself a mug of extra-strong, extra-sweet tea, then settled in front of his laptop. His hands roamed idly over the keyboard. Bruich padded through and curled up in his lap.

It was not until Sam found himself on the Edinburgh University website that he even realized that he had typed Nina Gould's name into his search engine. Well, he thought, she must have made more of an impression than I realized. He clicked through to her staff profile on the university's website.

Nina is originally from Oban. She completed a BA (Hons) in History at the University of York, then an MSc in Contemporary History at the University of St Andrew's before undertaking her PhD at the University of Edinburgh. Her thesis explored the role of propaganda in fiction in Germany prior to World War II. She is currently the Martha Allbright Foundation Research Fellow. She is currently working on "Glaube und Schönheit: The Bund deutscher Mädel and Gender Politics in the Third Reich."

It took Sam's barely awake, slightly hung-over brain a few moments to catch up with his eyes. He had the nagging sensation that he had just stumbled across something important, or at least useful, but he could not quite put his finger on it. Thinking hard, he took another slurp of tea.

"German history?" Sam's brain finally woke up. "She studies German history?" He leaned around in his seat, trying to remember where he had dumped the strongbox that Mr. McKenna had given him. It was over by the living room door, where he had put it down as soon as he got home. The key was hanging on the corner of his laptop screen. Fortunately it had not yet occurred to Bruichladdich to play with it. Sam picked it up and looked around for his wallet. When he found it, he tucked the key in beside his emergency credit card. Then he turned his attention back to the computer and began writing an email.

Hi Nina,

Nice speaking to you at the Braxfield Tower opening yesterday. Sorry the vox pop didn't work out!
Hope you don't mind me getting in touch, but I found your email online and realized that you're a German history specialist. This might sound like a weird request, but I was recently given a box full of documents that used to belong to a Nazi scientist. Right now I'm trying to figure out what they are and whether there's a story in them, but I don't really speak German. Would you be interested in taking a look at them?

Sam Cleave

The time it took to type those two paragraphs was sufficient for Sam's eyeballs to start throbbing. Unsure whether it was hangover or eye strain, he decided his best course of action was to pour another whisky, lie on the couch, plug his headphones into his ancient stereo system, and lose himself in whichever Johnny Cash album happened to be in the CD player. Slowly, unexpectedly, he felt himself drifting back into sleep.

When Sam awoke, the first thing he saw was his open laptop, with Nina's message waiting for him.

Hi Sam,

Thanks for contacting me. It was good to meet you. I'd like to know more about these papers. I'd invite you to my office, but as I was ranting about yesterday, I no longer have one. Could we meet at the National Library some time? I'll be finished with teaching for the semester after today, so I can meet any time that's convenient to you. It would be great to do this some time before Christmas.
Let me know.

Nina

CHAPTER 3

WELL, THEY'RE DEFINITELY army documents," Nina said. Several pairs of eyes glanced at her with disapproval, but she paid them no attention. Sam, on the other hand, felt a little intimidated. He was used to having people look askance at him, wondering who the disheveled drunk was, but the reading room at the National Library made him feel even more judged than usual. All of these serious, studious people seemed to be doing work that was far more legitimate than his was.

He had not always felt this way. During his time at the Clarion he had been in and out of the British Library in London, checking out old stories and researching people's backgrounds. But in those days he wore shirts with all their buttons still attached. He shaved every morning and only drank in company. His work felt important. No one questioned his legitimacy then. Just eighteen short months ago . . .

"Sam?" Nina's voice called him back to the present.

"Uh, yes," Sam pulled himself together. "Army documents. That's great. Any idea what they're about?"

She pointed to a sheaf of typed papers. "These are in some sort of code. They refer to some kind of base in New Schwabenland. It's not entirely clear—there are several abbreviations and military acronyms that I don't understand —but I know that the Nazis hoped to establish a whaling base there. They needed whale oil for things such as soap, margarine, god knows what else. And they were thinking of setting up a naval base there. They got as far as charting some of the territory—I think that's what some of these handwritten notes refer to—but then it became clear that Germany was going to war, so setting up remote ice stations wasn't really a priority. It's strange, though, because some of these notes make it sound like some sort of base had actually been established and the writer—Harald Kruger, did you say? —was working on something there."

Next, she tapped the little pile of notebooks. "These look like some sort of journal. Again, there are a lot of abbreviations and acronyms, but I should be able to translate them if you don't mind leaving them with me." She glanced up, her brown eyes sincere. "I promise I'll take perfect care of them."

Sam allowed himself a small smile. He wondered for a moment how Nina imagined him taking care of the box's contents. She'd probably be horrified if she saw my place, he thought. "Sure," he said, "as long as you're careful."

"Thanks." Nina looked genuinely excited at the prospect of spending her Christmas holiday translating old Nazi letters. "I will be." Carefully, methodically, she took out the metal parts and laid them in a row on the table. There was a cog, small in diameter but thick and heavy, a flat disc with a tiny hole in its center like a miniature CD, an inch-long cylinder, and a strange ring with a row of bulbous protrusions along the top. "Any idea what these are?" Nina asked.

"Not a clue," said Sam. "Just bits of metal as far as I'm concerned."

"I thought as much. Do you want to hang on to these for now? There's not much I can do with them, but I'll let you know if I find any reference to them in the notebooks. Now, shall we get out of here? If we talk for much longer these people are likely to turn violent."

"We'd better, then," Sam agreed. "Some of them have staplers. They could do a lot of damage."

He watched as Nina folded the papers and slipped them back into the strongbox with care bordering on reverence. She took the key from him and was just about to lock it when she paused. "You know what?" she said, "If I just take the notebooks and leave the papers with you, I could put you in touch with someone who might be able to decode them."

"Who's that?" Sam asked.

"His name is Dr. George Lehmann," Nina said. "Here, I'll write down his number. I'd call him myself, but . . . well, I can't. Here. Tell him I sent you."

"And who exactly is this guy?"

"Another German scientist. You'd be surprised how many were spirited out of Germany during Operation Paperclip. He was a friend of my supervisor's, he helped me with some research for my doctorate and I've kept in touch ever since." She gathered the notebooks and put them carefully in her handbag, then locked the strongbox and handed it back to Sam. He could not help noticing that her tone of voice had become suspiciously calm. A spark of mischief flared up in him and he decided not to resist it.

"So . . ." he said casually. "How come you can't contact this Dr. Lehmann? I mean, I'm very happy to do it—thanks for the contact and everything—I'm just curious. Wouldn't it be better for you to talk to him, one expert to another?"

Nina's mouth folded into a hard line. "It's complicated," she said. She made her way out of the reading room and headed down the stairs, Sam at her heels.

"How so?" Sam asked, deliberately keeping his voice as

light as he could.

She stopped dead, spun around and looked Sam straight in the face. "Is this any of your business?" she demanded. "Ok, you really want to know? Dr. Lehmann lives with his son, Steven. When I went down to Berkshire to interview Dr. Lehmann, Steven and I . . . hit it off, shall we say? We had a kind of on-off affair for a couple of years. Then last year, Steven's wife found out. She wasn't particularly happy to find out about me. To be fair, I wasn't particularly happy to find out about her . . . But apparently they've worked things out. Dr. Lehmann wrote to me recently to say that they'd had a baby. I have a feeling that a call from me wouldn't be appreciated right now, even if it wasn't Steven I wanted to talk to."

"I see." Sam could see that Nina was scrutinizing his face for any hint of judgment. He kept his expression neutral. These things happened, he knew. Patricia's ex-husband hadn't exactly been thrilled when Trish packed her bags one night and headed straight for Sam's place.

"So, I'm sure you can understand why I would rather have you call him. You're less likely to get his wife accusing you of trying to destroy her home." She turned away and continued down the stairs, stopping at the bottom to put her coat on.

Sam caught her up and stopped beside her to wind his scarf around his neck. "Sorry," he said.

Nina glanced back over her shoulder at him and Sam caught a hint of a smile. "No you're not," she said. "You're a journalist. Prying is your job. And everyone loves gossip, don't they?" She slung her bag over her arm and patted it. "I'll get on with translating these. Give me until New Year's Day. We can meet up after that. I'll talk you through whatever I've found and you can tell me if Dr. Lehmann could clear anything up regarding those papers. Bring wine." She strode off toward the door.

"Sam, what the hell is this?"

Sam's mind raced as he tried to figure out who was speaking. One of these days, he promised himself, I am going to get myself a phone with caller ID. He seldom felt the need for anything more sophisticated than his old brick of a phone, but moments like this made him wish that he knew who was calling so that he could avoid answering the call. A quick process of deduction, running through the list of people who could possibly be pissed off with him, brought him to the conclusion that it was his editor, Mitchell Scott. "What's up, Mitch?"

"This piece you wrote about the Braxfield Tower opening." Mitchell was exasperated. "What am I supposed to do with this, Sam? There's hardly any information about what the new building's for, who built it, who paid for it, anything. You give us a brief hint that the staff aren't happy about the design, but then you don't go into it—no quotes, nothing! The whole thing just reads like you don't give a shit. I'm going to have to do a massive rewrite. Basically, this is going to end up as a rehash of the press release."

The reprimand was not entirely unexpected. Sam knew full well that his article was lackluster. He knew that Mitchell would rewrite it. He also knew that he should care, but he just couldn't find it within himself. He made some apologetic noises, but Mitchell was in full flow.

"Are we back here again, Sam? Really? I'm trying to be supportive, I really am. I know you've got a lot to deal with. And it's not that you're not good. When you're on form, your work's fantastic. The Queensferry murder piece was phenomenal. Seriously. I loved it. Figures for that day were amazing. We were ahead of the Guardian, the Times—all the nationals. But then you give me something like this. Any teenager with a blog could do better than this. What's the matter, Sam? Are you ok? Is there anything you need?"

"A lifetime supply of single malt wouldn't come amiss." Sam leaned back in his chair and lit a cigarette.

"Oh, Sam," Mitchell sighed heavily. "This is serious. I'm really concerned about you. Look, why don't you take some time off? Have a bit of a break. I can sort you out some paid leave. Maybe just relax until after the new year, get your head together a bit."

"Gardening leave?"

"Don't think of it like that. I'm just concerned about your well-being, Sam. Are you seeing anyone? Such as a therapist or someone? I know it's none of my business—I'm not trying to be nosy, it's just that if you need a recommendation I know a couple of people . . ."

Sam sighed. If only Mitchell weren't so nice. Most people who had tried to recommend therapists to Sam had been told to fuck off, or worse. He couldn't say that Mitchell. "That would be great, Mitchell," he conceded.

"Fantastic!" Mitchell's tone brightened at once. "I'll email you their details. And if there's anything else, anything at all, just you let me know. I'll drop you a line after Hogmanay and we'll have a chat about what to do going forward. Don't you worry about a thing."

"That's great, Mitchell. Thanks." Sam let Mitchell twitter for another couple of minutes before hanging up. Then he took a lengthy puff on his cigarette. Well, he thought, no more local interest stories for a bit. Now what am I going to do to ignore the run-up to Christmas?

Sam decided that concentrating on the strongbox and its mysterious contents was his best option. He opened his search engine and looked up Schwabenland, taking a few guesses before hitting on the correct spelling. He clicked his way through link after link, flipping among sites that looked legitimate and sites that were clearly hosted by deranged conspiracy theorists. His favorites were the ones that insisted that Hitler had not died at the end of the Second World War but was still alive, even in 2012, at the grand old age of 124. Many of these suggested that he had been spirited off to Antarctica, leaving a look-alike to shoot himself in the bunker. Some even stated that Hitler was still there, cryogenically frozen, waiting in suspended animation until the Nazis regained power and revived him. The more Sam drank, the more entertaining his search became.

Eventually, countless conspiracy theories later, Sam grew curious about Dr. Lehmann. He could find nothing about the scientist online, apart from a couple of mentions in the thanks sections of academic papers. This annoyed him. He liked to find out a bit about people before he contacted them.

He also liked to be a little more sober than he currently was, so he headed to the bathroom and took a shower. The water was bracingly cold, which was good for sobering him up but also indicated that the boiler was on the blink again. He toweled himself off at top speed, threw on some nearly clean clothes and had a mug of tea and half a packet of chocolate digestives. As soon as his head began to feel a little clearer, he dialed the number on Nina's note.

It was a woman who answered. "Lehmann residence."

"Could I speak to Dr. Lehmann, please?" Sam did his best to sound professional.

"May I ask who's calling?" The female at the other end of the phone did not seem particularly friendly.

"My name is Sam Cleave; I'm with the Edinburgh Post. I'm working on a story about a scientist whom I think Dr. Lehmann might have known, so I'd like to ask him a few questions."

"Hmm. Right. I'll see if he's available. One moment."

Sam waited while the woman went to find Dr. Lehmann. The house sounded chaotic, judging by the noises he could hear at the other end of the line. Two male voices were raised in a heated argument, at least until the woman's voice cut through them, and a baby was wailing in the background. That's what Christmas is going to sound like, Sam thought glumly, recalling his sister's invitation to stay with her, her husband, and their two-year-old daughter. Maybe I'll just stay here and pretend it's not happening.

"Hello," a man's voice this time, "George Lehmann speaking." His speech bore only faint traces of his German accent. If it had not been for his pronunciation of his name, retaining the hard G, Sam might not have noticed it at all.

"Hello, Dr. Lehmann. Thank you for speaking to me," Sam said. "I'm Sam Cleave, I write for the Edinburgh Post. I was given your number by Nina Gould at Edinburgh University. She thought you might be able to give me some information about a story I'm working on."

"Indeed." Dr. Lehmann's voice remained neutral at the mention of Nina's name. "And what is this story about?"

Sam explained about the death of Harald Kruger, omitting the gorier details. Dr. Lehmann did not appear to have heard about the murder, though he admitted to a passing familiarity with Kruger's work. It was not until Sam mentioned the strongbox that a trace of excitement crept into his voice.

"And you say these notes pertain to some kind of Antarctic base?" Lehmann asked. "But no name is given?"

"That's right. Or at least, Nina says it's right. But she can't tell me more about it because the notes are partly in code. She said you might be able to help with that."

Dr. Lehmann broke into a loud, unexpected laugh. "She did, did she? Yes, that sounds like her. There's always a way to get the things she wants. Well, I would need to have a look at these papers before I could tell you how much help I can offer."

"I could scan them and send them to you," Sam suggested. "Do you have an email address?"

"Mr. Cleave," Lehmann replied with a chuckle, "I am 97 years old. How likely do you think it is that I have an email address?"

"Point taken," Sam shrugged. It was rare that he met anyone less up-to-date with modern technology than he was, but this time it seemed that he had. "Should I put them in the post?"

"No." Lehmann's tone was emphatic. "Definitely not. These are valuable artifacts, or at least they might be. If they were to be lost or damaged . . . No. Would it be possible for you to bring them to me, or entrust them to someone in whom you have the utmost faith? If it were remotely possible for me to come to you, I would—but I find myself less able to travel these days."

Sam considered it. His gut reaction was to say no. It was a long way to go, a journey that would cost money he didn't have. What am I doing with this story anyway? Sam wondered. I don't do this kind of thing anymore. I'm supposed to be leaving the investigative stuff to other people these days.

"Yeah, go on then," said Sam.

CHAPTER 4

BY THE TIME Sam had taken the train down to London, changed for a local train, and made his way to Thatcham, his emergency credit card was beginning to smolder. This is turning into a very expensive trip, he thought, as he handed over a ten-pound note for a railway station sandwich and weak tea. He got very little change. Once he had eaten, Sam went in search of a taxi. A lone minicab was waiting at the rank.

"The Old Rectory, The Ridge, Cold Ash, please," Sam said to the driver. They set off. The driver was pleasantly taciturn, leaving Sam to stare absently out of the window at the Berkshire countryside. Beyond the little town lay rolling fields, lush and green, dotted with chocolate box cottages and farmhouses. Despite its picturesque beauty, the landscape made Sam melancholy. He had not been back to England since he had moved home eighteen months earlier, and it was strange to see this kind of pastoral prettiness again.

Cold Ash was barely a village. The main street consisted of a few shops, a school, and a couple of pubs, and The Old Rectory was nowhere near the main street. It was a sturdy Victorian building with a gravel drive and seemingly endless gardens. Sam paid the cab driver, ignoring his grumbling about being given Scottish banknotes, then scrunched his way across the gravel to knock on the door.

Steven Lehmann answered the door with difficulty, holding a baby on his hip and a bottle in his free hand. "Oh. You must be the journalist," he said dismissively. "I suppose you'd better come in." Sam stepped into the cozy hallway, feeling out of place amid the expensively shabby Welsh dressers and occasional tables. I'm the wrong kind of shabby, Sam thought, shrugging off his battered black leather jacket and draping it over his arm. He was freezing after his journey, but this place was distinctly overheated.

"Dad's upstairs," Steven said, indicating the direction with a jerk of his head. He was just about to turn away toward the kitchen when he stopped and suddenly stared intently at Sam. "What was your name again?" he asked. "Dad did tell me, but . . ."

"Sam Cleave," said Sam. Then, because Steven's gaze was making him uncomfortable, he continued. "From the Edinburgh Post."

"Hmm." Steven nodded slightly, then continued as if nothing had happened. "I've got to get Lavinia down for her nap, but I'll bring you two some tea in a minute. Just head up. It's the first door on the right."

People are weird, thought Sam, as he climbed the stairs. When he reached the first door on the right he knocked. A muffled voice called from within, so he pushed the door open and stepped inside. He found himself in a small, book-lined study with a tiny coal fire. Dr. Lehmann was seated in a dark-green wing chair by the hearth, leaning forward on his walking stick.

"Ah, Mr. Cleave," he greeted Sam. "So good to meet you. Thank you for coming all this way. Do have a seat."

He directed Sam to a leather chair identical to his own. Sam gratefully settled into it, stretching his frozen feet out toward the fire. Before they could get talking, Steven appeared. "Tea, Dad?" he asked. Dr. Lehmann nodded, then turned his attention back to Sam as they heard Steven's footsteps on the stairs.

"Please, Mr. Cleave," Dr. Lehmann said, "do tell me about this story you are writing. How did you come into possession of these papers? I am a little confused. They belonged to Harald Kruger, you said, but you never met Mr. Kruger."

"That's right," Sam replied. "I got them from a Mr. McKenna, another resident in the retirement home. He told me he was looking after them for Mr. Kruger. He seemed quite worried about what would happen to him if he hung on to the papers, but I got the impression that he wasn't the trusting sort."

And neither are you, Sam thought, as Dr. Lehmann suddenly raised his finger to his lips. The old man began chattering inconsequentially—about Sam's journey, the expected snowstorm, the cost of train travel, anything at all. At first Sam could not understand the change, but then Steven appeared with the tea tray. Interesting, he thought, Lehmann doesn't want his son hearing about this stuff. Sure enough, the stream of chit-chat continued until Steven was back down the stairs, safely out of earshot. It took an agonizingly long time, since instead of going straight back down, Steven chose that moment to stop and fiddle with the plug socket on the landing. After several minutes he got up and left. At once, Lehmann dropped his doddery old man act.

"May I see the papers?"

"Sure," said Sam, reaching into his bag. The folded papers were tucked into a notebook for safekeeping, because Sam had thought it best not to lug the cumbersome strongbox all the way to Berkshire. "I've got some of the metal things that were in the box too." He pulled them out of the zip section and spread the complicated bits of brass on the table while

Dr. Lehmann poured tea.

"Please, help yourself to milk and sugar," the old man said, picking up a couple of the machine parts. He turned them over and over, scrutinizing them. "Wolfenstein?" he muttered to himself. "And this . . . No . . . no, I'm afraid these are unfamiliar to me. As I recall, Mr. Kruger and I were in very different fields at Peenemünde. What was it he did, aeronautics? Ballistics? They could be bomb parts, I suppose. Rocket science was my field. I had the immeasurable privilege of working with Wernher von Braun, you know . . ."

He picked up the typed papers. "Ah, yes, I recognize these. This one is notifying Mr. Kruger that he will be posted to a new location at the beginning of 1939. I can't tell you where, since that part is in code and I'm afraid it's not somewhere I knew the code words for. It may be possible to work it out—this little note in the margin here, it's a number puzzle. We used to come up with these as a way of disguising the—"

The door opened again. Dr. Lehmann immediately went silent. He shot a look at the papers. Sam could have sworn that he was looking for a swift way to hide them. He found himself getting ready to lunge forward in case the old man threw them on the fire.

Steven Lehmann strolled in, a plate in his hand. He set it down on the tea table. "Forgot the biscuits," he said with an icy smile. "Mr. Cleave?" Steven turned his attention to Sam.

"I believe you're here because Nina Gould sent you?" He looked Sam up and down, presumably jumping to conclusions about Sam's relationship with Nina and not liking them. "Hmm. Well, when you see her, tell her I send my love, won't you?"

Sam had never heard a greeting that sounded so much like a threat, not even from people who had been pointing guns at him at the time. He and Dr. Lehmann watched silently as Steven slipped out of the room again, leaving the door slightly ajar.

"My son is not a happy man," Dr. Lehmann said softly. "I wish it were otherwise. But he has made . . . unfortunate choices. I believe that he regrets not having the nerve to leave his wife and marry Nina when he had the chance. If, indeed, he did have the chance . . . I do not think that Nina trusted him after she learned that he had lied to her about being married. A pity. I should have liked to have her for a daughter-in-law. I do sincerely hope that you will be able to make her happy."

Sam nearly leaped out of his seat. "What? Me and Nina? No, sorry, Dr. Lehmann, I think you've got the wrong end of the stick. I've only just met her! No, we're just friends. Well, acquaintances. I ran into her at a university thing and ended up telling her about these papers in the hope that she'd help me. She's translating Kruger's notebooks at the moment."

"His notebooks? There are more?"

"Yup. She's only had a brief look at them, but she said his notes were about some kind of Nazi ice station that they were going to build for whaling or something. Does that sound about right?"

Dr. Lehmann was still and silent for a long moment. Sam watched with growing concern. Is he ok? He's very still. Should I get his son? Is he having an aneurysm or something? Then at last, he picked up his cup and took a slow sip of tea.

"Mr. Cleave," he said gently. "I would advise you and Nina not to pursue this any further. I can tell you that there was an attempt to build an ice station in New Schwabenland, and that many have died attempting to uncover its location. To do so now would simply be folly. It is perhaps the most hostile terrain on Earth. A station abandoned in 1945 would leave very little trace by now. Your safest bet is to leave well enough alone. There are secrets that are best left as secrets."

I bet there are, Sam thought. He could feel this case tugging at his interest despite his determination to keep his distance. Stop trying to recapture the glory days, Sam, he told himself. You don't have the balls for the investigative stuff anymore. If this gets any more challenging than chatting to old men about their wartime experiences, you'll be curled up under the nearest table, sobbing like a baby.

"Purely academic interest, I promise," Sam reassured the

old man, sliding the handwritten papers toward him. "Can you tell me anything about these?"

Dr. Lehmann did not even lean forward this time. He cast a cursory glance over the top sheet, then shook his head. "No," he said sadly. "I cannot help you with these. My eyes are not what they used to be, and the writing is too cramped. I am sorry."

Nothing further came of Sam's chat with Dr. Lehmann. They made polite conversation as they finished their tea and biscuits, but no matter how hard he tried, Sam could not draw out any further information about the contents of the strongbox. Still, Dr. Lehmann seemed a nice old boy, and he told Sam a little about his experiences after Operation Paperclip. He had worked for the Americans, he said, as they battled to win the space race. When Armstrong had landed on the Moon, Lehmann had celebrated with so much champagne that he finally worked up the confidence to propose to Steven's mother. As old men's reminiscences went, Dr. Lehmann's were among the more interesting. Sam listened, trying not to give in to drowsiness in the warm study.

He was not the only one feeling tired, though. Dr. Lehmann was clearly flagging. "I hope you won't think me terribly ill-mannered if I bring our interview to a close," he said, stifling a yawn. "I shall ask my son to drive you back to the station, if that is where you're going."

As little as Sam relished the prospect of half an hour in the car with Steven Lehmann, he was not in a position to turn down the lift. He waited beside the family Volvo while the two Lehmann men conversed in hushed tones in the doorway. Sam was prepared to bet that they were not discussing feeding times for little Lavinia. As he waited, his phone began to ring. He slipped it out of his pocket and went to answer it, then thought better of it. What if it's Nina? Sam wondered. That's a can of worms I'd be best not to open right now. He rejected the call and put the phone away again.

At last they were on their way. Steven's face was inscrutable, but his dislike for Sam was palpable. Sam sneaked a look at him out of the corner of his eye. Steven was a man in the early stages of losing his looks. Mid-forties, with the excesses of his earlier years starting to tell on him. Dissatisfied with life, as his father had said. Sam wondered what his relationship with Nina had been like.

"I hope you got everything you needed from your talk with my father, Mr. Cleave," Steven spoke for the first time as they approached the station. "Because I would appreciate it if you didn't come back. As a matter of fact, I don't want you contacting him again. Under any circumstances. My father does not need to relive his Nazi days. My family does not need to be reminded of where it comes from. And my wife and I certainly do not need anything else to do with Nina Gould. She had her chance. "

He pulled up outside the station. Sam, who could not think of a satisfactory response to Steven's strange outburst, simply climbed out of the car and thanked him for the lift.

"One more thing," Steven leaned out of the car window, the engine purring. "I'd advise you to stay away from Nina too. Both of you would be better off keeping your heads down. Best not let her drag you in too deep. Just a friendly warning."

"Errr . . . right." Sam said, wondering just how much of a weirdo this man really was. "Thanks."

Once Steven's car had disappeared around the corner, Sam remembered the phone call. He decided to find out whether his assumption that it had been Nina was correct.

"Nina Gould." Her voice was cool, professional. Maybe she doesn't have caller ID either, Sam thought.

"Nina," he greeted her. "Nice bunch of crazies you sent me to see."

"Hello Sam," she said. "Well, if I'd told you that my ex was a weirdo, would you have believed me?"

"Probably not. Did you call me earlier?"

"Yes, and it wasn't good news. Sam, I'm so sorry . . . it's the notebooks. I was looking after them, I promise, but I was out this afternoon and when I got home, someone had broken into my flat. The police have been around and they think it was just bad luck. Someone who knew what they were doing saw me going out, forced the lock and went for my computer. It looks like it was very clean and efficient, like they just shoved everything on my desk into a bag. And that . . . that included the notebooks. I'm really sorry. I can't believe this happened, right after everything I said about how I'd look after them."

Sam made shushing noises. "It's ok," he reassured her. "It's fine. Are you ok?"

"Yes."

"Then that's the important thing."

"If it's any consolation, I got a lot of work done on them over the past couple of days. That first night, I barely even slept. All of that work is in my notebooks, not my laptop. They weren't on my desk, I've still got them. And I had scanned a few bits and pieces and emailed them to myself, so I can retrieve them. Look, I have to go just now—I'm expecting the police to call me back any time now. Can we meet up once you're back?"

"No problem," Sam said. "I'll be home tomorrow. I'll give you a shout."

Then, since the last train for London had already left and

he was not sure that the emergency credit card would stretch to cover a hotel room, Sam slunk into the station's waiting room, found a bench and settled down for the night.

CHAPTER 5

WE SHOULD PROBABLY just pack this in," Sam said, setting down a round of drinks. Nina accepted her rum and Coke gratefully. "You think?" she said.

"Well, we seem to be drawing a blank. Dr. Lehmann clammed up when I mentioned the notebooks and the ice station, and now the notebooks are gone, so it seems to me that we don't really have much to go on." Sam took a sip of his whisky, letting the bitter, malty taste spread across his tongue. "Unless you found something useful before the notebooks got stolen."

In the fifteen minutes since they had met in the pub, Nina had done nothing but apologize for failing to protect the notebooks. Now, for the first time, her remorseful expression was replaced by a slow smile spreading across her face. "You know, I think I might have," she said.

"You remember those little number puzzles in the margins?" Nina asked, "the ones that showed up in the typed sheets too? Well, I figured out what they are. Some of the people working at Peenemünde used them as a way of referring to places that couldn't be mentioned by name. When Kruger jots these little puzzles in the margin, it's a reminder of where the events he's writing about took place. He takes the coordinates of the place and multiplies the number by the age he was when he began working for the Reich Air Ministry. So if you know what age he was, you have the key to working out the coordinates."

Sam was impressed. He clinked his glass against Nina's in a brief salute. "How the hell did you figure that out?"

"Kruger might have been a brilliant scientist—and he was, because you didn't get recruited straight out of university if you weren't—but literary subtlety wasn't his thing. I put the notebooks in chronological order and started at the beginning. The first entry in the first book consists of Kruger writing about how amazing it was to be chosen for the team at Peenemünde at the early age of 22, and how 22 would always be his lucky number. So I started playing around with the numbers in the margins. I must admit, I was expecting it to be a bit more complicated than this, but I suppose Kruger wasn't anticipating that anyone would read his notebooks. Or perhaps he wanted anyone who read them to be able to figure it out. I don't know.

"He writes from time to time about how he loves mystery novels, so I could believe that leaving clues would appeal to his imagination. Anyway, the first set of coordinates was for Peenemünde. Then later, when Kruger took a couple of trips to Kummersdorf, its coordinates start showing up. There were a few other places—Berlin, La Coupole in northern France, Kohnstein. All the coordinates checked out. Except one."

Nina pulled her own notebook from her bag and flipped it open to show Sam a page covered in scribbled numbers. Her writing grew less neat and more frustrated as it progressed down the page. Near the bottom, where her patience had run out, the strokes of the pen nearly tore through the paper. "I just couldn't figure this one out," she sighed. "It only shows up toward the end of the notebooks, from around 1943. So eventually I just divided by 22 and searched online." She took a folded sheet of paper from the back of the book and spread it open for Sam to see.

"What am I looking at?" Sam was perplexed. "It's nearly all white."

"Exactly," said Nina triumphantly. "It's Antarctica. Specifically, it's New Schwabenland. It's exactly the area that the Nazis were considering as a possible Antarctic base . . . and Kruger seems to be claiming that he'd been there. This is the most compelling evidence I've seen that there genuinely was an attempt to set up a base there. Look at this—it was one of Kruger's last entries."

Sam squinted at the page she indicated, struggling to decipher Nina's spiky writing. He had expected Harald Kruger's writing to be dry, academic, and full of advanced theories that were impossible for nonscientists to understand. Instead, what he found was something whimsical, something that read more like fiction than the thoughts of an eminent intellectual.

It shall be the greatest of adventures! Worthy of Holmes, of Nemo, of Doctor Moreau! Since it now seems inevitable that the journey must be undertaken, it behooves us to approach it with [zeal? unclear]. Hidden away in that most remote of places, we few may discover the means by which we shall snatch victory from the jaws of defeat. To be personally selected by F [Fuhrer?] and entrusted with the richest of our nation's treasures . . . It is my fondest wish. I feel the call of the vastness once again and can only hope that I shall be permitted to answer it. Wolfenstein, I am for you!

Sam wrinkled his nose. "Wee bit purple, isn't it? What's he referring to?"

"It certainly is," Nina replied with a roll of her eyes. "I

think . . . and this sounds crazy, but bear with me . . . There's a little-known theory that several Nazi scientists and a whole lot of the Reich's treasures were sneaked out of Germany when it became clear that the Allies were going to win. Some people even think—"

"That Hitler was spirited away as well, and that his death in the bunker was faked?" Sam chipped in. "Yeah, it's not as little-known as you think. I got that from a stroll around the Internet."

Nina took a deep breath before replying. "Perhaps I should have phrased that differently. There might be plenty of people who are familiar with the theory, but there are very few reputable historians who take it seriously, so in academic circles it's barely considered. Without evidence that the ice station—Wolfenstein, as he seems to be calling it—in New Schwabenland even existed, there was no reason to believe that any attempt was made to secrete anything there."

"Hasn't anyone ever, you know, gone out there to look for it?" Sam asked.

"Sam, look at the map!" Nina said. "We're talking about somewhere incredibly remote, it's not like you can just drive by and check it out. You've got to know what you're doing to survive in that environment—or have the resources to hire someone who knows. Mounting that kind of expedition costs, I don't know, tens of thousands? Maybe hundreds?

And that's before . . ." she trailed off, a thoughtful expression on her face.

"What?"

"I have an idea." Nina was suddenly alight with excitement. "I have a friend, another academic. She's a marine virologist, and she's part of an expedition to Queen Maud Land—better known to you as New Schwabenland—early next year. I wonder . . ."

It took Sam a moment to catch up. "You're not trying to get yourself to the Antarctic? Nina, that's insane."

Nina shrugged. "Is it? It's not a huge amount of evidence, I know. But that's how discoveries are made, isn't it? If I wait for someone else to get out there and prove there's an ice station to be discovered, it won't be me making the discovery. And I'm just spinning my wheels here. I'm teaching stuff I could recite in my sleep, I'm writing papers I don't give a toss about just to keep my publication record up to date. Frankly, if there's a chance to do something exciting at this point in my life, I'm damn well going to take it." She drained her glass and slammed it down on the table. "What did Dr. Lehmann say about the ice station?"

"Not much," said Sam. "Just that it existed—he called it by name, so he's clearly heard of it—and that we shouldn't look for it. Then he got caught up thinking about you and his son and I couldn't get any more out of him."

"Ugh, his son," Nina shuddered. "How is dear Steven?"

"Jealous, I think," Sam said. "He didn't seem to like me very much. Seemed to think you and I had something going on."

"Sounds like him." Nina's rosebud mouth gathered into a scowl. "Never mind the fact that he's got a wife and baby and that I finished things over a year ago. Sorry if he made things awkward for you. People skills aren't really his thing, as I'm sure his wife could attest."

"Sounds like there's a story there."

"I don't want to bore you."

After all the puzzles and confusion of the past week, Sam was more than ready for a tale of a simple relationship drama. Besides, Nina looked like she needed to unload. He listened as she poured out the story of how she had met Steven Lehmann when she was visiting his father. She had mistaken his coldness for mystery, his desperate need for fulfillment for love. Up to her eyes in stress during the final year of her doctorate, eager for excitement and purpose, Nina had persuaded herself that she was in love with Steven.

For two years they had met up in hotels, spent weekends abroad together, he had visited her at her flat. All the while, Dr. Lehmann had warned Nina to be careful of his son. Gradually she had come to realize that Steven was a strange, cold man whose pleasure was derived from control. When she had finally learned of the existence of his wife, she had only been half-surprised.

Since their relationship had ended, Nina had learned that Steven had no intention of letting her go easily. "I think he thinks he's some kind of mafia boss," she snarled, draining her third rum and Coke. "You know—sending messages and all that nonsense. For a while I kept finding shredded violets on my doorstep. He knew they were my favorite flower, so he'd have them ripped up and sent to me. Once he texted me and said he'd heard that I was seeing someone, and that I'd better not be or he'd do something about it.

"It would be funny if it weren't for the fact that he genuinely has some scary contacts. Not underworld, or anything like that—he's far too posh. But he's friends with some worryingly powerful people. You remember that arms dealer who got arrested, the politician's son? Charles Whitsun, I think? He was one of Steven's friends. They'd been at school together. Apparently they used to get drunk and—Sam, are you ok?"

Sam was not ok. He had finally realized where he and Steven Lehmann recognized each other from. Charles Whitsun was a name that no one had said in Sam's presence since the investigation into Patricia's death had ended. Charles Whitsun and his arms-dealing cronies were the reason she was dead, and Sam Cleave's testimony was the reason why Charles Whitsun had been sentenced to thirty-eight years in prison. Not that he served them. He had blown his own brains out rather than face jail. No wonder he wasn't happy at the idea of me and Nina getting together, Sam thought.

"Sam?" Nina's voice called him back to the moment. She looked worried. While Sam had been having his moment of unpleasant realization, it seemed she had been having one of her own. "Sam . . . I don't suppose Steven knew what you were discussing with his father, did he?"

Automatically, Sam shook his head. Yet as he did so, he remembered Steven Lehmann hovering outside the study, fooling around with a plug and socket. He remembered that something had caught his eye as he left the room, though he had been too tired to recognize the lumped shape of the device plugged into the wall just a few feet away from where they had been sitting. Of course Steven had heard their conversation. That device was a baby monitor.

CHAPTER 6

NINA,

You've already had your house burgled. Was that not enough of a warning? Tell me you're not still planning to go looking for this fucking magical imaginary ice station? Even if it did exist once, it's probably just a few shards of rusty metal sticking out of the ice now. Wouldn't someone have flown over and seen it, if it was really still there? Honestly. Just leave it.

Sam

Nina read the email while she drank her coffee. The time stamp read 04:07. Just a few hours earlier, Sam had been worrying about her. She felt a little bit guilty. It had not been her intention to worry him when she told him that she had applied for emergency funding for the Antarctic expedition.

It was just that she had no one else she could tell. Her

relationship with her fellow academics was not close, and the relationship with Steven had cost her the couple of good friends she'd had. Sam Cleave might be a new acquaintance, but he was currently the closest thing to a friend that she had. A damaged, heavy-drinking friend. A match made in . . . somewhere, she thought.

A little time online had revealed a lot about Sam Cleave. Nina had tried to resist the temptation to pry, but what had begun with looking for his Braxfield Tower story had ended with her reading all about his days as a prize-winning investigative journalist. She had not seen him during the past ten days, since their conversation in the pub, but she had been steadily working her way through every article she could find regarding his role in smashing that international arms ring.

Sam had really been through the mill, it seemed. His work on the arms ring story might have netted him a Pulitzer, but it had almost cost him his life when he got caught in the crossfire between the arms dealers and Interpol. A fellow journalist had been shot right in front of him. Nina could only imagine what that would have done to him. It certainly explained the drinking and his sudden cold feet about continuing to investigate Harald Kruger's evidence.

For the past ten days, Sam had contacted her on a daily basis to ask her to withdraw her application for emergency funding. He was convinced that the notebooks had been stolen on the orders of Steven Lehmann and that digging any deeper would bring her into danger. Nina was equally convinced that he was wrong. She could believe that Steven would threaten and bully and throw his weight about, and she could easily imagine that it was concern about this that had stopped Dr. Lehmann from talking. However, Steven had never gone further than that. For all his powerful contacts, Steven was held in check by his own sense of limitations. Nina knew him better than anyone. She was sure she was right.

The alarm on her phone beeped. She silenced it. Ten minutes until she needed to leave the house. Just enough time to send Sam a quick reply.

Sam,

I should find out about funding today. If I get it, I'm going. Stop worrying. I'll let you know how it goes.

Nina

She hit Send, drained her coffee cup, pulled on her coat, scarf, and gloves and headed off to meet her department head.

"Dr. Gould." Professor Frank Matlock leaned forward, his elbows on his desk and his fingers steepled. Nina bit the inside of her cheek, refusing to be intimidated. She remembered this tactic all too well from the early days of her doctoral research, before she had been reassigned to a different supervisor.

"Allow me to make sure that I have got this straight," Matlock sighed gently. "You wish the department to grant you emergency funding so that you can join an Antarctic expedition. This expedition may or may not be going to a place where you believe there to be the remains of a secret Nazi ice station. Wolfenstein, I believe you said? How melodramatic. And this ice station is so very secret that there is, in fact, no definite proof that it exists—apart from a collection of notebooks which you alone have seen, but are unable to present.

"The theory of the lost ice station is one to which no reputable scholar gives credence, but one which is beloved of Internet conspiracy theorists. Yet you believe that in a matter of a few days, you have been able to establish its exact location, and you are willing to stake a great deal of money—the department's money—on your accuracy. This," he brandished the printed map on which Nina had marked the station's location, along with a note of its coordinates, "is the only surety you offer."

Nina folded her hands in her lap. She had been in Professor Matlock's office many times, but it never ceased to intimidate her. There were books on his walls that were worth her entire salary. His desk featured prominently displayed photographs of him with various famous historians and literary figures. The latest addition, hung proudly above his leather armchair, showed Matlock at the summit of Piz Roseg, the culmination of a summer holiday spent with his dear friend Jefferson Daniels—who just happened to be a famous explorer. Even Matlock's holiday snaps were status symbols. The entire room seemed to be designed to make her feel small, insecure, insignificant, and unlikely to amount to anything academically.

"I'm aware that it sounds far-fetched, Professor Matlock," she said. "But I am certain that—"

"Dr. Gould," Matlock interrupted, "I hate to doubt your—dare I say it?—feminine intuition, but you must understand that the department simply cannot give out funding—especially in the kind of sums you are requesting—based on nothing more than a hunch."

"I understand that, Professor," Nina was finding it increasingly difficult to stay calm. She had spent the past hour outlining her case, and now she could see quite clearly that Professor Matlock was going to dismiss it with only cursory consideration. "I understand that this is unorthodox. But you know me. You've known me for years. I'm not impulsive or fanciful. I wouldn't make a request such as this without being absolutely sure of what I'm doing.

"I wish I could show you Mr. Kruger's notebooks, but as I said, they were stolen. I can show you the police report if you don't believe me. I would hate to pass up an opportunity to make such an important breakthrough just because a few thugs chose to rob my flat at exactly the wrong moment— and I'm sure you wouldn't want the department to miss out for such a silly reason either."

The moment Professor Matlock got to his feet, Nina knew she had lost. This was a favorite trick of his and she knew it well. He would stroll casually around his office, nonchalantly laying hands on the many status symbols that he kept scattered around. He would perch on the edge of his desk, looking relaxed and confident, a man who absolutely belonged in this place. For the person trapped in the uncomfortable captain's chair in the center of the room, it was unnerving—and Matlock knew it.

"Nina," he addressed her in deliberately warm, reassuring tones. "I can see you feel strongly about his. I know. Believe it or not, I was once a young academic myself. I remember what it was like to feel unsettled and eager to prove myself. I know you are keen to get tenure, and no doubt you think that something wonderfully high-profile will give you the boost that you need." He whipped off his glasses and began to gesticulate with them. "Trust me. You're a bright girl, a very bright girl. You'll get there. Perhaps not here, but there are plenty of universities and many would be delighted to have you, when you're ready. Give yourself time and the right line of research will present itself. You don't need to go rushing around chasing after Internet rumors and conspiracy theories. You're an academic, not a journalist."

He leaned forward and tapped Nina on the knee with the leg of his glasses. She fought the impulse to scream with rage. "Tell you what," he dropped his voice to a conspiratorial whisper. "Let's meet in the new year, shall we? You and I can have a little chat and perhaps I can help you find some research topics that would be of interest to you. I could put some editing your way. You might find that stimulating. Or perhaps you might be able to help me with the book I'm working on."

Matlock got to his feet again and returned to his chair. "In the meantime," he said, sitting down heavily, "I am afraid I shall have to deny your request for funding. I do hope you will have a happy Christmas." He uncapped his fountain pen and drew a pile of papers toward him. Years of being a student had trained her to interpret this kind of professorial body language. It was an unmistakable dismissal. She got to her feet.

Then, just as she laid her hand on the door handle, she turned around. "Professor Matlock," she said. "May I ask—if you had discovered evidence of the ice station and it had been stolen, would you have been denied the funding?"

Matlock stared at her over the top of his glasses, unaccustomed to being addressed by someone he had dismissed. "If I had discovered it, Dr. Gould, I would have been seeking funding as an established academic with three decades' worth of reputation behind me, not as someone who has only just finished her doctorate. It makes a great deal of difference, as you may someday find out." He looked down again. "And believe me, I have access to funding streams far superior to this."

"Then you think that making important discoveries should be left to academics at the end of their careers, not the beginning?" Nina was aware of the harsh tone in her voice, but she was beyond the point where she could do anything to control it.

Matlock looked up again, and this time his eyes were steely. "Dr. Gould." His voice was smoothly menacing. "I have given you my decision. Unless you wish to become an academic at the end of her career before you have even got started, I would advise you to leave my office. Now."

With a white-knuckle grip, Nina turned the handle. She

forced herself to smile sweetly and thank Professor Matlock
as she walked out of the room.

"Oh, and Nina?" he called after her, "Let's have that chat
after the new year!"

By the time she got out of the building and onto the street,
Nina was shaking with rage. She had known all along that
the funding application was a long shot, but Matlock had not
just rejected her. He had patronized her. He had humiliated
her. He had made it clear yet again that the only way to rise
within his department was to suck up to him.

She walked through George Square Gardens, trying to let
the icy beauty of the place calm her down. When that did not
work, she found herself a quiet corner and smoked two
cigarettes in quick succession. Then she pulled out her phone
and rang Sam's number.

"Hello?"

"Sam, it's Nina. Look, the funding interview . . . it didn't
go well."

"Ah, well," Sam did not sound disappointed. If anything,
he sounded relieved. "Never mind. Other things will come
up."

"Mmm." Nina refused to be comforted. "The thing is, I've

got this stupid benefactors' ball to go to tonight. The entire department's going to be there, and by this evening they'll all know about my application and the head of my department will be taking the piss behind my back. I really can't face it."

"So blow it off."

"I can't. I'm crap enough at networking as it is. If I don't turn up it'll look really bad, especially after today. Come with me?"

Sam snorted. "Well, you've really sold it to me!"

"I know," Nina groaned. "Sorry . . . I wouldn't ask, but the invitation is a plus one and I'd feel a lot better about going if I had someone I got on with there. There'll be free food. And lots of free drink."

She was sure that she could hear Sam's shrug over the phone. "Well, if there's free drink . . ." Sam said. "Go on then. Where is it? Do I have to dress up?"

"Old College," Nina grinned. "Black tie. Do you have a suit?"

"Somewhere."

"Dig it out, then. I'll meet you in Dagda about half past seven."

CHAPTER 7

SAM LINGERED BY the bookshelves in the Playfair Library, clutching his champagne glass as if it were a shield. From time to time, eager young research fellows would mistake him for someone important and attempt to strike up a conversation, at which point Sam would develop an instant fascination with the books that lined the alcoves.

The sweeping central aisle had been designated as a dance floor, where Nina was allowing the head of the classics department to waltz with her while the string quartet played. Sam had no intention of being dragged out to dance, so he identified the optimum position for accosting the waiters who wove in and out of the shelves proffering drink and canapés, and remained there.

Nina scrubs up well, Sam thought, watching her swirling gracefully in the arms of the elderly academic. Her dark-red cocktail dress flowed as she moved, and she danced well. Sam found himself wondering about her. We've never really talked about anything other than the ice station stuff, he realized. I don't even know how old she is. Early thirties, I'd guess. I wonder what she's done with her life, other than have an affair with a married man?

He glanced down at his own attire. It wasn't full black tie—Sam had never owned a tuxedo and never intended to—but it was a suit rather than a pair of jeans. His shirt was ironed and he had managed to borrow a black bow tie from Paddy. He was clean-shaven for the first time in a long time, and he knew himself to look passable.

"Ugh, I hate dancing." Nina appeared at Sam's side, two fresh glasses of champagne in her hands. "Schmoozing is horrible enough at the best of times, when all you have to do is stand around and chat. But all the pawing . . . ugh."

"But you dance so well," Sam teased. "From what I could see, your footwork is much better than your conversation."

"Shut up or I'll tell them you're a gatecrasher and they'll make you pay for your booze," Nina shot back. "Oh, god, he's coming over—quick, pretend we're in the middle of a really intense conversation."

"What? Who is it?" Sam scanned the room and spotted a tall, thin man striding purposefully toward them. "Who's he?"

"Dave Purdue," hissed Nina. "He's one of the benefactors. At last year's ball he backed me into a corner and tried to get me to go home with him. I really don't want a repeat performance."

Sam did his best to look as if he and Nina were having a deep and meaningful discussion, but he found that his mind had gone completely blank. He began talking at random about the library, the Old College, the construction of South Bridge, anything he could dredge up from the depths of his memory. Nina hung on his every word, doing a good impression of being fascinated.

It did not work. "Nina!" Dave Purdue cried out as he approached. "Lovely to see you again!" Ignoring Sam completely, he took Nina's hand and pressed it to his lips.

"Hello, Dave," Nina said with a strangled smile. "Good to see you too." She detached her hand as subtly as she could and wrapped it around Sam's arm. "Have you met Sam Cleave?" she asked. "He's . . ." Nina's sentence ground to a halt as she realized that she and Sam had not prepared for this eventuality. Sam was tempted to help her out, but far more interested in finding out what she would say unprompted. "He's here with me," she finished lamely.

Dave Purdue peered at Sam with quizzical detachment. "Is he your lover?" he asked Nina.

"What? No!" Nina was taken aback. "He's a friend, that's

all."

"Good," said Purdue. He appeared to consider the matter closed. "Did you say Sam Cleave?" he asked. "Of the Edinburgh Post?"

"That's me," Sam said. Might as well work the advantages while I still have them.

"How fortunate. I was hoping to meet you in the very near future." Purdue registered Sam's bemused expression. "Your paper's editor was in touch with me recently asking for an interview, since I have recently made Edinburgh my permanent home and he seemed to consider this noteworthy. I have yet to agree or disagree, but I had promised myself that I would allow it on the condition that you were the one to write about me. Will you do it?"

Sam was taken aback. "Thanks," he said, "but it's not really my decision to make. If the editor's been in touch, he probably has someone in mind. I just go where I'm sent."

"Don't spin me a line, Mr. Cleave," Purdue fixed Sam with a hard stare. "Bullshit is beneath you. I am well aware that you have a great deal of leeway at the Post. It's a piffling little paper and they know they are lucky to have you. If you want to profile me, and I want to be profiled by you, I doubt they will stand on procedure. Now will you do it?"

Sam shrugged. He was not sure whether he found this stranger's directness refreshing or irritating. Judging by the look on Nina's face, which she was trying and failing to conceal, she found him irritating. "Go on then," said Sam. "I might as well."

"Hmm. Good." Purdue gave a small, contented nod, then demanded that Nina join him on the dance floor. With a despairing look at Sam, she complied.

Sam had expected that Purdue would eventually leave them alone and choose to mingle with the other guests, but he was wrong. Purdue attached himself firmly to Sam and Nina and refused to be separated from them. Nina was clearly feeling the pressure of having to be nice to the man with all the money, and while Sam felt a little sorry for her he also had to admire Purdue's tenacity. He ignored any subtle hints about circulating and stuck close to Nina. Any suggestion that Sam and Nina might be planning to leave together went straight over his head, or at least appeared to.

Purdue's presence had a couple of major benefits, though. First, it kept anyone else from trying to engage Sam in conversation and absolved him and Nina of the need for any further socializing. Second, Purdue was clearly another heavy drinker. No champagne tray was allowed to pass without new glasses being collected, and Sam found himself beginning to get a little dizzy. Whisky he could handle, but his system was not use to champagne. He scrutinized Nina in case she needed help, but despite her petite stature she was holding her drink better than Sam was. Perhaps if you have to go to a lot of these things you build up a tolerance, Sam speculated. Either that or Nina just happened to be remarkably hardheaded.

Several glasses and increasingly clumsy dances later, Purdue suddenly announced that he wanted to go home.

"Are you sure?" Nina asked. "I know the dean of faculty was particularly hoping to speak to you and I don't think he's had a chance to catch you yet."

Purdue glared over at the dean. "Nonsense," he said. "If he needs to contact me, he can email me. I've had enough of crushes for tonight." He reached for his mobile phone. The device he pulled out looked the way a Smartphone might be expected to look in fifty years. It was smart and shiny, nearly paper thin. Purdue held it delicately in his hand and spoke into it. "Call driver," he said, then looked up. "There. We will be on our way shortly." A brief moment later it beeped in confirmation that Purdue's driver was indeed on the way to collect him.

"Now," he said, draping one arm around Nina. "All I need to make tonight perfect is for you to join me for a nightcap. Don't worry. I shall have my driver drop you off at home afterward."

Sam hurried forward, certain that Nina's look of apprehension was not motivated by concern about travel arrangements. He laid a hand on Purdue's arm. "Sorry, Mr. Purdue," he said gently. "But I promised Nina that I would see her home. I really can't let you . . ."

"Nonsense." Purdue's look of annoyance gave him the air of a discontented heron. "She will be perfectly safe with me. I shall make sure that she gets home in one—"

"Excuse me," Nina piped up. "I'm quite capable of seeing myself home. Thanks, Mr. Purdue, but I'm really not looking for anyone to go home with. Thanks all the same." She disengaged herself from Purdue's hold, but he caught her by the wrist.

"Forgive me, Nina," he said. "I believe you have the wrong impression. I am not asking you to join me for a nightcap because I hope that you'll sleep with me, although I would be delighted if you would. No, I am asking you because there is something I need to discuss with you and do not wish to do so here, surrounded by prying eyes and ears." Sam thought he detected a sidelong glance from Purdue.

"What is it you need to discuss?" Nina asked suspiciously.

"Your Antarctic expedition."

Nina gaped at Purdue. Sam caught himself doing the same. How does he know about it? he wondered.

"Now if you will come with me, I can discuss it with you."

Nina was torn. On the one hand, she clearly did not want to go with Purdue and find herself at a disadvantage, stuck in a strange place with a man who had been making his intentions clear all evening. On the other, she did not want to reject the possibility of help. As subtly as she could, she gave Sam a nudge.

"What? Oh, errr—yes." Sam stuttered. "Look, Mr. Purdue, I really did promise Nina that I'd get her home safely, so maybe—"

Purdue cut him off. "As the lady herself has said, she is more than capable of looking after herself. However, since you feel so vehemently about protecting her, why don't you come too? If you're going to write about me you might as well see my new place, and my driver can just as easily take two of you home."

So Sam and Nina found themselves in the back of Purdue's 4x4. "Less stylish than a limousine, I know," he said, as the driver moved aside to let Purdue climb into the front and take the wheel. "But you'll see why I prefer this when we get to my place. Especially if it keeps snowing."

Sure enough, a thin layer of snow had settled over the Old

Town while they had been at the ball. The snow was intermittent, taking the form of occasional swirls rather than anything heavier, but Sam guessed from Purdue's words that they would be going out of town. Even on the cobbles of the city center, the four-wheel drive was proving its worth. Sam had never traveled in such a comfortable vehicle.

They wound through the city streets, sparkling with fairy lights as the tourists poured in for Christmas, then out through the quiet suburbs. Eventually they sped out of the city entirely, tearing along the main road toward the Forth Road bridge. I'm hardly ever out this way, Sam thought, but that's twice this month. This was the route he and DCI Smith had taken on their journey out to the retirement home. Only at the end of their journey did the 4x4 turn in a different direction, heading off the main road and onto a series of twisting dirt tracks.

"This isn't the actual road up to the house, of course," Purdue called back over his shoulder. "But it's by far my preferred route. I do hope you're both properly strapped in back there."

As the car swung gut-churningly off the main road, Sam noticed a light coming from behind them. He craned his neck to look behind and saw another 4x4 hot on their heels. "Is that other car meant to be following us?"

Purdue stared at his rearview mirror for a moment. "Yes,"

he said. "That's Blomstein. My bodyguard. Discreet, isn't he?"

"Has he been around all evening?" Nina asked. "I didn't notice a bodyguard at the ball."

"I asked him to keep his distance. He's rather imposing, and I didn't want you to think that you had no choice about accompanying me here."

Despite the car's excellent suspension, Sam and Nina were bounced about until their teeth rattled as Purdue raced along the dirt track. Ditches and potholes only encouraged him to go faster. "This is why I love private roads!" he yelled. "Welcome to Wrichtishousis!"

They rounded one last bend at high speed, then screeched to a halt before an impressively grand house. Sam guessed that there were about fifty windows on the front side of the central building alone. Other buildings sprawled out to the sides, but he could only guess at their function. Stables, perhaps? Servants' quarters?

He and Nina climbed out onto the gravel while Purdue tossed the keys to his driver and instructed him to come back when called to take the guests home. The driver nodded and took off again, steering the 4x4 around one of the adjoining buildings and out of sight. Blomstein, the bodyguard, simply swung his car into place in the driveway and left it there. As he climbed out Sam and Nina could see what Purdue had meant about Blomstein's presence making people feel they had no choice but to do as Purdue wanted. He was a tall, stocky man with scornful eyes, and his nose and cheekbones had clearly been broken several times. His jacket flapped in the wind as he stepped out of the car, giving them a brief glimpse of the gun in the holster at his hip.

"This way!" Purdue called, showing Sam and Nina into an imposing hallway. Staircases swept up the walls on either side, supported by elegant white marble pillars. Thick red carpet lined the floors. "The tour would take far too long," said Purdue, "so you will have to come back for that. For now, let's go to the conservatory."

Both Sam and Nina had pictured a small glass structure when Purdue mentioned his conservatory, but their expectations were far too small. After cutting through several large rooms containing strange, oversized sculptures, lavish modern furnishings, and discreetly concealed technology, they arrived in Purdue's library. "It's up here," he said, sliding open a hidden door to reveal a spiral staircase. They followed him up.

Purdue's conservatory contained nothing but the tiniest of plants. A painstakingly cultivated collection of bonsai trees was lined up against the back wall. The rest of the room was given over to large, luxurious couches, all arranged to face the windows. Even for a cynic like Sam, the view was breathtaking. South Queensferry was completely obscured by the woods surrounding Wrichtishousis, and beyond that lay the vast expanse of the River Forth, inky black beneath the clear night sky. Beyond that, the hills of Fife, impossibly white with snow. All three stood quietly, looking out at the panorama. Their silence had the muffled quality that only a snowy night can provide.

It was Purdue who eventually broke the silence. "I am glad that you seem to enjoy the winter scene, Nina," he said. "You'll be seeing plenty of it in Antarctica."

"What?" Nina whirled around and stared at him. "What are you talking about?"

"Have you changed your mind? Do you not still want to go? I believe you did earlier today."

Nina stormed across the room and slammed her fists into a sofa cushion. "That bastard!" she snarled. "It was Matlock, wasn't it? I bet he just couldn't wait to tell anyone who would listen about my stupid application."

Purdue crossed calmly to a section of wall and pushed it to reveal a well-stocked drink cabinet. "Professor Matlock did mention your application to me," he said. "But I have other sources of information. Now let me guess . . . a whisky for you, Mr. Cleave? Lagavulin? And Nina, for you . . ."

"Whisky," she said, "straight. But if it wasn't Matlock who mentioned Antarctica to you, who was it?"

"The important thing is not where my information comes from, but the fact that I have it. You are seeking a lost Nazi ice station. I find these things fascinating. I have never been to Antarctica, and for a man such as me this is a most serious omission. I have done most things, you know. I've leaped out of planes, I have climbed mountains, and I have taken submarines to the deepest parts of the oceans. I have a place reserved on the first commercial spaceflight. I've designed nano-electronics and software that you both use daily, though you don't realize it. I have made myself extremely rich. And yet I have never been to Antarctica. So I would like to join your expedition." For the first time, Purdue began to look less like a mechanized heron and more like a human being. In fact, he was beginning to remind Sam of a toddler becoming overexcited.

"Mr. Purdue," Nina said softly, "I wish I could help, but there is no expedition. My application for funding was turned down. Besides, I wasn't in charge of it. It was being led by Jefferson Daniels and the lead academic was Fatima al-Fayed."

"I am aware of all this, Nina," Purdue replied, settling himself on one of the couches with his whisky. "And I know that you are a friend of Dr. al-Fayed. So I have a proposition for you. If you can persuade Dr. al-Fayed to allow you, me, and a few carefully selected companions to join the expedition, I will meet the cost of the whole thing."

Nina stared at him. "Have I had too much to drink?" she wondered aloud. "No, scratch that—I know I've had too much. You're seriously offering to pay for the expedition on the condition that you can bring a couple of people along?" Purdue nodded. "Well," said Nina, "I'll have to think this through. This really isn't a decision I can make after quite a lot of champagne. And I'll have to ask Fatima. I'm sure she'll appreciate the offer to pay, but I don't know how she'll feel about having a group of tourists in tow."

Purdue sipped his drink, a contented smile playing around his lips. "Oh, I'm quite sure that when she considers the sum involved she will find it in her heart to accommodate us." He turned to Sam, who was trying not to doze off on the comfortable couch. "And you, Mr. Cleave—will you join me?"

"What, in Antarctica?" Sam laughed. "I can just see me thriving there. I'd get eaten by a polar bear or a penguin or whichever it is that they have there."

"I promise that you won't be eaten by penguins," Purdue said solemnly, "and there are no polar bears. We will need someone to document our adventures, and I feel in my gut that you would be just the man to do it, Mr. Cleave."

Sam was quiet for a moment. He rolled his head back to look at his surroundings. I'm sitting in a billionaire's pad, watching snow fall on the Forth and talking about a wee trip to Antarctica, he thought. A trip with this fucking weird billionaire, Nina, and a marine biologist or virologist or horologist or whatever she is. How the fuck is this my life?

"What the hell," Sam said. "Yeah, I'll come."

CHAPTER 8

"MR. CLEAVE?"

Sam felt a gentle pressure on his shoulder as the young woman shook him back to consciousness. He turned his head on the pillow, rubbed the matter from his eyes and squinted at her, trying to wake up enough to focus on her glossy blonde hair and sweet, regular features. He had caught a glimpse of her just as he had drifted off to sleep and cursed his brain for letting him think for a moment that it was Patricia.

"We're just starting our descent into Ushuaia, Mr. Cleave," she said softly. "Time to sit up and fasten your seatbelt."

"Thanks." As Sam spoke he noticed how dry his mouth was. "Could I have another whisky?"

"It's 7:00 am local time, Mr. Cleave," the stewardess pointed out, the merest hint of disapproval in her voice.

"That makes it 10:00 am Scottish time. Perfectly acceptable

time for whisky in my culture."

The young woman nodded, confirmed his order and moved away. Somewhere behind him, Sam heard her waking Nina. He dragged himself into an upright position and fumbled with the seatbelt until it clunked into place around his waist. Beyond the window he could see a vast expanse of cloud tinted pink by the early morning sun. Objectively he knew that it was beautiful, but after more than twenty hours on the plane he had lost his ability to be impressed by clouds.

"Good morning, good morning!" Dave Purdue glided into the cabin, clearly firing on all cylinders. Sam wondered whether the man ever slept. "I hope you both slept well? Not long to go now! I'm sorry you won't get a chance to explore Ushuaia, but I've had a message to say that the others have all arrived safely and are waiting for us on the boat. We had best not keep them waiting."

As Purdue settled into one of the plush plane seats and proceeded to talk about his previous experiences of visiting Ushuaia, Sam noticed that he did not seem to be bound by the same rules as his guests regarding seatbelts. Even Ziv Blomstein, Purdue's bodyguard, was safely strapped in at the far end of the cabin, but Purdue himself was unfettered. Must be an unrewarding task, being bodyguard to a hardcore thrill-seeker, Sam thought. Yet if Blomstein found his job a hardship, he did not show it. He was completely inscrutable and almost always silent, a tall, taciturn figure usually found at Purdue's shoulder.

The stewardess reappeared with Sam's whisky along with coffee for Nina and Purdue. As they drank and half-listened to Purdue, both Sam and Nina watched the changing view from their windows as the plane dipped below the clouds and they caught their first glimpse of the world's southernmost city. From their vantage point it looked like a small handful of colorful buildings arranged haphazardly on a fragmented piece of land, surrounded by snow-capped mountains. The airport's landing strip jutted out into the ocean, giving Sam the unpleasant feeling that the plane was going to drop straight into the freezing water. His heart rate did not return to normal until they were all off the plane and speeding away from the airport in a hired car, destined for the port in the center of town.

"Enjoying yourself?" Sam asked Nina. "If you keep pressing your nose against the window like that it'll stick."

Nina didn't even glance at him. She was determined not to miss a thing. "This place is amazing," she said. "Just look at it! This is the End of the Earth, the Land of Fire—Darwin sailed from here, and there use to be a penal colony that was considered to be the most remote in the world. Can you imagine being sent here to live out the rest of your days? It's so bleak, but it's so beautiful. I hope we get to spend a little more time here on the journey home."

For a moment Sam remembered when he had experienced that same romantic sense of wonder. There had been a time when he had been unable to believe his luck at having a job that took him to all sorts of interesting places. In fact, he had always felt that way, even when he had simply been discovering new areas of London. Investigative journalism had spoken to the adventurer in Sam—but now, that adventurer was gone. Now all that remained was an apathetic, broken man who would rather be dragged along on some hare-brained Antarctic caper than spend Christmas with his sister.

After such a long flight on Purdue's luxurious private jet and a short trip in the hired limousine, the ship that they boarded was something of an anticlimax. It was a sturdy vessel, clearly intended for work and harsh conditions rather than for pleasure cruises. It looked like an overgrown fishing boat covered in tarnished blue paint, with its name picked out in white on the prow. Unfortunately, since the name was in Russian, Sam could not decipher it.

"What's this thing called?" he asked Purdue, as they climbed the metal steps to the deck.

" No idea" Purdue replied. "I don't speak Russian! Ask Alexandr, he'll know—he's the one who hired it."

"Alexandr?"

"Yes!" Purdue reached the top of the stairs and stepped aboard, turning back to face Sam and Nina. "Here he is. Alexandr Arichenkov—this expedition's fearless leader!"

"May the gods help you all," Alexandr smirked, then lunged forward and grasped Purdue's hand, shaking it firmly. He did the same to Nina, then to Sam. At once Sam noticed the familiar tang of spirits on the man's breath. He knew that he ought to find that alarming, but instead he found himself oddly comforted. The Russian man was wiry, a little on the short side, with pale blue eyes and a deep scar across his left cheek. He turned to Purdue, flipped him a mock salute and clicked his heels together. "Ready when you are, sir!"

Purdue clapped his hands, his long face alight with schoolboy glee. "Then let's get going at once! The sooner we leave, the sooner we'll be there! Sam, Nina, come with me." He strode off toward the deckhouse while Alexandr turned away and began yelling orders at the crew.

Sam and Nina hurried along in Purdue's wake, following him into the deckhouse and through its corridors. Soon Purdue flung open a set of double doors and led them into a large room overlooking the prow of the ship. It had clearly been decked out to function as an observation lounge, similar to the one Purdue had at Wrichtishousis, but the overstuffed couches and slick bar setup were at odds with the utilitarian vessel. It seemed strange, Sam thought, to smell expensive spirits and furniture polish mixing with engine oil and salty air. Still, he did not object—there would be plenty of discomfort ahead of them, he knew, so best to make the most of these luxuries while they were still available.

"What the hell is he doing here?" Nina hissed. Sam dragged his attention away from the bar and followed her line of vision over to one end of the vast window. Two men were standing together, both dressed in expensively casual winter clothes. One had white hair, worn slightly long, with a short, neatly trimmed moustache and beard. The other had unnaturally dark hair and craggy features that had clearly improved with age. Sam vaguely recognized them both.

"What's who doing?" Sam whispered back, but before Nina could answer they were interrupted by a tall Arabian woman who rushed over to them and grabbed Nina in a tight hug.

"It's so great to see you!" The woman embracing Nina had a slight American accent, Sam noticed. "It's been way too long!"

"I know," Nina said, not letting go of her friend. "It shouldn't have taken an Antarctic exhibition for us to have a proper catch-up. Thanks for letting us come along, Fatima— though I'm sorry that you seem to have got stuck with a few extra guests along the way."

Fatima grimaced as she released Nina and the two of them glared over at the men by the window. "It's ok," Fatima said. "I'm sure it'll be fine. It's tough terrain, but I've visited worse. Between me and Jefferson we should be able to keep you all straight. I'm just a little nervous about doing this with such a big group, especially when so many of you haven't been to Antarctica before. This Purdue guy does know that it's not a skiing vacation, right?"

"Who knows?" said Nina. "I've been afraid to ask. I've been trying not to think too much about him and his motives for offering to pay for all this."

Fatima snorted derisively. "His motives? Yeah, he made those pretty clear when he told me what the deal was. It's partly the billionaire equivalent of hiring a stretch limo to pick you up for prom, and partly him wanting to be Indiana Jones. He'd like to get into your panties and he thinks that buying you the Antarctic trip that you want is the way to do it. And he wants to be here so he can have an adventure and you can swoon into his arms or some shit. I don't know. No one ever spends that much money trying to get me into bed. The most I ever got from Evan was a steak dinner and a four-star hotel, and I thought I was doing well!" She nodded toward Sam. "Is this the journalist? Purdue said there'd be one."

Nina swiftly introduced Sam to Fatima al-Fayed, telling him how they had once been roommates during their undergraduate years and had stayed friends even though they now lived on different continents. Sam listened to Nina's description of him with a strange sense of detachment. He understood the words—"prize-winning investigative journalist"—but did not feel as if they really applied to him. There was no mention of his drinking, his disorganization, or his inability to run his life. He knew that Nina was aware of these things. She was too smart to have missed them. Yet here she was, introducing him as if he was a functioning human being.

Suddenly Sam realized that Fatima was asking him a question. He shook off his self-critical reverie and did his best to pay attention.

"I asked why you're here," Fatima repeated herself. "Are you writing something for your newspaper or what?"

"I wish I knew," Sam said. "I know it sounds crazy, but Purdue wasn't exactly clear about why he wants me here. Said it was 'to chronicle his adventures,' so I'm guessing it's going to be for a memoir or something. Either that or it's the most extreme profile ever done for a local paper . . . Mind you, for the amount of money he's paying, I'll do pretty much anything he asks!"

"Well, that makes two of us, at least," Fatima sighed. "He's covering pretty much all of this trip and sprung for a serious upgrade to our equipment, so if he wants it to be a history field trip as well as a virology expedition, then that's what it is."

"You don't sound too happy about it," Sam observed.

"Would you be?" Fatima cast a glance around the room. "You two will be ok, and Jefferson knows how to handle himself. Matlock's pretty fit and at least he's done a couple of mountain climbs. And I guess Purdue's bodyguard isn't going to let him get into too much trouble. Even the change of guides shouldn't be too much of an issue. It's the old guy I'm really worried about." She pointed to a man Sam had not spotted before, sitting alone on one of the couches with a glass of whisky in his hand. He looked frail, pensive, and far too old to be taking his first Antarctic trip.

"He does seem like a strange addition to the expedition," Nina agreed. "Did Purdue bring him aboard?"

"Yes," said Fatima, "but that's all I know—I don't even know the guy's name yet. I tried to talk to him just before you guys arrived, but he just sat there staring at his drink and wouldn't say a word to me. It was kind of weird. I guess he's probably just nervous. He'll loosen up during the trip, I bet. Maybe you can get him talking—it'll beat making small talk with your boss, right?"

As Nina made a small noise of disgust, the pieces fell into

place for Sam. Of course, he realized. Matlock. The guy with the white hair. He works at the university, that's why I know his face. But he's the guy who turned Nina down and told her the ice station is a fairy tale? Weird.

Then Purdue strolled over, accompanied by a waiter carrying a tray of drinks, and Sam stopped thinking about the strange old man and the presence of Nina's boss. All his energy was required for ignoring Purdue's flirtations with Nina and Fatima—and, of course, for drinking. He took his champagne and stood alone by the window, tuning out the chatter and watching the horizon as the ship plowed on into the strange half-light that passed for night.

CHAPTER 9

URING THEIR FIRST few days aboard the ship, Sam saw very little of the other members of the expedition. The icebreaker may have been excellent for breaking through ice, but its hull was not designed for the choppy seas they encountered.

As the ship pitched and heaved on the rolling waves, Sam found his stomach doing the same. He had only lasted a few hours at the drinks gathering on the first night before the seas had become rough and sent him staggering toward his cabin. Since then he had not left it.

"Are you still malingering?" Nina's voice was loud and clear on the other side of the door as she knocked.

Sam shifted on his narrow bed and squinted blearily at his alarm clock. 10:30. Far too early to be awake unless it was for breakfast, drink, or a cigarette, and he knew he would not be able to handle any of the three.

"Yes, I am," he called back. "Go away."

The door swung open and Nina stepped in, looking trim and elegant in a snowsuit. Her pale face was flushed slightly pink with the cold, and the faint smell of a recently-smoked cigarette hung around her. The aroma made Sam's nostrils tingle with longing. It had been two days since his last cigarette. He had been able to stay vertical for long enough to attempt to smoke one in the bathroom in his cabin, but all that had got him was an alarm going off and a crew member lecturing him in Russian and confiscating the packet. The combination of sea sickness and withdrawal was hitting him hard.

"You look like shit," Nina said, eyeing Sam distastefully. "Are you feeling any better? Want me to get someone to bring you some food?"

"No," Sam groaned. "No food. I'll puke."

"Here." Nina pulled a small thermos flask from the deep pocket of her suit, unscrewed the cap and filled it with a pungent amber liquid. "Ginger tea. It'll settle your stomach."

Sam sniffed it suspiciously. It smelled warm and comforting, but after three days of illness he was in no mood to be comforted. "That's not proper tea," he grumbled. "I don't need any herbal nonsense, I just need flat seas. Or preferably land."

The look on Nina's face was less than sympathetic. "Well,

tough luck," she said. "We won't reach land for another few days, and Alexandr doesn't think the seas are going to calm down any time soon. So you can either lie here and feel sorry for yourself, or you can give this a try." She pushed the cup into his hand. "Come on, Sam. What's the worst that could happen? You puke it up? But on the other hand, if it makes you feel better, you can come and have a smoke with me. Come on. Drink up. There may be nicotine at the other end of the tunnel."

Sam took a small, grudging sip of the ginger tea. It tasted surprisingly good. He took another. With every mouthful he felt a tiny bit less nauseated. It's psychosomatic, he told himself. Apparently I'm more attached to the old nicotine than I thought. By the time he had finished the contents of the little cup, his stomach had settled sufficiently that he could sit up.

"I'll find you something to wear," Nina said, rifling through the small chest of drawers in the corner. "Not that the filthy long johns don't look great on you, but it's much colder now that we're farther out and you're going to need extra layers." Sam looked down at his makeshift sleepwear. At home he always slept in his boxers, assuming he remembered to get undressed, but attempting to do that here had led to him waking up shivering on his first night. He had dug out the ancient thermal underwear that he had had since his youthful (failed) attempt to walk the West Highland Way. After three days of covering his seasick carcass, the thermals were beginning to reek.

Watching Nina pulling garments from the drawers, Sam felt confused. "Have I got someone else's clothes by mistake?" he asked as she flung one thermal layer after another at him. "I didn't pack any of this. Look at it—most of it's designer stuff, I don't own anything like that!"

"You do now." Nina opened the wardrobe and took out a brand new parka. "Purdue kitted us out, remember?" She saw Sam's blank face and rolled her eyes. "Didn't you read any of the emails he sent us? This was part of the deal. When he said he'd pay for everything, he really meant it. You've got a whole new winter wardrobe here, and we're getting close enough now that you're going to need it. I'll be waiting outside when you're ready. Now get a move on, I'm bored out of my skull."

As soon as Sam was dressed, Nina led him toward the stern where she had found a quiet spot where they could smoke without getting underfoot or into trouble. On the way, she slipped into a supply cupboard that she had found and liberated a packet of saltines and couple of bottles of Coca-

Cola. "The other miracle remedies for settling your stomach," she said as she handed a bottle to Sam.

"I thought it was the other way around," Sam said, following her along the narrow corridors. "That you weren't supposed to drink this stuff if you're seasick?"

Nina appeared to consider this for a moment, then twisted the top off her own bottle. "Kill or cure, I suppose," she replied, and took a long swig.

Sam had to admit that the fresh air, the cold, and the cigarette between his lips were doing wonders for his nausea and his state of mind. "So is everyone else laughing at me for being such a big softie?" he asked. "I bet you they're all fine."

"Not in the slightest," Nina said. "That's why I'm so bloody bored. Practically everyone else is seasick to some extent. Even Fatima gets it quite badly, and you'd think that she'd be used to it considering the amount of time she spends on ships. It's really just me, Alexandr, Jefferson Daniels, and that hulking bodyguard of Purdue's who are still on our feet. I've got no one to talk to—or at least, no one I want to. Jefferson's only really interested in talking about how great he and his expeditions are, and the bodyguard doesn't talk at all."

"What about Alexandr?" Sam asked. "I didn't get to speak to him much that first night, but he seemed like he might at least be interesting."

"He's ok," Nina conceded. "But in small doses. He's intense. Besides, he seems to be in charge of the ship as well as the expedition, so when he's not yelling at the crew he's off bickering with Jefferson or Fatima." She blew out a long stream of smoke and watched it drift away from the ship. "It seems they have very different ideas about what the purpose of this little jaunt is. At least that's not our fault—she's got serious scientific stuff in mind, and all Jefferson cares about is photo opportunities and being covered for TIME Magazine or something.

"I think she regrets agreeing to join forces with him even more than she regrets letting Purdue get involved. All she wanted to do was trek out to the middle of nowhere and find out what nasty things are living in the ice, but she couldn't do that without selling her soul to someone with money. This, Mr. Cleave, is the parlous state of academic funding today. Fucking ridiculous."

Sam nodded in sympathy. Life was one long round of selling out to someone or other, and he knew Nina was still smarting a little from Matlock's harsh rejection of her application. "How does Fatima feel about having us along?" he asked.

"She doesn't mind that too much," said Nina. "At least I'm here because I have work to do, not because I'm thrill-seeking or because I want to flash my overly whitened teeth on a magazine cover. But she's not thrilled about having to bump a few of her own people to make room for Purdue and the old guy. I think she's feeling a bit lost in this group, and Purdue's bodyguard is not helping."

Sam could not imagine that Blomstein would ever help anyone to feel at ease. The bodyguard did a great job of being large, silent, and imposing in his sharp suits and yarmulke, and Sam had no trouble believing that he was more than capable of keeping Purdue alive. Why Blomstein should trouble Fatima in particular, however, was a mystery to him. "Is there some history there?" he asked. "Or does she just not like the strong, silent type?"

"I thought you were supposed to be politically engaged, Mr. investigative journalist?" Nina said through a mouthful of saltine. "He's an Israeli Jew. And Fatima . . ."

"Is an Arab?" Sam took a cracker and nibbled it, still wary of incurring his stomach's displeasure. "But I thought she was American?"

Nina shook her head. "She's from Jordan originally. If Blomstein's a decent bodyguard he'll have checked out the other people aboard and he'll know that. Her family immigrated to Canada when she was still quite young, hence the accent. Incidentally, if you tell her you think she's American she'll probably throw you overboard. Assuming Blomstein hasn't already done the same for her. I doubt the two of them will be bonding any time soon. He's already made it pretty clear that he's not happy about being on the same ship with her. Yesterday he had to climb down a ladder that Fatima had just used and he actually stopped, took out a handkerchief and wiped the handrail clean before touching it. Fatima didn't say anything, but I could tell she was furious. Should make for a pretty cozy Hogmanay . . ."

"Do you reckon we'll have made it to land by then?" Sam asked. "I'd really like to start next year on solid ground."

"Alexandr thinks so," Nina said. "He was saying something about seeing in the new year at Novolazarevskaya, so—" She was cut off as a huge wave sent the ship rolling upward and then plunging back down so that a shower of icy salt water sprayed over them both. Nina's first reaction was one of dismay as she realized that her half-smoked cigarette had not only been extinguished but soaked beyond use. Then she saw Sam lurching toward the rail and heaving his upper body over it as he spewed the barely-digested crackers into the sea. She went over to join him and stood at arm's length, giving his shoulder an encouraging pat—or at least as encouraging as she could manage. "Not to worry," she said with forced brightness. "We'll be back on land soon. Or ice, at least. But it'll feel solid enough, one way or the other. Come on. Let's get you back to your cabin. At this rate I doubt you'll be in a fit state to celebrate anything by New Year's Eve."

Sam had never been so grateful to feel solid ground under his feet, and to judge by their faces, neither had many of the others. Alexandr stood at the head of the group, watching with amusement as they disembarked and, one by one, nearly collapsed as their legs tried to adjust to being back on land. Even Purdue, dressed in an understated but stylish snowsuit and clutching a walking pole to help him balance, had to cling to Blomstein to remain upright. Fortunately the bodyguard seemed as unperturbed by the thick ice as he was by everything else, and with the assistance of a pair of hefty crampons he moved steadily across the glassy surface. Three small hovercrafts were waiting to collect the party.

"Welcome to Antarctica!" Alexandr called, striding steadily across the ice as the others scrabbled to their feet and adjusted their backpacks. "You may perhaps be finding it a little chilly here, yes? Well, here the lowest temperature ever was recorded—minus 89.2 degrees Celsius, so you will want to stay wrapped up in the lovely snowsuits provided by Mr. Purdue. We will not be staying here long, just enough time to load the hovercrafts and then be on our way to our destination because Mr. Purdue has requested that we press on. First a refueling stop at Novolazarevskaya, the most isolated research station in the Antarctic—as I am sure you will imagine, that this is saying something! It is early yet, so we might make good time and begin the new year at Neumayer Station IV. You shall have the honor of being the first party to visit the new station."

He was interrupted by a muffled cry as Sam lost his footing and landed hard on his backside on the packed ice, yelling into the thick hood of his parka, which was pulled tight to protect his face. "You have not got your land legs back yet, Mr. Cleave?" Alexandr inquired politely. "Think yourself lucky that you arrived by icebreaker—the alternative would have been the airstrip at Novo, but it is made of solid ice. If you are finding it difficult to retain your balance on your feet, imagine how nerve-wracking it would be attempting to balance a whole plane, knowing that the tiniest error on your part would bring the whole thing crashing to an explosive end! Now, the hovercrafts are wasting fuel while we talk, so we must get ourselves aboard and leave."

CHAPTER 10

THE EXPEDITION PARTY had been divided into groups of three for the trip, because each vehicle had space for one pilot and three passengers. Apparently the groups had been decided in advance by Alexandr, who was traveling with Nina and Fatima. Dave Purdue, accompanied as always by Blomstein, was sharing his transport with the mysterious white-haired old man, leaving Sam to travel with Jefferson Daniels and Professor Matlock.

Sam shot Nina a despairing glance as he climbed into the hovercraft. Nina tried to give him a sympathetic look in response, but all she could manage was a smirk as she tried not to laugh at the thought of Sam stuck between Daniels and Matlock for the duration of the ride. She could not imagine that he would enjoy their conversation.

Alexandr climbed into the front seat, next to the pilot.

Apparently they knew each other from previous expeditions, and they settled down and started chatting in Russian. Nina scrambled into the back, then Fatima followed her in and the door slid shut behind them and locked with a clunk.

"I'm glad you're in with me," Fatima said, buckling her safety belt. "I thought for sure that you'd be sharing with Purdue. What's the deal with him, anyway? I mean, I know he's trying to impress you and all, but . . . is it working? Do you like him?"

Nina sighed. "Ugh, it's a hell of a way to get what I want, isn't it? I know it seems really sleazy, but he's not all that bad. He's always been upfront about the fact that he wants to get me into bed, but he's been equally clear that he doesn't expect sex in exchange for funding this trip. He's always been disarmingly straightforward—I never told you about the first time I met him, did I?"

"You mentioned him, I remember. Wasn't it at some college thing?"

"That's right. It was last year's benefactors' ball. You know what I think of those. Anyway, I got chatting to him for a while and he was getting all excited about some kind of microscopic medical camera he'd been working on. I thought he was just another boring rich guy, albeit a slightly younger model than the rest. You know what it's like, usually they just ramble at you for a while and eye you up, but they never have the nerve to say or do anything. Well, he did. I had just about zoned out when he told me he had a suite at the Balmoral and wanted to know whether I would be interested in joining him there, since I seemed to be, and I quote, 'the perfect encapsulation of intellectual and erotic fascination.' No, seriously, that's exactly what he said! Stop laughing!"

Fatima could not help herself. She shoved her gloved hand against her mouth and tried to stifle the giggles, but her eyes were screwed shut and her shoulders were shaking. Nina smiled. She had fond memories of these giggle fits. Fatima felt everything very deeply, and when something amused her, it kept her entertained for ages. Hours, sometimes.

She remembered a particularly fraught time during finals fortnight when she and Fatima had been revising into the early hours. Having reached a point where even black coffee wasn't keeping them alert any more, they had each taken a handful of caffeine pills. Far from aiding their revision, the intense caffeine hit had sent both of them spinning off into such a wired, jittery state that neither of them had got any further work done. They had, however, spent the rest of the night laughing hysterically at a number of inconsequential things, while chain-smoking in an attempt to calm themselves again.

At length, Fatima's hilarity subsided and she let out a long sigh and settled back into her seat. "I needed that," she said.

"I'm getting too old for all this expedition stuff, Nina."

"Bollocks. You're thirty-five."

"Yeah, but you know what I mean. I feel too old. I've done seven trips out here in the past nine years, and I've overwintered twice. That's a lot of time to spend in the Antarctic. I'm beginning to think that maybe it's time for me to hang up my cleats and maybe spend a whole year in one place. I think I'd like to work in a lab that's not in the middle of nowhere. Somewhere I could finish work at the end of the day, get in my car and pick up a pizza on the way home, you know? And I could make plans to hang out with my friends in Starbucks instead of on Skype. Wouldn't that be amazing?"

"I suppose," said Nina, picking at the skin around her fingernails. "Although I've got the opposite problem. I kind of envy you being out here, getting to do work that you actually care about. You're actually making a difference to your field. People take you seriously. I'm still spinning my wheels. Honestly, if I have to write one more stupid fucking conference paper on some bullshit topic that no one actually cares about but everyone writes about because it's fashionable . . . I will break something. Or someone.

"I don't mind teaching, but my schedule's so heavy most of the time that it doesn't leave a lot of room for writing anything that's important to me. I can hardly even remember the last time I got to do some proper, in-depth research rather than just rehashing part of my doctoral thesis and smearing it with a thick layer of whatever bullshit theoretical stuff happens to be popular at the time." She tipped her head back and stared at the roof of the hovercraft, watching the black canvas shudder as the vehicle whirred along. "It sucks. I'm actually considering getting out of academia altogether."

"What?" Fatima stared incredulously at Nina. "You can't be serious, Nina. You're good! You know you are! And you've come so far."

Nina laughed. "Have I? I don't know. Remember when we used to talk about how our lives were going to be, and you were going to be off unlocking the secrets of the permafrost and I was going to be writing books that would change the way the world thought about the past? God, I sometimes wonder what happened to those girls. I barely recognize myself these days."

"Everyone feels that way, Nina," Fatima said.

"Do they? Do you?" Nina shook her head. "I don't see why you would. You're actually doing the stuff you said you'd do. You get funding, you publish work that actually makes a meaningful contribution to your field . . . While I, apparently, can't even scrape together one lousy field trip unless some billionaire decides he's got the hots for me and bankrolls the whole thing. I just feel so . . . I don't know.

Undermined, I suppose. I mean, I should be elated, right? We're here! We're in Antarctica!"

She gestured expansively at the whiteness beyond the narrow windows. "This is just the kind of research trip we all dream of, isn't it? The places we'd never have got to go if we'd had different jobs. This is supposed to be the payoff for all the hard work, the crap pay, and the constant neck pain from living behind a laptop screen. Our reward is that we get to make new discoveries and breakthroughs, right? And that when we do, we know it's because we worked so hard and earned the right to be there. Well, that's not how I feel just now. Right at this moment, I feel as if the only reason I'm here is because I've got nice tits, which makes me feel like a huge failure professionally."

"Hey now," Fatima chided. "Don't you talk like that! So you're finding that life isn't working out exactly the way you thought it would when you were young and naïve, so what? Mine isn't either. I was going to be Miss independent, remember? I was going to overwinter every winter because I could deal with the isolation and I didn't need other people in my life. Now look at me! All I want is to get to a point where I can settle down, stabilize my life, marry Evan, and live a happy, boring life. It's just what people do, Nina. There's nothing wrong with it." She glanced out of the window and caught sight of a familiar handful of buildings on the horizon.

"Now lighten up—we're nearly at Novo, and if you're going to stay all whiny I'm going to switch places with Purdue. Ever had sex in a hovercraft?"

"No!"

"Me neither. It probably wouldn't be that great. My first boyfriend's car had a bigger back seat than this. But, you know, you and Purdue could find out what it's like. Totally out of academic interest, right? What was it again? A perfect combination of the erotic and the intellectual? You see? He didn't buy you into this trip just because he's hot for you— he's into your intelligence as well!"

Nina pulled a face as they slowed down and the buzzing of the hovercraft diminished. "Well, that makes it all better," she said. "Thanks, F. You're a real help!"

There are telephones in this building here—" Alexandr gestured at one of the handful of tiny prefabricated structures behind him—"and you may use them while we refuel if you wish. I believe Mr. Purdue has supplied a phone card in each of your packs, and this will be the last opportunity to telephone home before we reach Neumayer, where there is not yet a terrestrial phone connection. The satellite phone is not ideal for chit-chat calls, it is for emergencies only."

Roughly half of the little group shuffled off toward the phones. Fatima disappeared to speak to some of the Novo team members whom she knew already, taking Nina along to introduce her. Purdue collared Alexandr and demanded to be shown the hovercrafts at once, as impatient as a schoolboy. Jefferson Daniels and Professor Matlock, who both had wives and children back home, took the opportunity to seek out the phones, as did the elderly gentleman. For want of anything else to do, Sam tagged along behind them. With every step he took in the thick, fleece-lined boots and unfamiliar cleats, he cursed his decision to join the expedition.

When his turn on the phone arrived, he rang DCI Patrick Smith. There was no one else to call apart from his sister, and he had spoken to her on Christmas Day, just before leaving for the airport. She had been disappointed not to have her brother spend Christmas with her, but he could hear the relief in her voice when he told her that he was joining an expedition to research something he couldn't really talk about. That, she had said, sounded like the old Sam Cleave. A return to form. The first signs of Sam getting over what had happened that day in that warehouse.

Sam was glad that she had taken some comfort in what she had heard rather than worrying about his safety in such hostile terrain, but he had nothing further to say to her at present and he lived in dread of her tendency to put the

toddler on the phone. "Uncle Sam" had little to say that he
thought would be a suitable topic of conversation for a two
year old. He had little to say to Paddy either, but at least he
could check how Bruichladdich was doing.

"Aye, he's fine," Paddy's voice was distant over the crackly
phone line. "Bruich's just fine. Thinks he's on his holidays. I
come home after work and get a big ginger lump sat in my
lap while I have my tea, and he gets a bit of whatever I'm
having. It's a good system."

"That's good," Sam said with a smile. He knew that Smith
would spoil the cat rotten before his return. "Thanks for
looking after him. I'll probably be out of contact until we get
back to Novo, so don't worry if you don't hear from me—I'm
not planning to die out here and stick you with the big ginger
lummox indefinitely. Scratch him behind the ears from me.
I'll be back when I'm back, and in the meantime, Happy New
Year."

"Happy New Year, Sam," said Paddy. "Hope you're having
a good time out there. Stay safe."

Sam stepped out of the rickety booth and braced himself
for another crunchy, slippery trip across the ice to rejoin the
group by the hovercrafts. As he took his first steps he noticed
the old man in the next booth, with the phone pressed to his
ear and a blank expression on his face. Sam paused for a
moment. The man did not appear to be engaged in a

conversation. He did not look as if he was listening to someone on the other end of the phone. He simply looked as if he was not present.

Should I knock on the door? Sam wondered. See if there's anything I can do? He tried to watch surreptitiously, out of the corner of his eye, but it was difficult to be subtle in such an empty place. There was nothing he could pretend to read or be preoccupied by, no reason he could think of for continuing to stand there. Maybe that's just what he's like, Sam thought. Maybe he's talking to someone who just likes to ramble on and he's not really listening. Maybe that's the kind of relationship he's got with his wife, or his kids, or something. Or maybe he's just pretending to be using the phone so that people won't think he's lonely. Kind of like what I was doing, I suppose . . . except without Paddy as a convenient cover. He wouldn't thank me for pointing that out. I should probably leave him be. I've been here long enough that if he wasn't ok, if he needed any help, he'd have said by now.

Sam turned away from the old man in the booth, left the ramshackle building, and picked his way across the ice toward the three waiting hovercrafts.

"And then I told Ran that you can't let these little things get you down, you just have to go for it," Jefferson Daniels was in full flow as the hovercraft sped over the ice, sweeping away the kilometers beneath its thick cushions. "I mean, yeah, of course his family is going to worry about a man his age setting out on that sort of expedition, but they were worried the first time he climbed Kilimanjaro and he was fine. If we all let ourselves be held back by our families, nobody would ever achieve anything!"

Sam leaned his head against the cold windowpane and stared out at the endless ice. He had expected there to be lots of snow in Antarctica, but all he had seen so far was ice— vast, dense sheets of it, all the way to the horizon where it met a slate-grey sky. A little way off he could see one of the other hovercraft buzzing along. He wished he was aboard it, rather than trapped in this confined space with Jefferson Daniels and Frank Matlock.

"That's why I told Paige that we can't stand in Henley's way," Jefferson droned on. "She's sixteen now, and if she's ready to compete we have to let her."

"Quite," Matlock chimed in. "Remind me though, what's her sport again? Skiing, was it?"

"Snowboarding. She was real close to the halfpipe speed record last summer, but then she broke her collarbone and now Paige is worried and thinks we shouldn't let her train any more. But I said to her that the girl's a natural, and if we take that away from her we'll just be mean old mom and dad, and what will it do to her competitive spirit? She's a great kid, and she gets that you have to work hard and push yourself to get ahead. Undermining that right now would be the worst thing we could do."

"Well, indeed. How is Paige, by the way? You must give her my love. I can hardly believe that it's been a year since I saw her last. The memory of her excellent New Year's Eve dinner lives on." Professor Matlock drew a deep sigh. "I think we can say with certainty that this year's celebration will not compare. What's happening here?"

Sam turned his head to look out of the window on the other side of the hovercraft. Following Matlock's line of vision, he saw that one of the other vehicles, the one which had been farthest ahead, was rapidly slowing down. "Looks like they have a problem," Jefferson said, as their own transport began to decelerate.

They came to a halt a short distance away. Partly curious and partly just bored of his companions, Sam wanted to climb out and find out what was going on, but the passenger door did not open. Only the pilot got out, returning some minutes later with Alexandr

"We have what you might call a minor issue," Alexandr announced, pushing his ski goggles up onto his forehead as he climbed into the cramped vehicle. "And we have what you might call a major one. The hovercraft in which Mr. Purdue is traveling is experiencing some slight difficulty with one of its air cushions. This is nothing that I cannot repair, but for that I would require time. This, unfortunately, we do not have. The Neumayer Station has alerted us that we are in the path of a storm, so we must make camp and wait it out before we continue our journey. Gentlemen, if you would be so good as to step outside, we shall erect the Space Station. With any luck, we shall be at Neumayer this time tomorrow." Abruptly, with no time for questions or responses, Alexandr ducked out of the passenger door and set off toward the remaining hovercraft.

Sam, Jefferson, and Matlock glanced at one another. "Best do as he says," Jefferson said. "Last thing we need is to get caught in a storm with no shelter. Antarctic weather gets pretty vicious." For want of a better idea, Sam obediently followed the other two out onto the ice, where Jefferson made a beeline for an orange duffel bag lying on the ground nearby. Sam wondered what was so important about it, but it quickly became clear as Jefferson tugged it open and began to take out canvas and an assortment of poles.

"That's the Space Station?" Sam was incredulous. "How is that going to keep us safe from a snow storm?" He lifted the canvas and rubbed it between his gloved fingers. "I've been to a T in the Park festival in sturdier tents than this."

"I doubt it," Matlock scowled. "Didn't you do any research before coming on this trip, Mr. Cleave? Ah, forgive me, that's a silly question to ask of a journalist."

Jefferson handed Sam a pole. "Here. Link this up with the other ones of the same color. You're looking at the last word in expedition technology, son. These tubes are reinforced scandium. You could drop an avalanche on this sucker and we'd all be safe inside. It's coated with titanium oxide, too, so you're safe from radiation down here where the ozone layer's at its thinnest. Trust me, if we're not going to make it to Neumayer today, there's nowhere I'd rather be than in a Space Station."

Not even the pub? Sam thought. All he needs to do is grin into the camera and let the light flash off his teeth and he'd be the perfect commercial for whoever makes these tents. With clumsy hands he fitted the poles together while Jefferson and Matlock laid out the canvas and prepared the guy ropes. Within a few minutes they had been joined by Alexandr, Nina, and Fatima, and between the six of them they made short work of getting the tent up.

Sam had to concede that it looked a lot more impressive once it was up. The strange apricot color was a little incongruous with the white surroundings, but it was comforting to see something so obviously built by humans in the vast expanse of nothingness. As the wind began to pick up around them, the little group filed gratefully into the tent. It was spacious inside, with more than enough room in the semi-sphere to accommodate everyone's sleeping bags, and although Sam did not relish the prospect of sharing a communal sleeping space with so many near-strangers, he was glad of their body heat as the air temperature inside began to creep upward.

Alexandr had just set up the little Jetboil stove and began to heat some water when Purdue, Blomstein, and the old man arrived. It made sense to Sam that the old man had waited in the hovercraft while the tent was erected, but he thought it was a bit rich that both Purdue and his bodyguard had not come over and helped. Still, any animosity was quickly dispelled by the prospect of food—he was beginning to realize how quickly he was burning off calories in the Antarctic, and it felt like a long time since the PowerBar he had snacked on at the start of the hovercraft journey. He never would have imagined that rehydrated macaroni and cheese could smell so appealing, but as soon as the boiling water hit the sachet of dried food, his mouth began to water and he gripped his spork tightly in anticipation. Alexandr passed the sachets around, followed by steaming metal mugs of tea, and for a while the tent was silent apart from the sounds of titanium cutlery scraping silicon dishes.

"Well, that might not be the fanciest New Year's Eve dinner I've ever had," Nina commented as she drained the last of her tea, "but it was certainly the most welcome."

"You get used to the high-fat, freeze-dried stuff pretty quickly," said Fatima. "It's when you get home and have to go back to a normal diet that the trouble begins. The first time I came here I prepared by drinking pints of extra thick cream to get my weight up, then when I got back to British Columbia, I didn't have an excuse to down four thousand calories a day anymore."

Sam thought back to the diet he had been on for the past few weeks, prior to their departure. He had received a delivery the day after he had agreed to join the expedition—Purdue's doing, of course—full of high-fat, high-calorie foods, a diet sheet and a note reminding him that the harsh conditions they would face would require him to bulk up. Although he was a wretched cook and disinclined to eat anything other than cereal at home, Sam had a policy of never turning down free food. He had devoured everything Purdue sent with a will, but his metabolism was still swift and he had not managed to gain more than few pounds by the time they set off.

He had also been instructed to lay off the whisky, but that was never going to happen. A period of few weeks was nowhere near enough for Sam Cleave to quit smoking or drinking. He had made the decision that he would just have to take his chances. Of course, when he had done that he had imagined the Antarctic to be more or less like Scotland but with more snow. Here in this frozen wilderness, where the snow did not lie in fluffy drifts but whistled like bullets around the outside of the tent, he began to wish that he had had more time and inclination to prepare. Looking around the group, he wondered whether any of them—with the exception of the seasoned Antarctic explorers—were anywhere near tough enough to be making this crazy trip.

CHAPTER 11

S AM HAD NEVER really cared for Hogmanay. Seeing in the new year, bidding farewell to the old . . . it seemed so arbitrary to him. The first of January never felt all that different to the thirty-first of December, except that his hangovers were usually a little worse on the first. Patricia, in her endless optimism, had loved it.

She said that the Scots knew how to celebrate properly. On the one New Year's Eve that they had spent together, two years earlier, she had insisted on honoring as many traditions as she knew. They had waited for the bells, toasted the new year with whisky, then she had made Sam open the living room window to let the old year out while she opened the door to welcome in the new. Sam had tried to persuade her to come to bed and spend the first hours of the year making love, but she had recently learned about first-footing and was determined that they must take coal and shortbread around to Paddy's to ensure a lucky, prosperous year for them all.

So much for that little bit of superstition, Sam thought, shaking his head to rid himself of the images of Patricia, glowing with happiness at the prospect of starting the year with him, lying dead on a mortician's slab with most of her beautiful face missing fewer than six months later. He forced himself to concentrate on what was happening in front of him. Alexandr was making his way around the tent, weaving through the piled backpacks and sleeping bags spread out on the groundsheet, a small flask in his hand.

"For you, for you, for you," he said as he poured tiny nips of clear liquid into each person's mug. "Yes, we are not supposed to be drinking alcohol out here in such cold places, but what is a celebration without a little vodka? And not just any vodka. This is such pure, such perfect vodka as you have never tasted, distilled by my cousin, Ivan Yevgeny Ivanovich, who anyone will tell you makes the best vodka in all Siberia— and in Siberia is the best vodka in all Russia. Tonight we celebrate the dawn of a new year, but also the beginning of an adventure!"

As the minutes ticked away, getting ever closer to midnight, Alexandr began to regale the group with tales from his native Siberia. "There is a tradition which is, as far as any man knows, unique to my family," he half-whispered, forcing his companions to be silent and lean in to catch his words. "For where I grew up, deep in the remotest parts of Siberia, the Ke'let is known to walk. When I was only a small boy, perhaps five years old, my father explained to me that as the New Year was being born, the Ke'let would make his rounds. He walks surrounded by his pack of dogs, built like wolves with sabre-sharp fangs, their eyes glowing green in the black night.

"To look on the face of the Ke'let is the end of a man's life, for he is death to all who cross him. On the night of the New Year he goes out to select those who will die in the year to come, scratching his mark into the wood of their house with his long fingernails. So my father taught me that when the Ke'let walks, we must defy him. We must seek him out, him and his dogs. We must run bare-chested in the snow until we see the green glow of his hounds' eyes, and when we find him we must call out 'I am here, Ke'let! I claim my life for another year!'

"And when he turns, we must stand and face him bravely. If he uncovers his face then we shall be granted a swift and honorable death, such as was accorded to my grandfather who faced the Ke'let and was taken. But if he does not, then we know that we shall not die this year, for the Ke'let has looked on our face and granted us another year. So when midnight tolls, I shall go in search of the Ke'let and see if he has followed me here." Alexandr grinned at the group, the light from the alcohol burner casting demonic shadows across his face as if he were a child playing at ghosts. "And any who wish to join me and claim their lives will be welcome to do so."

For one spellbound moment there was silence in the tent. Then Nina laughed. "That's the best spooky story I've heard in years, Alexandr!" she said. "Bravo! But I don't think I fancy joining you out there tonight." She glanced toward the window. Although there was no true darkness in the Antarctic at this time of year, the thick grey clouds had obscured the daylight and all she could see was an unsettling, furious whirl of snow.

"Have it your own way," Alexandr replied, his customary smirk playing around his lips. "I will maybe put in a good word for you with the Ke'let." He glanced at his watch. "But it is close to midnight, and I must prepare."

"You're not actually going to do it?" Professor Matlock demanded. "You can't go out into that, you'll be dead in seconds!"

Alexandr slipped his thermal sweater over his head and shrugged, the lean muscles of his wiry body clearly defined under his pale skin. "When one grows up in Siberia one learns to handle a little cold," he said. "And my father was never clear on the matter of what will happen if we face the

Ke'let wrapped up warmly."

"I'm with you, Alexandr," Purdue, who had been sitting on his rolled-up sleeping bag, suddenly unfolded himself and stretched to his full, lanky height. "Let's face this Ke'let." Automatically Blomstein got to his feet, but Purdue waved a dismissive hand at him. "No need, Ziv, no need. I am not sure that your particular brand of thuggery would protect me against this mythical creature of Alexandr's, and I doubt anyone planning to kidnap or assassinate me will have followed us all the way out here. If they have, perhaps they deserve to hit their mark in reward for their dedication."

He unzipped his snowsuit down to the waist, letting the upper part fall around his legs, then stripped off the layers he was wearing beneath. Where Alexandr's body was wiry, Purdue's spoke of years spent behind computer screens and in libraries. Sam was relieved to see that he was not the only one who had failed to put on much weight ahead of their trip. Purdue stared intently at his watch, quietly counting down the last seconds of the year. "Midnight," he announced. "Happy New Year!" Then he and Alexandr crawled out of the tent and dashed into the storm, leaving the others to watch in disbelief.

"Well, Happy New Year," Sam said, clinking mugs with Fatima and Nina. "Looks like it'll be a short one, considering that our guide and our benefactor just ran off to sacrifice themselves to the gods of hypothermia." He knocked back the shot of vodka. It was certainly strong—he could feel it burning its way down his throat and leaving a slight sting at the back of his eyeballs. It had been a long time since any kind of alcohol had had that effect on Sam. Fatima choked slightly on hers.

It only took a few moments, less than a minute, for Purdue and Alexandr to return. They burst back into the tent, both tinged slightly blue from the cold, their faces flushed pink from the exhilaration of their mad dash. "I live for another year!" Alexandr cried, his fists clenched above his head, looking like a mad god. He seized his vodka flask and drained it, a crazed smile on his face.

Fatima leaned in to whisper to Nina and Sam. "Good to know we've got someone sane leading the expedition," she said sotto voce. "If he gets us all killed, I just want you to know that I had someone normal lined up to lead us. Happy New Year." With that, she turned away and burrowed into her sleeping bag, pulling it up over her head.

When the group awoke the next morning, the wind and snow were still howling outside the tent. So it continued the next day, and the next. Before anyone else was awake,

Alexandr would step outside and get on the satellite phone to communicate with the Neumayer station, who would give them the same information each day—they were to stay put. The hovercraft had been repaired, but the pilots agreed that it would be suicide to try to get through the storm. As long as the expedition was well-supplied and no one was in any immediate medical danger, their best move was to make no move at all. Once the storm had cleared, they would send a truck to rescue the party. Its caterpillar tracks would have an easier time of negotiating the snow than the hovercrafts would. Until then, the group could only wait.

Fortunately, despite the incredibly low temperatures outside, the tent was trapping the group's collective body heat and keeping their living space warm. They had plenty of food, and the newly fallen snow just beyond the outer door kept them supplied with water. Provided they stayed within the sturdy tent, they were not in any immediate physical danger.

The danger to the group's morale was another matter entirely. Sam, who had lived alone for so long and was accustomed to plenty of time with no one but his cat for company, was finding it hard to be trapped with eight other people in a space measuring no more than thirty square meters. Communal living did not suit him well.

In fact, it did not seem to suit any of them particularly well.

Alexandr seemed unperturbed, which Sam attributed to his not occupying the same reality as the rest of them. Fatima and Jefferson, who had obviously done this kind of thing before, were coping better than the rest, but even they were showing signs of strain. Fatima's calm self-possession had tipped over into withdrawing from the group and spending most of her time sitting on her own, scribbling and sketching in her notebook. Jefferson channeled his energies into regaling the group with tales of his previous expeditions and the well-known people he had traveled with. He seemed either unaware or unconcerned about the response of his captive audience. Professor Matlock had gone from joining in enthusiastically, matching each of Jefferson's stories with a name-dropping tale of his own, to listening politely without really responding, to not listening at all.

Purdue seemed to have abandoned his pursuit of Nina for the present—Sam guessed that this had something to do with the lack of both showers and privacy—and was spending much of his time chatting in low voices with the old man. I really should get to know his name, Sam thought. But how do I ask after all this time without making myself sound like a complete muppet?

Nina rolled onto her stomach and slapped a deck of cards down in front of Sam. "Right," she said. "Texas Hold'em. You're playing. Shuffle."

"Again?" Sam moaned. "But you cheat!" Still, he did as he was told and began to shuffle the deck.

"No I don't," Nina took the cards back from him and began to deal. "I'm just better at it than you. But look, I'm magnanimous enough to give you a chance to win your cigs back."

As Nina deliberated over her cards, Sam wondered how she was really feeling about their situation. On the outside she appeared calm and graceful. He had even seen her have a couple of conversations with Frank Matlock without rising to a single one of his barbs. She had asked him politely how he had found the journey and commented on how fortunate he was to have a good friend like Jefferson Daniels, and she had made no mention of the fact that he had suddenly decided a trip to the Antarctic was in order after her meeting with him.

Sam knew from the torrent of fury she unleashed in whispers every time they huddled in the doorway to the tent for a smoke that she was still angry about it. He knew that she resented her superior's ability to use his rich, well-connected friends to get what he wanted, and she could see his attempt to steal her discovery for himself. But this was not the place to settle that score, and they all knew it. So Nina continued to feign serenity, letting off steam only when she was alone—or as close as they could get to "alone"—with either Fatima or Sam.

Even though Nina and Sam strung their game out for as long as they could, it still took less than half an hour for Nina to win the rest of Sam's cigarettes from him. "I'm not heartless enough to leave you with nothing to smoke," she said, pushing half of her winnings back toward him. "I'll keep a tally and you can pay off the balance when we're back in Edinburgh. Assuming we ever get back. Now come on. It's been nearly twenty-four hours since my last cigarette and I'm just about ready to strangle someone."

Bundled up in their warmest gear, they crawled out into the outer layer of the tent and unzipped the door to the outside world. Nina stuck her head out for a moment, then led the way toward the side of the tent that offered the most shelter from the wind. They fashioned gaps in their hoods and scarves to allow just enough space for their cigarettes to reach their mouths, then Sam flipped open his Zippo lighter. They each took a deep puff as the cigarettes lit, then paced themselves after that.

"Looks like it's letting up a bit," Sam bellowed optimistically, raising his voice to be heard over the whistling gale. "Maybe we'll get on our way soon."

"Hopefully," Nina yelled back. "I'm beginning to wish I'd never come. If I'd known it was going to be this uncomfortable I'd have left Matlock to get on with it."

"I was wondering," Sam said, "Do you know the old guy's

name? I never caught it and now I can't ask him or he'll think I'm an idiot."

"You are an idiot. That's the most British thing I've ever heard. Like the joke about the two men on a desert island who could never talk to each other because they hadn't been introduced."

"Hilarious. Now what's his name?"

Nina shrugged. "I don't know; I never caught it either." Even though hardly any of her face was visible, Sam could see her grin. "You'll just have to ask him yourself."

"I will, then," Sam said. "So have you and Fatima figured out how you're going to check out the ice station, then?"

"She's got friends at Neumayer," Nina nodded. "She reckons that once she's collected her samples and got everything set up in the lab, we'll be able to borrow some transport while her cultures develop. Then we can check out the coordinates and see if there's any sign of a structure having been there, and if there is we can photograph it. All I need is proof that the thing existed, or that the Nazis tried to make it exist, and I should be able to recruit some archaeologists and get together a proper, legitimate expedition—something with academic discovery at its heart rather than Dave Purdue's thrill-seeking."

"You'd do this again?" Sam was incredulous. "You're insane."

"If it got me what I wanted," Nina said.

"And what's that?"

Nina hesitated, the remains of her cigarette poised between her gloved fingers. "I don't know," she said at last. "Perhaps if I found it, I would."

CHAPTER 12

FOR CHRIST'S SAKE, why can't you just talk normally for once?" Professor Matlock was yelling at the top of his voice as Sam and Nina reentered the tent. They exchanged a brief, puzzled glance. Matlock and Alexandr were on their feet, a mug of coffee dashed to the ground between them. "All this nonsense about spirits and demons! Do you take this seriously, man? Do you? We are out here risking our lives, and we appear to be led by a lunatic!"

Jefferson Daniels stepped in and placed a calming hand on Matlock's shoulder, but it had exactly the opposite effect. Matlock shoved him off, though he did not have the physical strength to make much of an impression on his muscular friend. "Don't you try to defend him, Daniels!" Matlock shouted. "Can't you see this man for the dangerous imbecile he is? Surely you of all people realize the danger in being taken on a wild goose chase around the Antarctic by a man who is half-drunk most of the time?" With his Byronic white hair tousled and the bags under his eyes after a few nights of restless sleep, Professor Matlock looked quite mad himself as Jefferson attempted to restrain him gently.

"Mr. Matlock." Alexandr spoke softly, but at once all eyes were on him. "I appreciate that this is your first time in the Antarctic. I realize that to you, what I am doing must appear to be madness. When you have been here a little longer you will begin to see my reasons, you will learn that all have their ways to cope with this place. For me, it is more fun, more excitement to think of the storms and cold and perils of this place as gods and demons. For you, perhaps, this is not the case. But I do not insult your ways of handling things, and you will not insult mine. I do not question your expertise, and you will not question mine."

He looked straight into Matlock's wild eyes and walked toward him, then grasped the academic's hand in a firm grip. "I swear to you that I will get you home safely from this place. But for this you must trust me. What you are doing now, this is how madness starts. Do not give in to it. Do not trust it." Matlock cried out in alarm as he was dragged into a short, tight hug by Alexandr, who then turned his back and walked away, considering the matter ended.

Jefferson pulled Matlock over to the edge of the floor and

made soothing, placatory noises while Matlock continued to mutter, obviously rattled by Alexandr's little speech. Sam sneaked a look around the rest of the tent. Many of the others were hunched, tense, and obviously not happy. Conflict in such a confined space could only lead to more. He looked around for Nina's deck of cards, thinking that perhaps a game would distract everyone. He wracked his brain for a game that could accommodate so many players, preferably one for which he knew the rules.

Before Sam could come up with anything, Dave Purdue clapped his hands together. "Oh, I've always wanted to say this," he chuckled, then cleared his throat and assumed a dramatic tone. "I expect you're wondering why I have brought you all here!"

"Did he really just say that?" Nina whispered. Sam nodded. He wondered what Purdue was playing at. Was this his way of defusing the tension?

Purdue clicked his fingers and Blomstein reached into his pack and took out a large, folded piece of paper. He handed it to Purdue, who unfolded it and spread it in front of him, beckoning the others to draw near and see it. "This," he flung his hands out theatrically, "is the reason we are here. Look at it."

Sam, Nina, and some of the others huddled around. What they saw was a map of Antarctica, with several points marked on it in Purdue's emphatic, sprawling handwriting. Novolazarevskaya, the old Neumayer stations, and the newly opened one that was their destination . . . and also a large cross with the word Wolfenstein beside it. Sam felt Nina's fingers close around his arm. "I never told him the name," she whispered urgently. "Did you?"

"What name?" Sam hissed back. "What's the matter?"

"I owe some of you an apology," Purdue peered around the group. "I have brought you here on—well, not false pretences as such, but certainly distorted ones. We all came here in search of something. Dr. al-Fayed for the algae, Mr. Daniels for his memoirs, Dr. Gould and Professor Matlock for evidence that a Nazi ice station was once established here, and Mr. Cleave for the obscene amount of money he was promised to profile me on this trip. But all those things are nothing compared to our true purpose. We are here in search . . . of legend."

He paused for dramatic effect, watching his little audience carefully and monitoring their response. Had he been playing to a fresh crowd he might have had greater success, but after their long confinement the group was too fractious to respond well. Mutters rippled around the room, questioning what Purdue was talking about. Undaunted, he continued.

"First I must tell you a story," he said, settling onto his rolled sleeping bag. "Some of you will be familiar with the tale of Captain Alfred Ritscher, will you not? Nina? Professor Matlock? Oh, even you, Mr. Daniels. That's good. For those who are not, the hero of our little story began his career as a mere cabin boy, flew reconnaissance flights during the First World War, and by 1934 was executive officer in command of the German Navy. There he was entrusted with a very particular task by Herr Goering himself—to lead an expedition to the Antarctic, claim New Schwabenland for the Fatherland, and chart this desolate terrain so that it could be colonized.

"In 1938 he made an extensive aerial survey—the planes were brought from Europe by ship and had to be launched by means of a catapult because they had no adequate runway, can you imagine? I would have loved to do that . . . Where was I? Ah yes. The expedition was a secret to all but the German high command and a select few at Lufthansa Airways, who provided the ship, the Schwabenland.

"But why, you may be wondering, would anyone want to colonize such a remote, inhospitable place? The Nazis had no interest in Dr. al-Fayed's algae. The answer is twofold. First, the extensive conquests made by other nations, primarily the British, left them very few options for empire building. Antarctica was there for the taking. Second, whaling. Whale oil was a valuable commodity and one that Germany had to import. With war looking ever more likely, the official story was that they wanted to secure their own supply. This is clearly nonsense. Why, in the event of war, would it make sense to transport such a precious resource such a long way through hostile, submarine-infested waters? Surely it would be more sensible to channel their efforts into creating suitable substitutes, rather than into the costly and inefficient process of establishing a whaling base out here?

"No. The true purpose of the base they wished to establish was much more interesting. This was where the Nazis planned to build their impregnable fortress, their Shangri-la. It would be their fallback position should the tide of the inevitable war turn against them. It would be their first base of operations for the conquest of South America should things work in their favor. Controlling the northern hemisphere from Berlin and the southern hemisphere from their unassailable ice station, there would be no limits to their plans for expansion. While the Allies concentrated their forces on the war in Europe, Nazi scientists could work undisturbed in the Antarctic to develop military technology of a kind the world had never seen. This place would prove essential to the establishment of the thousand-year Reich.

"Of course, that is not how things worked out for them. They lost the war before their plans could come to fruition. However, there have always been questions about what happened to particular German treasures and indeed to a large portion of the U-boat fleet. More than fifty U-boats simply disappeared at the end of the war. Perhaps they were patrols that never made it home, blown up by mines or sunk by accidents and small natural disasters. There are many terrible things that can happen at sea. But could that account for so many? I doubt it. There are theories that the submarines that disappeared were evacuating Nazi personnel and treasures, spiriting them away to somewhere they would never be found. And where better than Antarctica? Where better than a series of secret tunnels hidden deep beneath an icy mountain range on a continent unoccupied by man?

"By 1945, rumors about this place were already circulating among the Allies—but when Germany surrendered in May of that year, there were more important things to do than investigate such rumors. Then, a few months later, a Nazi U-boat—U530—surfaced at Mar del Plata in Argentina. The commander was a tall, blond man who gave his name as Otto Wermuth, but he could produce no papers to verify his identity. Neither could his crew. Neither could the German female civilian who was inexplicably aboard.

"Soviet agents reported that the woman was Eva Braun and that Adolf Hitler was concealed among the crew. These reports were largely dismissed because the burned body found near the Führerbunker was believed to be Hitler's, but you may remember that a few years ago, DNA testing revealed that the corpse was in fact that of a forty-year-old woman. Where, then, was Hitler? Possibly Argentina.

"During the two years that followed, an incredible number of Nazi U-boats and other vessels appeared in the waters surrounding Argentina. Some surrendered, including U977. Others were sighted and vanished, with no convincing explanation given for their presence. Then, in 1946, the US Navy began Operation Highjump, which they described as a 'purely scientific expedition.' Now, perhaps the scientists among you can tell me whether this is a standard complement for a scientific expedition: an aircraft carrier, several destroyers and icebreakers, submarines, thirteen warships, fifteen heavy transport aircraft, long range reconnaissance aircraft, and about five thousand men? Our own operation feels dreadfully ramshackle by comparison.

"Anyway, Operation Highjump was beset with difficulties. Within three weeks, several aircraft and their pilots had been lost. A 'ship-unloading accident' killed numerous men and curtailed the Americans' intention to build an airstrip on the Ross Ice Shelf, roughly where the Pegasus Field would eventually be. Admiral Byrd ordered a sudden withdrawal of forces and they made a hasty retreat to the United States, leaving nine of their planes behind, just sitting on the ice. I'm sure you'll all agree, that is a particularly disastrous end for a 'scientific expedition.'

"I believe, as many others do, that the true purpose of Operation Highjump was to attack the Nazi fortress, which had been steadily developed here over the course of the Second World War. I believe that when the Americans realized that there truly was a Nazi base here, they saw the threat it posed to them and set out to neutralize it. I also believe that they failed, and that the reason they failed was that the technology they encountered was so advanced that their own forces were inadequate. They were driven out of Antarctica by superior might in the hands of the last remnants of the Nazi forces.

"For some reason, although they were able to withstand attack, those Nazi forces were never able to regain sufficient power to go on the offensive—and so much the better for the rest of us, perhaps. Yet there is no evidence to suggest that anyone dismantled the ice station—no sign of its equipment or transport being dumped or sold or otherwise disposed of. Which would suggest that it is still there, and that somewhere deep in the Antarctic there is a trove of Nazi technology, weapons, and treasure just waiting to be found . . . and as luck would have it, we are almost on top of it. Here," Purdue jabbed a pencil into the map, "is our current location."

Sam stared at the map. Sure enough, the little square marked Wolfenstein was just millimeters away from them.

"This," Purdue dropped his voice to a whisper, "is our true destination."

CHAPTER 13

ALEXANDR WAS THE first to laugh. "Very good, Mr. Purdue, very good!" he cried, slapping Purdue on the back. "Better even than my Ke'let story! Excellent!"

Fatima was sitting bolt upright beside Nina, her body quivering with tension. She gave a nervous chuckle. "You had me worried for a moment there, Purdue," she said. "I thought you were actually planning to change our destination in mid-trip! Your storytelling skills are amazing."

Delicately, Purdue adjusted the cuffs on his sweater. "Dr. al-Fayed, that is exactly my intention. Rest assured, we shall make it to Neumayer. Your research will not be abandoned, just slightly delayed. That is why, when we first corresponded, I was so keen to know whether your work was in any way dependent on the seasons. We could have gone to Neumayer first, but who could wait longer than they had to for discoveries such as these?"

"You've got to be joking." Fatima's voice was barely
audible.

"I am not."

Fatima stared wildly around the rest of the group. "This is
insane!" she cried. "We're in incredibly dangerous territory.
This is the kind of place where you survive by having a plan
and sticking to it. We can't just go wandering off into the
mountains, that's how you get killed." Now on her feet, she
whirled around to face the Russian guide. "Alexandr, back me
up here!"

Arichenkov made no reply but stood stroking his beard, his
eyes closed, apparently lost in a world of his own. In three
strides Fatima had crossed the floor and grabbed hold of his
shoulders, shaking him and yelling at him to speak. With a
laugh, he took hold of her wrists and stopped her. He looked
her straight in the eye. "Fatima," he said softly, "do you not
trust me to keep all of you safe? Would you not like to
explore new territory, perhaps find the thing that will bring
you back for your next voyage of discovery? You think this
story of a Nazi ice station is a fairy tale. So do I. But what if it
is not? Our supplies are plentiful, our equipment is excellent,
and we are well-placed to make such a detour."

"Well-placed!" Fatima erupted. "You're insane! Have you
looked at this expedition? Have you? Fewer than half these

people are prepared to be here at all, let alone to be going off the beaten track on some wild-goose chase. I guarantee you that if we go wandering off into those mountains, most— perhaps all—of them are going to die. Is that what you want? Is this some kind of suicide trip for you? How can you seriously be considering this?"

Alexandr shrugged. "I am paid to guide this expedition. Where it goes is of little matter to me. For the right sum, I will take you anywhere you like. And I will get you home alive."

Unable to believe the lack of support she was encountering from Alexandr, Fatima rounded on the rest of the group. "Why am I the only one who seems to have a problem with this?" she snarled. "Are you all completely suicidal? Or am I the only one who didn't know about this? Did all of you come here specifically to play Nazi hunter?" She turned a beseeching look on Nina. "Did you know?"

"I don't know anything more than I've told you already," Nina's voice was as calm as she could make it. "As far as I'm concerned, we're here in the hope of finding some evidence that there was an attempt to establish a Nazi base here. I didn't have any plans to drag you off course. But knowing what I do of Mr. Purdue, I'm not entirely surprised. I should have made it clearer to you that he's crazy and not overly concerned with anyone's safety. I didn't know about his plan, but I have to admit that now we're here . . . if it's feasible to investigate properly, I think we should do it while we have the chance. Especially if we're already almost on top of it."

Fatima threw up her hands in frustrated fury and went back to yelling at Purdue, demanding to know where he got his evidence and how he could justify doing this to the rest of the group. As she got close, Ziv Blomstein stepped silently forward and stood between them. Fatima dodged to one side, determined to get to Purdue, but Blomstein blocked her again. "Hands off, Arab bitch," he growled.

Sam lunged forward and grabbed Fatima as she shrieked with rage and her fist flew back to prepare for the punch. Nina had the same idea, and between the two of them they wrestled her away from Blomstein while Purdue watched with amusement. Crazy bastard, thought Sam.

"May I say a few words?"

They turned their heads in the direction of the unfamiliar voice. The white-haired old man was kneeling next to the alcohol burner, his air of quiet composure undisturbed by the tension in the rest of the tent.

"I can understand your alarm, Dr. al-Fayed," he nodded in Fatima's direction. "I can imagine that this must be a great shock to you, and that you may feel that there is not sufficient evidence to justify going in search of the ice station. But Mr. Purdue's tale, while very exciting and dramatic, is only part of the story. I can tell you more, if you are prepared to listen. But first, I would appreciate it if someone would make some tea. My hands are not as steady as they used to be and I am not confident of my ability to work the burner."

Glad of something constructive to do, Sam hurried over and fed a fuel tablet into the burner and filled the pot with melt water. While Sam added teabags and stirred the brew, the old man began to speak.

"I haven't been properly introduced to all of you," he began, "so for those of you who do not know me already, my name is Frederic Whitsun. Admiral Whitsun, if we're being completely accurate." Sam fumbled the pot and nearly spilled its contents, catching it by sheer good luck before the boiling water could end up all over the groundsheet. Nina looked at him quizzically, but she was the only one who paid any attention. Sam gave her a quick smile and she returned her focus to the old man.

"I can tell by the looks that some of you have been giving me that you are wondering why an old man such as me is making such a dangerous trip. Let me assure you that I'm not as frail as I look—and if it proves I have overestimated myself and am truly too old and infirm to survive this environment, Mr. Purdue and Mr. Arichenkov have strict instructions to leave me to my fate. I would rather die here than risk endangering any of you.

My father's name was Witzinger. As you can imagine from the name, my family was German. My mother and I fled our homeland when I was a boy, just before the outbreak of the war, and changed our name during our time in an internment camp on the Isle of Wight. My father, on the other hand, did not escape the grip of the Nazis. He was a brilliant chemist, and in the mid-1930s they recruited him to work at Peenemünde. You can imagine, I'm sure, that this was not the kind of job offer one could refuse.

"From Peenemünde he was transferred to another location —he was unable to tell us where, but I believe he spent some time as a doctor in one of the concentration camps. Then later, he was transferred out of Germany. My mother received a heavily censored letter from him, telling her that he was being sent to a remote location. Then we heard nothing from him again, apart from a letter informing my mother of his death. To the best of our knowledge, he died in that place where he was stationed. I have come here because it is important to me that I find my father's final resting place before I myself die."

The admiral reached into his pack and pulled out a small bundle of papers. "I appreciate that you may wish to know what evidence I have to suggest that my father ended up here. Please, feel free to examine these. Some are personal letters; some are the papers that were in with my father's belongings when they were returned to my mother."

"Oh, how could I have forgotten?" Purdue chimed in. "I was so wrapped up in my own story that I completely omitted one of the best parts! I have a little tangible evidence myself —something I obtained not long ago, just before we set off." From a concealed pocket he withdrew a small notebook and added it to the papers being passed around.

Professor Matlock stepped in and took charge of the papers straight away. With ostentatious care he unfolded letters and spread them out on a sleeping bag, laying the little black notebook beside them, then stood guard over them while the others crowded around to look.

"What are they?" Fatima demanded. "What are we looking at?"

"These are the letters to the admiral's mother," Nina explained, scrutinizing the papers. "I don't see much about where he's stationed—that will be under the blacked-out bits, if he wrote anything about it at all. But these are his notes here . . . That's the chemical symbol for mercury, and I think this is some kind of formula. Anyone understand it?"

Alexandr peered over her shoulder. "I am no great chemist," he said, "but I will guess that this is a type of fuel. Rocket fuel, perhaps?"

"That would make sense," Nina agreed. "If the admiral's father was at Peenemünde and then transferred down here, it seems likely that he was involved with either aeronautics or ballistics. These here are army documents, just like the ones I've seen before—and they're in the same kind of code. Now, let's have a look at this." She picked up the notebook and opened it to a random page. Sam saw a look of puzzlement cross her face. "Ok, it says . . . It shall be the greatest of adventures . . . Worthy of Holmes, of Nemo, of Doctor Moreau . . ." Her face was white as she shut the book. "Purdue, where did you get this?"

Purdue faced her calmly. "I have a wide range of sources, Nina. When I began to prepare for this expedition I asked a few associates of mine to obtain material like this for me, at any price. Why do you ask? Is it something I'm not supposed to have?"

"This notebook . . ." Nina paused, confused, searching for a solution in her head. "This notebook belongs to Sam, by rights. This is one of the notebooks that was stolen from me after he gave it to me to translate. Who did you get it from?"

"I'm afraid I can't remember off the top of my head," Purdue said dismissively. "I do keep a database of these things, but as you can imagine I would struggle to check it just now. Once we return to Scotland I shall find out who supplied it and see if I can trace the thief, all right? Will that do?"

Nina nodded, but Sam could read the suspicion on her face.

She was not happy with Purdue's explanation and neither, in truth, was he. When he said he had sources who had told him about Nina's funding application, I thought he meant other people in her department, Sam thought. Did he know about all this before she even applied? What the hell is going on here? And why the hell am I in the same tent as Admiral Whitsun?

The academics continued to pore over the evidence for a while and eventually concluded that the papers and the notebook corroborated each other on the likely existence of the ice station and its coordinates. The admiral's father had had a map in his pocket, which looked like nothing more than a few squiggles at first glance, but on closer inspection revealed markings indicating all the topographic features of the area and the location of something marked "W" with a few scrawled numbers around it. The numbers correlated to the coordinates Nina had pulled from the notebook. When they realized this, most of the group gasped, but Purdue sat smugly, certain that the evidence was in his favor.

"For me, that's sufficient evidence to justify investigating," said Nina. "But that's just me. Judging by these coordinates and the map, we wouldn't have to cross the mountains or even enter the mountain range. The entrance is marked as being right at the edge, about a kilometer from our current location. Having come this far, I would hate to turn back without having checked out whether this place is real and whether we can find it. But I can only make a decision for myself, not the rest of you. So I suggest we put it to a vote. There are nine of us. Shall we say that more than six counts as a majority? Is everyone happy to go with a majority vote? Or should we agree that if it's not unanimous we proceed with the original plan as most of us understood it and go straight to Neumayer IV?"

"I'm not exactly thrilled either way," said Fatima, "but I trust most of you to have some sense of self-preservation. If there's a majority vote in favor, I'm happy with that. I just don't want to be dragged off on the whim of one maniac."

Once Fatima had spoken, no one else spoke up against the idea of a majority vote. Nina asked those in favor of looking for the ice station to raise their hands, then counted herself, Sam, Purdue, Blomstein, Admiral Whitsun, Jefferson Daniels, and Alexandr Arichenkov.

"Those against?"

Fatima and Professor Matlock raised their hands. Alexandr offered to contact Neumayer and ask that the two dissenters be collected and taken to safety before the rest of the group began their hunt, but they both declined.

"I'm staying in case you need me," Fatima said.

"I am just making my feelings known," said Matlock. "If— or when—this expedition comes to a sticky end, I would like us all to remember at the last that I, at least, was not in favor of it."

CHAPTER 14

I T TOOK ANOTHER day for the snowstorm to calm down and allow the expedition to proceed. Sam woke on the fifth morning in the tent to the unfamiliar sound of silence—no howling wind, no delicate flutter of falling snow. The quietness seemed strange, almost unnerving after spending so long in a shrieking gale.

He did not realize how early it was until he noticed that the others were all still bundled up in their sleeping bags. Only Alexandr was up and moving about, and he was unzipping the inner door and making his way out of the tent. Sam caught a glimpse of the satellite phone in his hand. He must be going outside to get a signal, Sam thought. He vaguely remembered something Purdue had said about the phone requiring open sky to work. Sam burrowed back down into his sleeping bag, rubbing his chilly feet together for warmth.

A few moments later Alexandr returned. Sam was drowsy,

but not yet fully asleep. He half-opened his eyes to see Alexandr shaking Purdue's shoulder to wake him up. They had a brief, rapid conversation in whispers, then Purdue wriggled out of his sleeping bag, grabbed the snowsuit that was neatly folded beside him and quickly pulled it on. The two men headed back outside. Ziv Blomstein rolled onto his side, his eyes open, watching and listening for any sign of danger to Purdue.

Sam dozed again, and had no idea how long it was before he woke again. By the time he opened his eyes, several of the others were awake and dressed, and Jefferson Daniels was making coffee on the burner. Sam had never liked coffee, but the smell was amazing and when it came to hot drinks, he would take what he could get out here.

Because his cigarette consumption had been cut so drastically, he found himself turning to caffeine to compensate. He dragged himself out of the sleeping bag and began to pull his clothes on over his thermal underwear. I could do with a shower, he thought, accidentally catching the scent of his own unwashed body. If we find this ice station, I hope it somehow has hot water. He could only imagine how bad the tent would smell to someone walking into it for the first time, because none of the expedition members had been able to have more than a sponge bath since they left the ship.

"Good morning!" Nina trilled, seeing that he was awake. It

was her turn to make the rounds that morning, doling out breakfast sachets and hot water. "And what would sir like for breakfast this rather fine morning? We have porridge with blueberries, porridge with strawberries, butter flavored scrambled eggs, or scrambled eggs with potato and mixed peppers. Which would you prefer? All equally high-fat, high-protein, and lacking in any kind of flavor or deliciousness."

"How come they don't have just porridge-flavored porridge?" Sam asked. "Normal porridge that I can put a wee bit of salt in. Why does everything have to have berries in it?"

"We're stuck in a tent in Antarctica and you're complaining about the food being too luxurious?" Nina ripped open a sachet of porridge with strawberries. "The berries are to stop you from getting scurvy."

"Whisky would stop me from getting scurvy. I'm sure I read that somewhere."

"Probably in an article you'd written yourself." She poured hot water on the freeze-dried oats and handed the sachet to Sam before moving on to offer the breakfast selection to Admiral Whitsun.

Once everyone was awake and finished with breakfast, Purdue clapped his hands for attention. His long face looked more than usually solemn as he glanced around at everyone to make sure they were listening. "I have some news which is . . . a little alarming, possibly," he began. "This morning

Alexandr attempted to make contact with Neumayer Station, as usual. Unfortunately, he found that the satellite phone was not operational. I have examined it, and we have tried again a number of times since, but it continues to fail to detect any signal. I believe that a small piece of hardware has malfunctioned within it, making it unlikely that we will be able to repair it."

"Well, that's it, then," said Fatima. "We'll have to go to Neumayer and not this ice station. We can't go traipsing off into unknown territory with no means of contact with the outside world. That would be insane."

"It is true," said Alexandr. "It would be insane. But is this not what the great Scott of the Antarctic did, so many years ago? Is this not was Alfred Ritscher did? Not one of them had the benefit of satellite phones. When they went into uncharted territory, they took their lives in their hands!"

"So that we wouldn't have to!" Fatima wailed. "Is that what this is all about? You want to be like them? Is this all about your ego?"

Sensing another argument in the making, Sam caught Nina's eye and mimed smoking at her. She nodded and pulled on her snowsuit, and the two of them crept out and left Alexandr and Fatima to battle it out.

"It's not so bad without the wind chill," Nina remarked. "Pity the snow's a bit too deep for running around. We could have had an epic snowball fight."

"You're insane," said Sam, flicking open the lighter.

"Probably. I think I'm just glad to be out of there. I can see Fatima's point, but I just don't think we should squander this opportunity—broken satellite phone or not."

Sam's eyebrows shot up. "You really are insane. You think we should keep going?"

"Why not?" Nina asked. "It's not like we'll actually be going into the mountains or anything, and I'm not sure there's any point in chickening out on the grounds that it's not safe. It's the Antarctic, for Christ's sake. It's never going to be safe. Fatima knows that. She's just freaking out because she doesn't trust Purdue or Alexandr. Do you, by the way? I'd love to know."

Sam shook his head. "Not really. I think they're both kind of crazy. Though I would trust Alexandr to keep himself alive, and I suppose that for as long as we're with him that probably means he'll do the same for us. Purdue . . . I don't know. I've got a feeling he'll run headfirst into danger and take us all with him."

Nina closed her eyes and exhaled. "I suppose this means we'll need to do the vote again. Does that mean you're going to vote to head for Neumayer, then?"

"I'm here to profile Purdue," said Sam. "Where he goes, there go I."

"Really?"

"Yeah."

"Crazy."

"Yeah."

They stood in companionable silence for a little while, concentrating on their cigarettes and trying not to overhear the argument going on inside the tent.

"Nina?" Sam said eventually.

"What?"

"I was wondering . . . what did you make of all that stuff with the phone?"

She shrugged her shoulders. "I don't know," she said. "Shit happens, I suppose. Phones break. It's unfortunate, but it's just one of those things. Why, do you think it's something sinister?"

"Hmm." Sam took a contemplative puff. "It's just . . . it seems a bit weird. Coincidental. That's the second important thing to break down, despite the fact that Purdue paid top dollar for all this stuff and probably invented that phone. Did you not think it was a bit odd that the hovercraft blew a cushion when we were right on top of this supposed Nazi ice station? Kind of convenient, wasn't it?"

"I suppose so," said Nina. "I did think it was a bit weird. But I haven't been able to come up with a plausible explanation for why anyone would go to that much trouble. I mean, if it was Purdue, he could just have had the hovercraft drop us off and said 'Right, we're not going to Neumayer, we're going Nazi-hunting, everyone out.' We're here on his money, after all. It's not like we'd have had a huge amount of choice."

"I don't know," Sam stared out across the snow, trying to work it out. "On the one hand I agree with you. It's a hell of a faff when he could just have made us all do what he wants. But on the other hand, look at him. He likes drama. He likes putting on a bit of a show. For someone who can be so zipped up the back, he certainly likes to be the center of attention. I'm not sure what to believe. But as you say, we're here now. The opportunities aren't going to get any better. I'm trying to live by the motto I had when I was a teenager: just because you can doesn't mean you should—but you might as well."

"Fair enough," said Nina. "Well, if he's that determined to get us to do what he wants, there doesn't seem to be much sense in resisting—it's what we're here for anyway. Now, I've been meaning to ask, what happened to you yesterday? When Admiral Whitsun was talking, you nearly dropped the tea. I wanted to ask, but judging by the look on your face it wasn't anything you would have wanted to talk about in front of everyone else."

For the first time in their short acquaintance, Nina saw Sam withdraw into himself completely. His eyes went blank and his face hardened a little. She could hardly believe that she was looking at the same man whose sardonic smile she had grown so use to seeing during the past month.

"I'm sorry, Sam, I shouldn't have asked—"

"No," he said quietly. "It's fine. I just hadn't realized it was him. I'd never seen him before. His son got busted for running an international arms-dealing ring. Killed himself rather than face a trial. It was me that broke the story. Really, it was me that discovered that Charles Whitsun was involved."

"Charles Whitsun?" Nina was suddenly alert. "Steven's friend?"

"Yes. Sorry, I had forgotten there was a connection there. Well, I don't know whether Admiral Whitsun knows who I am yet, but I can't imagine that he's forgotten that I was largely responsible for getting his son arrested. He hasn't said or done anything to suggest that he's figured it out, but it's got to happen at some point and it's going to be pretty bloody awkward when it does."

Nina gave a long, low whistle. "It certainly will," she agreed. "Look, Sam, I don't know the ins and outs of the case

. . ."

"No reason why you should," Sam said. "There wasn't that much coverage, seeing as how there was no trial. There were a few mentions of the arms ring in the coverage of his suicide, but only in the tabloids, really. The broadsheets thought it would be a bit insensitive. Rich, powerful families get that kind of consideration, apparently. The rest of us don't."

"I'm sure you did what needed to be done, Sam."

"I did." The light drained from his eyes once again. "And everybody paid the price for it." He fell silent, staring out at the soft drifts of snow. Nina watched him, intrigued, trying to judge whether she could get any more out of him or whether she would stir up too many painful things. She concluded that she would, and that she should leave him alone.

When Sam and Nina returned to the tent, the argument seemed to have blown over. Fatima still did not look happy and the tension was almost palpable, but at least no one was yelling at anyone else any more. It was Fatima herself who brought up the matter of the vote. She said that once again, she would abide by the majority's decision, but she thought it was only fair that those who had voted in favor of searching for the ice station before should be given the chance to revise their choices in light of the problem with the phone.

Not a single member of the group decided to change his or her vote. Professor Matlock remained sulky and reiterated his previous point, that he would continue if the others did but wanted his reticence to be noted. Fatima, likewise, voted to go straight to Neumayer, but refused to leave the others. The decision remained unchanged. With or without the satellite phone, they would go in search of the ice station. As soon as they had repacked their equipment and provisions, they would make a start.

CHAPTER 15

I THOUGHT THERE would be penguins," Sam mused idly. He was tagging along at the end of the column, where Professor Matlock and Jefferson Daniels were bringing up the rear. Mixed in with the soft whistle of the wind and crunch of their shoes, Sam heard the satisfying sound of Matlock's jaw grinding.

"For the last time," Matlock said, barely containing his annoyance, "we are inland. We are hundreds of miles inland, at the foot of a mountain range. Why on earth, Mr. Cleave, would there be penguins here?"

Sam scuffed his feet along the ground, or at least gave an approximation of doing so. Winding up Professor Matlock made him feel like he was fourteen years old again and getting a rise out of his teacher. "Dunno," he said. "Don't penguins like mountains?"

"They eat fish, you fool! How do you suppose they would

feed themselves so far from the sea?"

"They could eat us," Sam suggested. "I'd do that if I were a penguin. Never mind eating fish, I'd be hiding out in the foothills eating lost expeditions."

"We're not lost."

"Then where are we?"

Just as Matlock was on the point of losing his cool completely, Jefferson stepped in and laid a hand on his shoulder. "Simmer down, Frank," he said. "I think Cleave's just trying to get a reaction. We all know we're not lost. We're not even that far from the campsite. I could still get us back there without even having to use a compass." He flashed his tombstone smile, evidently picturing himself as a movie star.

Sam waited until Matlock had finished grumbling and Jefferson was congratulating himself on a mediation job well done, then dropped in one last facetious remark. "I bet there's polar bears around here."

The explosion Sam was anticipating never came, though. It was averted by Alexandr calling the group together. They gathered into a rough circle, but as they shuffled into place Purdue hauled Alexandr aside and the two men began an intense conversation in heated undertones. Sam took the opportunity to chat to Nina, who had been up at the head of the party since they left the base camp. She was carrying one of the three metal detectors that they had brought, with Blomstein and Alexandr wielding the other two.

"How are you getting on with that thing?" Sam asked, pointing to it. "Found any buried treasure yet?"

Nina rolled her eyes. "Not yet, no. I don't know how far we're going to get with these things. We might be looking for a needle in a haystack here."

"How's that? I thought we were looking for an ice station? How do you miss that? Come to think of it, how come we're trying to find it with tiny wee metal detectors?"

"From Kruger's notes, I wouldn't expect to find it up here. There should be an entrance somewhere around here, but it's concealed. The ice station itself would be underneath us, built into the tunnels."

"So we're looking for a door?"

"Not quite. Well, kind of. If that's what we find, then that would be great. But no, the reason we're using these is that we're looking for the markers that the Nazis left here to claim the land. You know how you're meant to claim territory by sticking a flag in it, right? Well, that wasn't incredibly practical here—it would have meant getting people onto the land and faffing around with poles and suchlike. So instead, they did a flyover and dropped a whole lot of iron swastikas in lieu of a flag. Apparently we'll find the entrance wherever we find the iron swastikas. But I don't even know what size they are, or how many were dropped, or even whether they were definitely iron. So basically, I have no clue. But we're in the right place, so if there's anything to find—"

She was interrupted by Alexandr turning back to the group, waving them toward him while Purdue stormed off, closely followed by Blomstein.

"Mr. Purdue and I, we are in the middle of a slight disagreement," Alexandr announced. "I am of the opinion that the storm that kept us trapped for so many days is not finished with us yet. I look at the sky, I feel the quality and taste of the air and I believe that there will be more snow within hours, so we must make our way back toward base camp and be prepared to set up a temporary camp if necessary. Mr. Purdue, however, does not believe this. He wishes to continue. So he and Mr. Blomstein have elected to continue their hunt a little longer and find their own way back. As for the rest of us, we shall head for shelter and resume our search when the storm clears again. This way!"

Sam looked in the direction Purdue had gone. He and Blomstein had vanished into the snowdrifts, and Sam could see nothing but their footprints. If the crazy Russian guy wants to turn back, it must be pretty dangerous, he thought. I hope Purdue will be ok. He's a mad bastard too, but I wouldn't like to think of him freezing to death out here. Then he turned around and shuffled off in the same direction as the rest of the group, covering the ground slowly, restricted by the pace of the group's slowest member, Admiral Whitsun. The old man was coping well with the strenuous hike over the frozen territory. He was evidently in excellent shape for his age, but there was no denying that his exertions were taking a lot out of him. Getting him back to the safety of the base camp before he ran out of energy seemed like a very good idea.

"WAIT!"

They spun around to see Purdue lurching across the ice with his clumsy, gangling gait, arms flailing. Once again, Alexandr was first to reach him, but this time their conversation was short and characterized by considerable amounts of wild gesticulation. Then Purdue propelled himself forward, into the thick of the group, and ripped off his goggles to reveal his flushed, exhilarated face.

"It's over there," he yelled, waving madly. "We found the iron swastika! And I think there's a door, we can see it through the ice—come on! We've going to need help getting through this!"

He was clearly expecting the whole group to follow him at once, but no one did. They stood and exchanged confused glances.

"Dave," Nina said. "Are you being serious? You actually found an iron swastika?"

"Yes!" Purdue cried. "You could see it for yourself if you would only follow me!" He grabbed her hand and pulled her along behind him, and the rest of the expedition began to follow. Sam took up his usual position toward the rear. It was only now that Purdue claimed to have found something that Sam realized that he had never expected their search to lead to anything other than frostbite and frustration. Yet when they rounded the snowdrift, there was Ziv Blomstein holding a titanium shovel—and next to him, half-buried in the frost, was a large, crooked iron cross.

Within seconds, barely even aware of what he was doing, Sam had flung his pack to the ground, hauled out and assembled his own shovel, and rushed over to Blomstein's side to help him dig. Moments later he was aware of Nina beside him, thrusting her shovel downward with all her strength to break through the ice. Sure enough, beneath the thick layer of ice and frost and snow, they could see something that looked remarkably like a circular metal door.

CHAPTER 16

THE FIRST HOWLING gust of sleet-laced wind tore across the ice field just as Blomstein hauled the heavy metal door open. It groaned and squealed, but it swung open with surprising ease. A dark tunnel lay beneath.

"Jefferson!" Alexandr called over the mounting gale. "If I lead the way, will you see that everyone is in safely?" Jefferson nodded and waved a thumbs-up in response, and Alexandr bounded forward and seized hold of the ladder enthusiastically. In just a couple of seconds he had vanished into the blackness.

Nina was right behind him, scrambling eagerly into the dark. Purdue followed with Blomstein, then at last Sam saw a flicker of light down below as someone switched a torch on. He waved at Admiral Whitsun to go next, thinking it would be a good idea to get the old boy out of the storm. His instinct was to send Fatima down next, but when he made eye contact with her she shot him an amused look. Sam remembered then that she had far more experience in the Antarctic than he did and was much better equipped for all of this, so he closed his fingers around the metal ladder and began his descent.

By the time Sam reached the floor there were several torches lit. Their thin beams showed that the group had arrived in a tunnel with arching corrugated metal walls. Shuffling to one side to make room for the rest of the party, Sam bumped into a banister set into the wall. A little more shuffling confirmed that the floor sloped downhill. Above his head he heard the ominous clang of the circular door being pulled shut. He had never been claustrophobic, but for the first time in his life Sam experienced a pang of nerves at being shut in an enclosed space. He was not the only one. From somewhere behind him he heard a quickly-stifled whimper from Nina.

"You ok?" he muttered to her.

"Yes," she snapped. "I'm fine. Why shouldn't I be?" She shone her torch along the downward slope. "I think we should go this way," she called. "If we head uphill all we're going to find is another exit. This must be the way toward the main complex."

They filed slowly down the corridor, Alexandr and Nina at

the front. The place had an odd smell of disinfectant, stale air, and dust, but the one thing that was missing was the odor of rusty metal. Sam directed his beam toward the walls and noticed that they were indeed rust-free. I wonder how that works, he thought. I'll have to ask Alexandr I'd have thought that if this place has been abandoned for so long it would be falling to bits by now. Ah well. I suppose we should just be glad that it isn't.

The corridor opened out into a large, hangar-like room where their footsteps and voices echoed and the torch beams stretched out into the distance. A little exploration revealed a number of massive engines, presumably designed to power the whole station.

"Let's find a way to get these running!" Purdue clapped his hands in delight. "Alexandr, what do you think? Between the two of us we should be able to find a way, should we not?"

"Certainly," Alexandr smirked. "You can smell the diesel, yes? I have never yet found a diesel engine that I could not make run." He pointed his torch toward the base of one of the engines, sizing it up.

"Purdue!" Jefferson Daniels' voice rang out, followed by the sound of a body slumping to the ground. The beams of light zoomed around in the direction of the voice, revealing Jefferson crouching beside the fallen Admiral Whitsun. Fatima was at his side in a second, scrutinizing the admiral's ashen face, wriggling her fingers into the neckline of his snowsuit to check his pulse.

"He's ok," she pronounced. "His pulse is steady; I don't think he's in any danger. He's probably just exhausted, and it's a lot warmer in here than outside, so he might be overheating. We need to find somewhere for him to rest and we can keep an eye on him."

"Very well," said Purdue. "The engines will wait, I suppose. Alexandr, can you take a few people and find us quarters of some kind? It's probably best if we don't drag the admiral along on the search."

Alexandr nodded smartly and pointed to Nina, Sam, and Matlock. "With me," he said, then turned on his heel and set off toward the nearest door. The trio that he had selected fell into line at once. Nina caught up with Alexandr and began discussing the probable layout of the ice station.

"If this is the main furnace room, there should be stairs to all the other levels nearby," she said. There was a tone in her voice that Sam had never heard before—a rushed, gabbling quality, slightly breathy, quite unlike Nina's usual controlled lecturer's tone. He could not tell whether it was simply excitement causing the change, or a touch of fear. "I wish I'd had a chance to copy more of those notes, because I'm completely working from memory here—but there was something in Kruger's notebooks about the main staircases, and one of them was right next to the engine room. So let's all keep a lookout—somewhere along here there's got to be a door."

Nina was right, of course. Her memory and sense of direction were both good. They had gone a little way along the corridor when they found the stairway and followed it down to the level below. A forbidding metal door stood in front of them, marked Schlafsale. Because Nina nodded and reached for the handle, Sam assumed that they had found the dormitories and followed her into a long, narrow, pitch-black room.

The walls were lined with slim bunks, stripped bare to reveal grey mattresses. Under normal circumstances Sam would have found them uninviting, but after a few nights in the tent and the long, choppy sea journey, he had to fight the impulse to hurl himself onto one and sleep for at least forty-eight hours. The beam from Alexandr's torch flashed back and forth as he made a quick inspection of the rest of the room. In the darkness there was the sound of a long-closed cupboard being yanked open.

"Blankets!" Alexandr's voice rang out. "We are in luck, my friends! Here, take this and make up some beds. I shall go and fetch the others." In a flicker of footsteps and torch beams he was gone, leaving Sam and Nina alone in the dormitory with their arms full of sheets and blankets.

Sam took his armload of bedding and dumped it on one of the bunks, then balanced his torch on the bunk opposite so that he could see what he was doing. The bedding had been neatly arranged in piles consisting of a white sheet, a pillowcase, and a grey blanket, though Sam's decision to toss them onto the mattress had sent this system into disarray. He unfolded item after item until he had a complete set, then began putting the sheet on the bed.

"Aren't these amazing?" Nina was in heaven, though her progress with the bed-making was slow thanks to her need to examine the sheets in detail. At least it kept her distracted, keeping her claustrophobia at bay. "All these things have been here since the 1940s, completely undisturbed . . . No one else has touched these, not since the people who staffed this base! We're going to be sleeping in their actual beds, in this actual dormitory—I know it's morbid and horrible, but there's something so incredible about being the first people to see these things and getting to interact with the artifacts this way! We need to photograph everything, absolutely everything. Look, the sheets are tagged with the serial numbers of the people they'd been issued to! We should be able to find out exactly who each of these sets belonged to— it's incredible!"

Sam fumbled with the stiff mattress, shoving the corner of the sheet beneath it. "So you're telling me that Nazis managed to build this station, but they couldn't manage fitted sheets? Do you know how to do corners?"

"Nope. Just tuck them in and hope for the best."

They continued making the beds inexpertly until they had prepared enough bunks for everyone. By that time the rest of the party had arrived, and Admiral Whitsun was very nearly back on his feet, being helped along by Jefferson and Professor Matlock. They eased him into the nearest bunk, then the group bedded down for the night, their torches blinking out one by one.

Sam flung his arm across his face as bright light flooded the room. In his semiconscious state he heard yells and groans from the others as they protested at the sudden glare. He tried to force his eyes open, but all he could see was painful whiteness. As he rubbed them and waited for the flashing behind his eyelids to stop, there was a rattle of footsteps dashing down the metal staircase outside. The door flew open and Nina and Alexandr tumbled in, giggling like schoolchildren.

"And God saw the light," Alexandr declaimed, flinging his arms wide, "and it was good, and he divided the light from the darkness! I told you that I had never yet seen the diesel engine that I could not make work! Not even after so many years of sitting idle!"

Sam hauled himself up onto one elbow and squinted at the Russian. "You got the lights working?"

Alexandr grinned and hoisted his flask in a salute. "Nastrovje," he smirked. "Miss Nina here could not wait to go exploring, so I had to provide her with light to see by. She was kind enough to translate a few things as we went along."

"It wasn't quite like that," Nina confessed, speaking low enough that only Sam could hear. "I'm excited, yes, but the darkness and the confined space were really getting to me. Alexandr was awake and overheard me trying to talk myself down from a claustrophobic freak-out, so he suggested that we go and see if we could make the lights work."

"Feels like you got the heat working as well," Sam observed. Nina shook her head.

"No. We can't take credit for that, I'm afraid. I don't think it's actually any warmer than it was last night, but we were all too tired and shivery to notice. There are radiators at intervals along the corridors, and all the pipes are warm. There's even a bathroom complete with hot water along the corridor. Just hot, though—no cold. There must be hot springs feeding the water supply, keeping the place warm naturally."

"Hot springs? In Antarctica?"

"You would be surprised," said Alexandr "There are several.

Many are below the glaciers, but some are accessible—on Deception Island there are beaches where the springs run so close to the surface that you can dig your own hot tub. It's not allowed any more, no one can legally disturb the ground . . . but it's still possible." Sam watched the devilish smile spread across Alexandr's face as he spoke. He got the impression that a little thing like the law would never stop Alexandr from doing precisely what he wanted.

"Come on!" Nina dragged Sam's blankets off, snatched up his pile of clothes from the end of the bunk and threw them at him. "Get up! We've got exploring to do and you need to bring your camera. There's something I really need you to get pictures of. It's kind of gruesome, though."

"What is it?"

"There's a furnace up in the engine room," Nina grimaced, "and it looks like someone had an accident up there. Alexandr was taking a look at it and he found a few buttons —someone had obviously burned some clothes, but the fire wasn't hot enough to melt the buttons."

"Wow. Buttons. Scary." Sam rubbed his eyes with the back of his hand and pulled on his sweater.

"Shut it," said Nina. "I haven't got to the creepy bit yet. We found bones in the furnace. Well, bone fragments. It's got a pretty big door. Some poor sod must have tripped and fallen into it."

"Or he got pushed," Sam suggested. "Maybe that's what happened to the Nazis here. Some big Agatha Christie—style murder mystery, but no one solved it so they all got killed. Maybe we'll find the rest of them while we're here, one by one, in all sorts of weird places."

"Grim way to go, however it happened. Now, are you ready? We've got lots to see."

"What about breakfast?" Still too sleepy for anything other than obedience, Sam began hauling his trousers over his thermal underwear.

"There's a sign on the stairwell that says the refectory's downstairs. Alexandr's going to head down and see if there's anything there that works, but we've got time for a quick look around while he gets things going. We won't go too far. Just up and down the stairs. We'll get a rough idea of what's on each level, then we'll head back right in time for a cup of tea and some delicious rehydrated mush. Come on!"

They clanked their way down the metal stairs, stopping on each landing to look down the long corridors. Next to the refectory were more dormitories, and on the level below were individual bedrooms. "Officers' quarters," said Nina, putting her head around a door. "There are plenty to go around. We should move down here and have rooms to ourselves."

Another flight of stairs took them to a corridor that appeared to be almost empty, apart from a single, unmarked door halfway along. Sam forced the stiff handle to turn, and they stepped into a vast, echoing room lit with eerie green light. Unlike the rooms above, its walls were not corrugated metal or wooden planks, but simply smooth rock. It looked as if the walls had been smoothed by prolonged exposure to water, but at some point that water had been drained or dammed leaving only this cave-like room . . . a perfect dry dock, designed to hold three U-boats. Two of the pens were flooded with icy water that lapped gently against the sides of the enclosures, but in the third, at the far end of the room, sat a majestic and menacing German submarine.

"Wow," Nina sighed, then strode along the narrow walkway that led from one pen to another. She reached the U-boat and laid both hands on the metal. "They actually did it, Sam. An Antarctic base. It's insane."

Sam searched his brain for a witty or insightful response, but in truth he was overwhelmed. It was one thing to agree to come to the Antarctic in search of this place, expecting it either to be a fairytale or to be nothing but ruins. It was quite another to find himself standing in a subterranean U-boat dock with incontrovertible evidence of the place's existence. He let Nina continue to chatter excitedly about the make and model of the submarine and speculate on what the implications of this ice station were for the rest of Nazi history, while Sam made himself useful and began taking as many photographs as he could.

CHAPTER 17

YOU'RE KIDDING?" Jefferson Daniels' eyes were wide and incredulous. "An actual U-boat? No way. That's impossible." A peal of laughter rang out, echoing around the metal-lined room. It came from Purdue, who was leaning against the wall in an attitude of careful casualness.

"Forgive me, Mr. Daniels," he said as all eyes turned toward him. "But surely you see the absurdity? No? You—all of you—have just spent the night in an ice station that you thought to be mythical. We are here in a place that you didn't believe existed, and now you can't believe that it could possibly have a U-boat in the dock?" He chuckled again and sipped delicately at his coffee. Jefferson scowled and shoveled another forkful of scrambled egg into his mouth. "Oh, don't sulk," Purdue chided. "I'm only teasing. Besides, you'll want to look your best when we head down to look at this fabled

U-boat—or weren't you planning to be photographed with it?"

Sure enough, after breakfast the group made its way down to the subterranean dock and Jefferson was first in line to have his picture taken with the metal leviathan. Sam unfolded his tripod and resigned himself to a morning spent playing photographer. One by one his companions posed beside the U-boat while Sam snapped away. Nina's pictures were endearingly enthusiastic. She could not tear her gaze away from the submarine long enough to glance at the camera, and her excitement was contagious.

At the opposite end of the spectrum was Admiral Whitsun, now recovering from the previous day's exertions and back on his feet. He simply laid a hand on the U-boat and stood in silent contemplation. Sam snapped away as unobtrusively as he could, eager not to disturb the admiral's reverie. At last, the old man straightened up and nodded, then stepped smartly away from the submarine. "Thank you, Mr. Cleave," he said softly.

"No problem," said Sam. "Do you mind if I ask, though . . . what were you thinking about? You don't have to tell me, it's just—it made for some really powerful images."

"No, no," Admiral Whitsun replied. His eyes were slightly distant and a small smile played around his lips. "It's all right. I'll tell you. I was thinking of my father. I was wondering whether this might be the very vehicle that brought him here. Assuming, of course, that this is where he ended up—and that he never left. I don't think I've felt so closely connected to him since I was a boy."

As Sam listened to the wistful old man, he felt a familiar prickle of guilt creeping down his spine. He still did not know whether Admiral Whitsun recognized him, or whether he would feel that Sam was responsible for the death of his son. Watching him seeking an answer to his father's fate, Sam could only assume that family was important to him, that he had probably taken the loss of his only child hard. Despite the fact that he had done nothing but bring an arms dealer to justice, Sam wanted to apologize. He longed to explain to the admiral that he had only wanted to make things better, that he himself had suffered a major loss, and that if he could go back and prevent himself from getting involved, he would. The two of them stood silently, each lost in their reverie.

"Nina!" Alexandr called out, making Sam jump. He looked around to see where their guide's voice was coming from, but he could not see him.

"Yes?" Nina yelled back. "What is it? Where are you?"

"Here!" Suddenly Alexandr's head appeared through a small hatch in the floor, barely visible in a dingy corner where the hole almost blended in to the rocks. "I found another room. Now I need you to translate something for me."

From the corner where he and Jefferson Daniels had been chatting in low voices, Professor Matlock immediately piped up. "Excuse me, Mr. Arichenkov—you may not be aware of this, but I am Dr. Gould's superior within the department. Should you require linguistic or historical expertise, your first port of call should really be me. I outrank her."

Alexandr looked Professor Matlock up and down. The expression on his face was impossible to read. For a split-second he looked as if he might explode at Matlock, then that look crystallized into something darker and harder, which was then replaced by a burst of laughter and a twinkling, mirthful look that was completely at odds with his expression of a moment before. "You can come too," he shrugged. "I like Nina. I trust her. She is the one I choose to help me, but I suppose two heads are better than one, are they not? This way."

He disappeared into the dark hole, followed first by Nina, then by Matlock. There was quiet for a few moments, just the sound of muffled voices coming from the new room, then the sound of Nina swearing and walking back toward the ladder.

"You ok?" Fatima asked, as Nina climbed back into the dock room.

"Yes, I'm fine," Nina rolled her eyes. "Just exasperated. We found a switch in there and Alexandr and Professor Matlock are both in favor of just flipping it to see what happens. I said I don't think we should, but they're determined. So I said we need to put it to a vote."

"It's clearly nothing harmful." Professor Matlock was next to appear. "Nina here is just being hysterical. Being surrounded by all of this is evidently a little too much for you, Dr. Gould—but then, I keep forgetting how few sites like this you've been on. It can be somewhat overwhelming until experience breeds level-headedness."

Nina gritted her teeth. "At risk of destroying my already tattered career prospects," she said with as much composure as she could muster, "Don't talk to me like that. It's not hysteria, it's common sense. We're in a building we don't know much about, we find a switch marked "power supply" even though we've already found and activated the power source, and you want to just flip this switch? Frankly, Professor Matlock, that's insane."

"Watch your tongue, Dr. Gould!" Matlock snapped. "I know a great deal more about this kind of setup than you, and our Antarctic expert agrees with me—don't you, Mr. Arichenkov?"

"Yes, Professor Matlock, I do," Alexander said, stepping off the ladder. "But not for the reasons you think. I believe that we should throw the switch precisely because we don't know what it does. It is the simplest way to find out. We know that it controls the power supply to something—let us find out what!"

"Yes, that's a great idea!" Nina threw up her hands in rage. "Let's all pile into the tiny, cramped underground room where we have no way of summoning help because we can't get a signal on the satellite phone, then we'll start pushing buttons! Am I really the only one who thinks that might go even slightly wrong?" She shook her head and grappled her temper back under control.

"Look, Alexandr, I take your point about it being the quickest way. But I'm really concerned that it might control the flood gate for one of these pens, or even some kind of emergency mechanism to flood the whole level. It's too much of a risk. Look, even if you're completely hell-bent on the idea, can't we put it to a vote? Please? At least give everyone a chance to have their say before they—"

She stopped dead as a dazzlingly bright light suddenly glared out from the hatch and the sound of clanking gears and grinding metal filled the room. Sam saw the horrified expression on her face and knew that she had immediately realized what was going on, but he had not. He stared wildly around at the rest of the group, hoping for a clue, but all he saw was face after face wearing a confused expression to match his own. The only person not looking confused was

Purdue—because Purdue was not there. A moment later, neither was Nina. She lunged forward and raced down the ladder into the newly lit room. It only took seconds for the others to follow Nina's lead.

The clanking and grinding were coming from a circular metal door at the far end of the room, which was slowly opening. Purdue was standing beside the switch, a look of manic glee on his face. She's going to wipe that smile off his face, poor bastard, Sam thought as he saw Nina storming across the floor toward Purdue. The noise from the mechanism was deafeningly loud, making it impossible for him to hear what Nina was yelling at Purdue, but their host did not look in the least disturbed. In fact he appeared to be laughing at her, which was just infuriating her all the more.

"—get us all killed, you fucking lunatic!" Nina concluded as the mechanism completed its process and the room went silent once more. They all stared at the open door.

"Well?" Nina fumed. "Since you're the one who's so determined to find out what's in there, aren't you going to lead the way?"

"Why, certainly!" The delight in Purdue's voice was clear. Either he was certain that what lay beyond the door would impress Nina to the point where she would cease to be angry with him, or he was simply incredibly sanguine about her wrath—Sam could not quite decide which he thought was the case. One way or the other, Purdue was clearly excited and champing at the bit to explore. With Ziv Blomstein at his shoulder, he strode into the tunnel. Despite the misgivings she had expressed, Nina was not far behind, and Sam decided that he had little to lose by following along with his camera.

What they saw was another rock structure, this one clearly manmade, because it lacked the watered smoothness of the main chamber. It formed a short tunnel, at the end of which was another circular metal door. It put Sam in mind of the doors you would find on a safe or a vault, complete with a dial waiting for a combination. However, it seemed that the combination was not the only thing required to unlock it. The handle itself was locked into a recess in the door, only to be released by means of a key—but clearly not an ordinary key. The object required to fit the keyhole would, it seemed, be something circular, but with bulbous teeth at the top. The shape seemed familiar, yet Sam could not place it . . .

"It might take a short while," Purdue was saying, still bickering with Nina, "but I could crack this combination. I doubt it would be more than a day."

"You know, if it keeps you occupied while the rest of us explore this place, leaving you here to fiddle with the lock probably isn't a bad idea. Perhaps that's what this room is—a crèche for dangerous idiots!" Nina stomped off to the other end of the room—a gesture that would have been much more powerful in a larger space. Sam and Fatima both went after her, leaving the rest of the group to gather around Purdue as he began talking them through the possible workings of the lock.

"I'm fine," Nina sighed, shrugging off the comforting arm that Fatima tried to put around her. "Honestly. I'm ok. It's just so bloody frustrating! First Matlock and the fact that everything that man does has to be a pissing contest, then Alexandr suddenly taking his side, then Purdue . . . I'm not crazy, am I?" She glanced imploringly from Fatima to Sam and back again. "It's dangerous. It really is. We're underground, we know there's got to be a flood mechanism for the pens, and we're just pushing buttons and throwing switches—am I the only person here who doesn't want to end up drowning under here? God, I need a cigarette."

"Me too," Sam said. "Look, let's go and take a few pictures of this door and then head back upstairs. We can shift our stuff into some of the officers' quarters and then you'll have somewhere to smoke."

"He's right, Nina," said Fatima. "It'll be good to break out into individual rooms, so we'll all have a little more space. Come and take a look at the door first, though. Sam will need you to tell him which details to focus on."

Biting back her anger, Nina pushed her hands through her

hair, took a couple of deep breaths and forced herself to look calm. Then she led Sam and Fatima over to the door, pushing past Purdue and the others with a swift, barely civil explanation that Sam should be allowed to photograph the door as they found it, before anyone started fooling about with it. Working to her instructions, Sam took shots of the door as a whole, of its hinges, its seals, the dial, and the strange lock. Then he, Fatima, and Nina left Purdue and the others to play safe-cracker while they went to claim rooms in the officers' quarters.

"That's better." Nina blew out a long stream of smoke and stretched out on the bottom bunk. She handed the cigarette packet to Sam, who was unpacking the contents of his rucksack into drawers. "So what made you choose this room? The ones at the other end of the corridor are nicer."

Sam shrugged. "The wee bit of me that's still six years old couldn't pass up the chance to get the top bunk. Besides, everyone will pick rooms at that end. I fancied a bit of distance."

"Makes sense. God, I love being able to smoke indoors." She eyed his attempts at unpacking with amusement. "Sam, is that what you call unpacking? If you're not going to organize your stuff, what's the point in taking it out of the rucksack?"

"There's a system!" Sam shoved a handful of socks into the bottom drawer. "Clothes in here, stuff that isn't clothes in the drawer above. Camera and general Nazi memorabilia stay on the top." He retrieved the little pouch that had belonged to Kruger from the depths of his pack. "Look, I could even make a little display with them." One by one, he took out the little brass pieces and arranged them on top of the pouch— first the tiny cog, then the thin disc, the cylinder, and the brass ring.

Nina picked the ring up for a closer look. "This is such a strange piece," she said. "It looks like a little one-finger knuckleduster, don't you think?" She slipped it onto the middle finger of her right hand and drew back her fist as if to punch Sam.

"You can take the girl out of the west coast of Scotland . . ." Sam teased. He caught Nina's hand as it arced in a lazy, slow-motion punch toward his jaw. Then his gaze fell on the ring, and realization hit him far harder than Nina ever would. "Is that . . . ? Give it here!" He flapped urgently at Nina, who tugged the ring off her finger and gave it back to him.

"What?" she asked. "What is it?"

Sam grabbed his camera and began flicking back through the images on his view screen. When he came to the close-up of the strange keyhole, he held it out to Nina. "You don't think this would fit, do you?" He held up the ring next to the little screen, inviting her comparison.

"I'm not sure." Nina scrutinized both the image and the ring. "It does look like it's about the right shape and size, and it's not as if we have any idea what else it does. Want to give it a try?"

"What did I tell you?" Purdue was yelling at the top of his lungs when Sam and Nina re-entered the tunnel. "I told you it would be easy!" He was capering from foot to foot, fists above his head in celebration, wearing a face-splitting grin. The others were cheering and congratulating him. Evidently he had cracked the code—yet the door remained obstinately closed.

"Surely that's a partial victory?" Sam could not resist playing devil's advocate for a moment. "It's still shut."

Regaining his composure, Purdue gave Sam a look of polite annoyance. "I did not say that I would open it, Mr. Cleave— only that I would work out the combination. That much I have done."

"But how do you know, if the door's still shut?"

"By the feel and the noise, Mr. Cleave. One by one I could

hear the tumblers fall into place, and now the dial has sprung forward ever so slightly. It is minute, but it is enough. Now all we need is to find something that can serve as a key and we can discover what—"

Without a word, Nina stepped forward and slotted her single-finger knuckleduster into the key slot. It clicked into place and the handle popped out, unlocked, and ready to be turned.

"Moment of truth, Dave," she murmured, looking Purdue straight in the eye and daring him to open the door. He shot his cuffs, stepped forward, and closed his fingers around the handle, drawing out the drama of the moment. The door creaked and complained as he tried to pull it open, protesting after years of not being touched. In the end, Ziv Blomstein had to step in and provide the muscle. At last, after a good three minutes of the two men working against the stiff hinges, it stood open before them, revealing a brightly-lit white corridor. No corrugated metal or smoothed stone here —this looked like a much better maintained and more permanent structure. With Blomstein at his shoulder, Purdue was the first to step through.

"Freeze!" A voice rang out from the corridor. "Down on the ground! All of you! On the ground right now!"

Sam saw a horde of black-uniformed soldiers sweeping toward the group from the other end of the corridor, wielding machine guns. Immediately obedient, he dropped to the floor and lay as still as he could while numerous pairs of heavy army boots tramped past his head.

CHAPTER 18

THE SOLDIERS SWARMED in and swiftly confiscated Blomstein's gun, the only visible weapon the group had. "Who's in charge here?" the major barked.

That's a good point, Sam thought. Who actually is in charge of this group? He raised his head as much as he dared to see who stepped up.

Purdue was the first to speak. "You can speak to me," he said. "I commissioned this expedition and am ultimately responsible for it."

"Then I'll ask you to get to your feet, sir," the major said. As Purdue straightened up, two soldiers briskly patted him down. "What is your purpose here, sir?"

"I could ask you the same thing," Purdue blustered. He waved grandly at the rest of the group. "We are a group of scientists and historians who came in search of Ice Station

Wolfenstein, to verify its existence and learn its secrets. And you are?"

The major regarded Purdue with a mixture of curiosity and disdain. "I am not at liberty to tell you that, sir. Please ask the rest of your party to stand so that we can check for weapons."

Purdue did not actually repeat the command, but everyone had heard it clearly and no one was in the mood to argue. Even Blomstein restricted himself to simply eyeing the newcomers suspiciously. The major began firing off questions about which countries they had come from, the exact nature of their business, and of course their names and professional capacities. One by one they answered, until he came to Admiral Whitsun. As soon as the old man gave his name, the major snapped to attention and saluted him.

"Might I be permitted to ask your name?" Admiral Whitsun asked.

"Major Erik Alfsson, sir!"

"Major Alfsson, could we speak for a moment in private? Perhaps we could step into the next room . . ."

For the briefest of moments the young major looked flustered. Encountering a man who outranked him was evidently not something he had anticipated. However, he pulled himself together and bellowed a few more instructions at his men, telling them to keep everyone else in the room and delegating his second-in-command to take the remaining names.

"This is so stupid!" Nina hurled a balled-up pair of socks at the wall, then tutted as they fell to the floor instead of bouncing back toward her. "We've come all the way here and now these soldiers or mercenaries or whatever they are aren't going to let us get anywhere near the most interesting stuff. What are they even doing here?"

"Don't know," said Sam. "I suppose the base is still operational in some way or other. Maybe scientific research of some kind."

"I wouldn't think so," Fatima chimed in. She got up from the bottom bunk, picked up the socks and tossed them over to Nina, who was leaning against the wall at the far end of the room. "I've been in plenty of research stations in my time, but they don't usually have soldiers crawling all over them. Not unless you're in an area that's on some kind of high alert."

"Could this place be on high alert?" Sam asked.

Fatima shook her head. "I don't know. I guess it could be. But I haven't heard of any territorial disputes or anything that would explain those guys. Word tends to get around among those of us who work at the bases. And those guys look serious."

Sam nodded. He did not want to mention his fears to the others, but he was growing increasingly concerned. If this place was crawling with soldiers, then someone, somewhere had something to hide. And if that was the case, then they were all too close to it for comfort. The smart thing to do would be to kill us all, he thought. We might not have seen whatever it is that they're hiding here, but we know this place really exists now and that's dangerous enough. The most sensible option would be to make sure we never get home. Just another expedition lost in harsh conditions. It happens. No one would question it much. My guess is that each and every one of us will get a bullet in our heads some time tonight.

They had been escorted back to the officers' quarters as soon as all of their details had been noted. The march back up the stairs had been brisk and efficient, but with no overt malice or threat from the strange soldiers. Once they reached the quarters they had been informed that they could move freely from room to room, provided they did not attempt to leave the corridor until further notice. At mealtimes they would be escorted to the refectory and back. This would continue, they were told, until orders came through. They had not said who these orders would be from. The rest of the brass pieces from Harald Kruger's box had been confiscated.

"Who are they, anyway?" Nina wondered aloud. "The one who was talking to us first, Major Whatshisname, he sounded American."

Fatima shook her head. "No, he sounded like someone who learned English from an American," she said. "I'd guess he's Scandinavian. But did you hear the others? It's a whole mix of accents—and languages. The two who are posted at the far end of the corridor, along by my room? They're Israeli. I heard them. With a mix like that, I would guess they're private military contractors—PMCs—like the Blackwater guys."

"That doesn't sound good." Nina reached for the cigarettes.

"Don't let it worry you!" Fatima was just a little too quick to reassure Nina, Sam noticed. "I know it all sounds shady as hell, but it's ok. I've been to a couple of places that had PMCs around and it was fine. Remember I told you about that time when I was working in the Indian Ocean, at that research base in Sri Lanka, and there were those endangered turtles and they were having real trouble with poachers? There was a PMC unit stationed there to keep the poaching under control. I talked to some of the staff at the base about it and they said it was fine. They still obey all the same rules as normal soldiers—you know, the Geneva Convention and international sanctions and all that stuff."

Sam silently accepted the cigarettes from Nina and lit one.

He had been meaning to talk to her about rationing their supplies, because they did not know how long it would be before they finally got to Neumayer and more cigarettes were available to buy. Now there seemed to be little point. Fatima may have been correct about the legitimate PMCs that she had encountered before, but Sam knew from his dealings with the arms ring that there were also shady, disreputable contractors who had little respect for the rules and would do whatever they were being paid to do, and they wouldn't balk at killing off a few academics and dilettantes who had been in the wrong place at the wrong time. If his experience of mercenary soldiers was anything to go by, they would be as well to smoke their cigarettes while they still could.

It was another hour before they were called out of their rooms and herded down the stairs. This is it, Sam thought. Either these guys like to eat their tea really early, or we're about to die. Bruich, I hope you'll be happy living with your Uncle Paddy. Trish . . . Looks like I'll see you soon.

His worst suspicions seemed to be confirmed when they were marched straight past the refectory and down toward the docking room. Sam's head was full of visions of them being lined up next to one of the flooded pens, ready to be executed. Their bodies would fall forward into the water, then the system would be activated so that the water flowed back out into the ocean, carrying their corpses with it.

Instead, they were taken through the room, past the U-boats, down the ladder, and back to the corridor where they had been stopped. They kept going, into the unknown corridors that they had seen so briefly. The image in Sam's head changed. Is there an exit down here? he wondered. That would be another way to do it. We don't even have our jackets on. If they kick us out into the snow we'll all be dead before long. Then, what, they scatter our stuff around and make it look like we were trying to set up a camp and didn't quite make it? Make it look like some weird, Dyatlov Pass kind of mystery? I'd have thought the ocean would be a better bet—a complete disappearance would be better than some big mystery. Unless they've got something they can use for easy disposal stashed around here somewhere. An incinerator, maybe? Who knows? I suppose it could be anything in a place like this.

Finally they arrived in a long, white room with a large table. It looked like some kind of meeting room, lined with notice boards that had been stripped of their signs. The group was instructed to sit and wait for Major Alfsson to join them. It was only then, sitting around the table, that Sam realized that Admiral Whitsun was not with them. He saw some of the others realizing the same thing, looking puzzled, displaying varying degrees of concern. Most of them were visibly alarmed by the presence of the soldiers, though Jefferson in particular was trying hard not to show it. Even Purdue looked troubled, although Sam suspected that this was more to do with being told what to do than anything else. Only Alexandr remained inscrutable and even slightly amused, but it seemed that danger brought him to life.

After several long, silent minutes, the door swung open and Major Alfsson appeared, along with Admiral Whitsun. The young soldier helped the old man into a seat, then sat down himself. It was Admiral Whitsun who spoke first.

"I fear I must apologize for keeping you all waiting so long," he said. "I realize that this is an alarming situation, and I am sorry to have been the cause of any delay—but I had another turn while Major Alfsson and I were talking, and he was kind enough to summon his company's medic and ensure that I was well. Unfortunately this detained him from communicating with his superior officers."

"I have now spoken to them," Alfsson said. "Our primary concern, of course, is to ensure your safety until we can establish contact with Neumayer Station and arrange your transport. But while you are here, my instructions are to ask you to share whatever information you have regarding this place. There are areas that we are still attempting to access and it seems possible that you might be able to help us. We had been working on the door that you opened for some time."

"Might we ask how long you've been here?" Purdue spoke up. "If we are to share information with you, it would be a gesture of good faith if you were to share yours with us."

"I'm sorry, sir," said Alfsson, "but I am not at liberty to disclose that information. All I can tell you is that we had been here long enough to get frustrated by some of the doors —but then, I am not a patient man."

"Then we've got that much in common," Purdue muttered to himself, leaning back in his chair and folding his arms sulkily.

"I have told Major Alfsson the basic details of our mission." Admiral Whitsun's breathing was becoming a little labored, though he remained sitting bolt upright and looking alert. "After a certain amount of negotiation, his superiors were willing to permit us not only to stay until our transport is arranged, but also to allow us to continue our explorations— provided we agree to remain under escort at all times. I trust we are all agreed?"

A ripple of nods ran around the table, punctuated by some relieved sighs as the less optimistic members of the group realized that they were not on the point of being shot after all.

"Great," said Major Alfsson. "Let's make a start."

CHAPTER 19

THE SECTION OF the ice station that was occupied by the PMCs was uniformly brighter and a little more modern-looking than the area occupied by Sam and the others. As they marched through the corridors Sam saw a couple of rooms that were clearly dormitories, but apart from the meeting room there was no sign of anything more interesting than living quarters.

Two stories up and along another passageway, they came to the door that had been causing the PMCs so much trouble. It was very similar to the one that they had opened earlier in the day.

"We've been working on this for some time," said Major Alfsson, patting the heavy metal of the door. "It seems to be resistant to more or less everything. We haven't been able to figure out the combination, and it seems to be impossible to wrench the thing open. Our next step is to try explosives, but

I would prefer that you take a look at it first rather than risk destabilizing the tunnels."

Purdue stepped forward and examined the dial. He laid his long fingers on it and gently, very gently began to spin it. His face was less than an inch from the steel, his eyes shut, his expression one of rapt concentration. Silently, Sam raised his camera and stole a picture. He had never seen Purdue looking peaceful before. As the first tumbler clicked into place, Purdue smiled in simple joy. It took him less time than the previous door. Sam wondered whether the combination was the same, but he never had a chance to ask. The moment Purdue cracked the lock, a cheer went up from some of the PMCs that drowned out Sam's attempt to speak.

"You next, Nina!" The look of manic excitement was back in Purdue's eyes. "Look at the lock; does it look the same to you as the last one?"

Nina looked back over her shoulder at Sam as Purdue grabbed her by the hand and pulled her forward. "That wasn't really my discovery," she said. "It was Sam who spotted the shape."

"No matter, no matter. Did you bring the key with you, or is it still in the other door?"

"It's here," Nina reached into her pocket and pulled out the ring with its strange, bulbous protrusions. She slotted it into the door and sure enough, the handle sprang forward. "You open this one," she said to Major Alfsson. "We got enough of a surprise with the last one we opened."

"Wow . . ." Before anyone could stop her, Nina charged into the new corridor. All the way along it were long, narrow windows looking into huge laboratories lined with sinks, gas taps, and burners, microscopes, and pieces of equipment that most of the group did not recognize. "I need a closer look at this." Nina moved toward the door, but Major Alfsson barred her way.

"With respect, Dr. Gould," he said, "we can't let you in there until our men have been in to make sure it's safe. Let's continue."

Nina looked disappointed, but chose not to argue. She rejoined the group members, but as they continued to march she could not resist staring longingly into each window that they passed. "We'd better bring a fresh SD card when we get permission to look around these," she whispered to Sam. "We're going to want to get a record of everything." Sam nodded. Despite his reservations about their safety, he was feeling those old pangs of satisfaction at being the first to see and record things. He remembered the excitement he had once felt when he knew that his camera contained the only evidence of whatever he had been investigating.

Back then, ambition had been a part of his life. He had planned to capitalize on his scoops and his success and become rich enough that he and Trish would be able to do whatever they liked. He had not imagined that he would ever experience even a flicker of that feeling again, but somewhere deep in the pit of his stomach he could sense that little thrill that came from having secret, potentially dangerous information.

At the end of the corridor they came to a set of double doors, which Major Alfsson wrenched open. Beyond the doors lay a vast cylindrical hangar, several stories high, reaching all the way up to what must have been the surface of the ice. Every level consisted of a narrow walkway all the way around the walls, all centered around the massive missile that stood partly constructed, awaiting completion.

There was complete silence in the room. No one had been expecting this, and very few of them had ever seen such a sight before. The missile was breathtaking in its sheer scale and terrifying power, even in its incomplete state. The skeleton of it was fully built, but its covering was not and its mechanisms were exposed in many places. On instinct, Sam lifted his camera and prepared the shot.

"Sir, you need to put the camera down!" Major Alfsson's voice was urgent. "You need to put the camera down now.

Everybody turn around and return to the corridor. This room is unsafe for civilian occupation and is off limits until further notice."

As he spoke, his fellow soldiers began rapidly shepherding the expedition party out of the missile hangar. Purdue was extremely reluctant to leave. Only when Major Alfsson stood in front of him and adjusted his gun with unsubtle menace did he finally drag himself away from the railing that separated the walkway from the missile.

Once they were back in the corridor, Major Alfsson ordered two of his men to stand guard at the double doors. "You are welcome to look around the rest of the facility," he said, addressing the expedition party, "provided you do so under escort." He signaled to a couple of soldiers who separated themselves from their platoon and joined Sam and the others. "We will ensure that you are safe at all times. Thank you for your assistance with the locks. Now, I will go and find out whether we've established contact with Neumayer yet."

Purdue stepped out from the group and attempted to take the major aside for a quiet word, but Major Alfsson did not respond well to Purdue's light touch on his arm. He stopped in his tracks and stood at ease, refusing to be drawn aside, forcing Purdue to state his business in front of the company.

"Major Alfsson," Purdue said quietly, "I realize the dangers of having a large group of people in that room, but I specialize in nanotechnology and have experience with ballistics, so having another look in there is of particular professional interest to me. I wonder if I might persuade you . . ."

"The hangar is out of bounds, sir. You are welcome to explore the rest of the facility. Under escort."

Purdue pinched the bridge of his nose in frustration. "Yes, I understand that. However, I am quite capable of taking responsibility for my own safety. Just five minutes, that's all I ask—no photography, no disturbance, just the briefest of looks—"

Major Alfsson raised a hand to halt Purdue's speech. Sam, who was pressed up against Ziv Blomstein in the crowded corridor, felt the bodyguard instinctively reach for the place where his gun had been. "Sir. The hangar is out of bounds. You are welcome to explore—"

"Damn it, man, I want to see what's in there!" Purdue exploded, his face flushing a sudden pink. "Do you have any idea what you're obstructing here? Let me in or I promise you, you won't—"

"Escort this man back to his quarters immediately." The major's tone was curt, dismissive. Instantly a pair of soldiers marched forward and stood on either side of Purdue, who gave an irritated snort but did not push his luck any longer.

He beckoned Blomstein to accompany him and allowed himself to be led away. Moments later Major Alfsson and the rest of his company disappeared back toward the control room, leaving only the expedition party, their guards, and the soldiers blocking the entrance to the hangar.

"Well, I don't know about you guys," said Fatima, as the sound of marching footsteps died away in the distance, "but I really want to see these labs. Come on."

The air in the laboratory was musty and still, apparently undisturbed for decades. For several long moments the group was completely silent, each lost in thought. Nina and Matlock briefly set their differences aside, united by the presence of their specialist subject all around them. They gravitated toward the neat stack of notebooks that sat at the end of the nearest workbench, but their hands hovered above the books, neither prepared to disturb them yet.

It was Admiral Whitsun who picked up the first book. He lifted it lovingly, holding it to his nose and inhaling the scent of old paper. "This may be the very laboratory in which my father worked," he whispered, half to himself. He opened the notebook. It was filled with labeled sketches of what looked like cells, accompanied by densely written paragraphs in tiny, neat writing. "It is one of my great regrets that I never learned the language of my ancestral country," the admiral mused, tracing his finger along a line of handwriting. "Professor Matlock, Dr. Gould—would you be so kind as to tell me what we have here?"

The two historians huddled around the book in the admiral's hands. "It seems to be the results of an experiment concerning a particular chemical compound," said Professor Matlock. "There's a hypothesis here concerning the use of sodium and . . . I'm not entirely sure of this, it's quite technical vocabulary . . . a couple of other elements. It's speculating about using this compound as an antidote to something. Then there's a description of how the experiment was carried out—lamenting the lack of suitable test subjects, I notice—and a note suggesting that it was inconclusive. Have you anything to add, Nina?"

"I don't think so," said Nina. "As you say, the vocabulary is quite technical and there are some abbreviations that aren't helping. I would need to spend a bit of time with these. But Fatima, you might be able to help."

"I'll try," Fatima said, approaching and leaning in to look at the books. "I don't speak much German, though. All I know is the really, really basic stuff."

"You might know what the drawings are, though," Nina suggested, handing the book over. For a few long minutes

Fatima studied the meticulous little sketches.

"They look like diagrams," Fatima said. "This one here is a virus—Filoviridae. Maybe that's what they were trying to find a cure for, although this seems like a really weird place to do it."

"Why is that?" Nina asked.

"Filovirus—it's stuff like Ebola, viruses that you find in places such as Africa. Countries near the equator, you know? I wouldn't have thought it would be that big of a problem here."

"I suppose if you're planning world domination, anything's fair game," Sam said. "I mean, you wouldn't want to get close to conquering the whole world only to have your army decimated by a virus, would you?"

Fatima looked skeptical. She was still flicking through the pages of the notebook, and with every drawing she looked at she seemed a little more concerned. "I'd love to think that it was as straightforward as that, Sam," she said. "But think about it—what's in the room next to these labs?"

"That rocket thing. A missile, was it?"

"Yes, a missile. An intercontinental ballistic missile, I think. So I'm guessing . . ." She trailed off and rubbed the heel of her hand against her forehead as if to soothe her brain. "Look, I'm sorry if this is going to sound alarmist, but . . . I think what we're seeing here is an early attempt at biological warfare. It looks like they were trying to find some way to engineer a virus that works something like Ebola, but more communicable and with a lower incubation time."

"And that means?"

"Well, it would mean that if that missile hit a populated area, in addition to the damage caused by the missile strike itself there would be an outbreak of a really virulent hemorrhagic fever. We're talking pain, nausea, diarrhea, respiratory tract hell, bleeding from places you really don't want to bleed from . . . not to mention probably hallucinations and delirium. It would not be pretty. And there would be no cure, so the mortality rate would probably be something like 70–80 percent."

Sam gave a long, low whistle as the thought of an attack on that scale sank in. Like any adult, he had always been aware of biological warfare—but only as a remote possibility, an abstract concept, a thought experiment played out in the conversations that followed zombie movies. He knew about the occasional training exercises that the emergency services carried out, but even those seemed more like games than serious preparation for a real attack. Even now, the idea of 80 percent of a place's population being swiftly wiped out by a disease seemed crazy—but standing in the laboratory, knowing that there was a partly-built ICBM in the next room, it suddenly felt like a more realistic and far more chilling prospect.

"That's sick," Jefferson said. His suspiciously golden tan had faded by a couple of shades. "Who were these people?"

"It's nothing that isn't going on now," Sam pointed out. "Your government's done it. Our government's done it. They're probably still doing it. There are certainly plenty of dodgy organizations experimenting with biological weapons. These guys were just ahead of their time."

"Are you making excuses for the Nazis?" Jefferson demanded, looking outraged.

"He's saying that war tends to involve unpalatable things, no matter who's doing them," Nina butted in. "But I wonder whether they really were ahead of their time, or whether this place was in use for longer than we originally thought. Look —there's a note here referring to the daughter of the scientist who owned this notebook. It refers to her as 'sie' instead of 'es,' but that German pronoun didn't change until sometime in the 1960s. Either people were using that form earlier than I thought, or someone was still working here after the change was made."

Fatima pointed toward a dispensing device poised above an Erlenmeyer flask. "And that's a digital titrator," she said. "It's pretty old, but they definitely didn't have those in the 1940s."

"They sure didn't," Jefferson agreed, stepping closer and examining the equipment. "I haven't seen one of these since I was at Yale! We had a whole bunch of them in the lab and my professors kept telling us they were state-of-the-art."

"And when was that?" Fatima asked.

"1977. My first year of pre-med." For a moment he stood in silent communion with the titrator, lost in memories of his early college years when the gloss of youth had been his by rights, not something he sought to recreate by means of surgical procedures and spray tans. "So what are you saying, Nina? This place was working all the way into the Cold War?"

"Possibly," said Nina. "I don't know. I don't have a working hypothesis yet. All I know is that what we're finding isn't what I expected. This place is more complicated than I ever imagined, and there's an incredible amount to document. Sam, does your camera take video footage? It might be quicker to film what we're seeing here than to shoot stills, and once we've got a record of everything as we found it we can get on with finding out what's in that pile of notebooks."

"And we can look for some safety equipment," Fatima suggested. "We don't know what's in this place, and I'd prefer it if we didn't take any unnecessary risks. We don't know how much of a scrub-down they did before they abandoned this place. It wouldn't hurt to take a few basic precautions."

"Good point," said Nina. "Everyone keep an eye out for

goggles and masks and the like. Now let's get moving. We don't know how much time we'll have before Neumayer sends transport for us."

The group got to work. Sam took as many images as he could of the equipment and the books, while Fatima, Nina, and Professor Matlock followed behind him, eager to get their hands on the artifacts once he was done with them. Jefferson and Alexandr tagged along behind them, but Admiral Whitsun wandered off alone. He trailed his fingers through the air an inch above the work surfaces, clearly longing to touch them. The youngest PMC hesitated, uncertain whether he should ask the admiral to rejoin the group. He shot a sidelong glance at his companion, who was evidently his senior.

"It's fine," the older man muttered. "Just keep an eye on him."

The young PMC strode across to the far side of the room and took up a position near the admiral, close enough to prevent him from going too far but distant enough to be respectful.

"This one is talking about Harald Kruger!" Nina jabbed at the page in front of her with her finger. "This note, here, look—whoever wrote this seems to have been dealing with Kruger for some sort of test. For a . . . a missile of some kind. Aggregat 13?"

"It's a type of ICBM, I believe" Professor Matlock said. "I have heard of the Aggregat series. The idea was to create a complement of rockets which, when used in conjunction, would have made the Nazis an unstoppable force. I was only aware of there being twelve in the series, though."

"It could be that we've come across something unknown outside of this station," Nina suggested. "Anyway, it looks like whoever was working in this laboratory had prepared something that was to be tested along with a prototype of this missile, but it didn't go to plan. Something didn't disseminate the way they wanted it to, and an area of land had to be put out of bounds until they could ascertain whether the container for this virus had been—"

"Sir!"

A crash of shattering glass pierced the silence. Admiral Whitsun was on his knees, coughing and wheezing. The young PMC rushed forward to help him. "Are you all right, sir?" he asked, giving the old man his arm.

"I'm fine," said Admiral Whitsun. "I'm fine. Please, don't make a fuss."

"Admiral, I'm worried about you," Nina said, coming round to support him from the other side. "We've only been here a day and a bit and that's the second turn you've had. I think you're overdoing it. Let's get you back to the meeting room and you can have a seat and we'll get you some tea."

"Honestly, there's no need to worry." The admiral's voice was as steady and reassuring as he could make it, though his hands were still trembling and Sam thought he could see the old man's legs shaking. "I would rather not cause any more hassle than I already have." He glanced down at the shards of glass lying on the floor. Judging by the little stand lying amid the wreckage, he had knocked over a handful of empty test tubes. "I do seem to have made a mess, don't I? I trust you did not cut yourself while helping me up, young man?"

The PMC shook his head. "No, sir."

"That is a relief, then. Do you have a name?"

"Private Hodge, sir." The PMC stood to attention.

"Well, Private Hodge, I wonder if you would be so kind as to escort me back to my quarters? I can hardly stay here if I'm going to prove such a liability to the others, and I am sure that Major Alfsson would prefer it if none of us wander the corridors unattended."

Again, Private Hodge stole a quick glance at his superior for confirmation, then said "Yes, sir" and set off, matching his strides to the pace of the frail admiral.

"I'm getting a horrible feeling that he's not going to make it back home," Fatima whispered, half to herself, half to Nina and Sam. Sam nodded. Whatever the state of the admiral's health on the journey, he seemed to be deteriorating rapidly now that they were here.

Pity, Sam thought. He seems a really nice old boy. Just a bit . . . broken, I suppose. Sad and reserved. I'm sorry I had to be part of that. I hope he's getting what he's looking for by being here. I hope he'll be ok.

CHAPTER 20

B Y THE END of the day, all the expedition team
had thoroughly explored the lab and exhausted
their patience with one another. Nina and
Professor Matlock were bickering with each other over the
contents of the notes and struggling with the highly specific
technical jargon. Fatima was doing her best to help, but since
she had the technical expertise but not the language, her
ability to break up the squabbles was limited. Jefferson
Daniels, who prided himself on his ability to mediate
disputes, apparently without justification, was attempting to
pour oil on troubled waters.

His work behind the camera done, Sam had decided to
sneak out. The sound of arguing voices was starting to give
him a headache and making him acutely aware that it had
been several hours since his last cigarette and even longer
since his last drink. Muttering some excuse about going to

find Purdue and work on his profile, Sam slipped out into the corridor. A moment later he heard the door open behind him and looked around to see Alexandr following him, with Private Hodge, who had returned to the labs, at his heels.

"I'm sorry, sir," Private Hodge said, "but I have to accompany you. Captain Hernandez's orders. Are you returning to your quarters?"

"Possibly," said Alexandr "Personally, I am going wherever the rest of the group is not. The amount of money that Mr. Purdue is paying me is obscene, but it is nowhere near enough to listen to any more of that."

"Well, I'm heading back to quarters," said Sam. "I suppose I should really go and talk to Purdue, but I'm not sure I can be bothered."

"Then don't."

"I really should, though," Sam groaned. "I'm supposed to be writing this stupid profile for the paper and he wants a longer version for some reason of his own, so he's paying me a stupid amount of money over and above what I'll get from the paper. I haven't even started the interviews I'll need yet."

Alexandr led the way back toward their quarters. "There is no rush, surely. Trust me, you have plenty of time. Even if the transport to Neumayer were to arrive right now, we would still have to stay there for as long as it takes Dr. al-Fayed to carry out her research. There will be many long days that will be much less eventful than this one, and you will be glad of having something to do. So for now, I suggest that you follow my lead. I have a far better idea than chatting with Mr. Purdue."

Sam had a feeling that Alexandr's idea might involve alcohol, and he was right. As soon as they got back to the corridor and Private Hodge departed, Alexandr slipped into his room and emerged a few seconds later with his flask. Sam wondered how the guide managed it—no matter how much he drank or shared, the flask always seemed to be full. Maybe it's the Ke'let, Sam thought, letting his imagination run free. Maybe it follows him around topping off his vodka. That would certainly explain why he's willing to rush off into the snow every new year. I'd do it myself for an unlimited supply of that stuff.

They repaired to Sam's room where they pulled blankets and pillows onto the floor and sprawled out. Not wishing to exhaust his supply of real cigarettes, Sam fished around in the deepest recesses of his backpack until he found his emergency pouch of loose tobacco and rolling papers. He held out the little packet of filters, but Alexandr waved them away and rolled himself a long, extremely thin cigarette.

"Expertly done," Sam said, marveling at Alexandr's speed and dexterity.

"You spend enough time out here, you become good at rolling these," Alexandr said. "The trick is to create as thin a line of tobacco as possible, but it must be unbroken and unfiltered. With such a thin line, if you use a filter you simply should not bother to smoke at all. It is the perfect balance of necessity and frugality, and if you do it correctly the result is close to art." Pulling his lighter from his pocket, he lit the cigarette and took a shallow draft. "Then you must inhale just deeply enough to get the benefit, but not enough to exhaust the cigarette too soon."

"I'm spoiled." Sam attempted to copy what Alexandr had done, but the line of tobacco was thicker than he would have liked and he lost a few precious flakes as he rolled the paper with clumsy fingers. "Well, close enough." He put his wonky creation between his lips and lit it. "This definitely wasn't how I thought I'd be spending the first weeks of this year."

"Nor I," Alexandr agreed, knocking back a shot of vodka and pouring himself another capful. "Never before have I seen an expedition pulled together so quickly, or with such strange purposes."

"Did you know what Purdue was here for? You didn't seem to when he told the rest of us, but I wondered whether you were just indulging his moment of drama."

"No, that was genuine. I did not know, and if I had known when he engaged my services I would have advised him against this search. Even though we have found this place, I doubt that every one of us will leave it alive."

Sam nodded. No one had drawn direct attention to the dangers the group faced since Admiral Whitsun had alluded to the instructions he had given that he should be left behind if his health failed. Yet it was always there—unspoken by some, unconsidered by others. Sam realized that only hours had passed since he had been waiting for the sound of a gunshot behind him and the sensation of oblivion. "We're in over our heads, aren't we? God knows what Purdue's dragged us into."

"We are. Something dangerous is going on here, of that there is no doubt." Alexandr's face hardened slightly, his expression darkening. "The key to surviving dangerous situations is to understand them. We do not. We are unaware of the true nature of our situation. This makes it unlikely that we will all get out alive. We may be lucky, perhaps, if any of us do."

Well, that took a turn for the morose, Sam thought. He tried to ignore the tingle of fear that was creeping up his spine. All through their time in the tent and their first hours in the ice station, Sam had been able to convince himself that as long as Alexandr remained sanguine there was really nothing to fear. But now . . .

"It's funny," Sam said, "I thought that I didn't want to live. My plan, back home in Edinburgh, was to drink myself to death eventually—and by eventually, I was thinking hopefully within the next couple of years."

"That seems a very complicated way to commit suicide." Alexandr's brow furrowed. "Why not concentrate it into a short period? Even a single night? It can be done."

Sam shook his head. "I couldn't. I wanted to—left to my own devices I'd just have got pissed and jumped off a bridge, but there was someone who would have been angry and upset if I'd done that. So I couldn't."

"And this person would not have objected to you drinking yourself to death slowly?"

"Probably. But if I did it over a long time, I could sort of pretend I was still trying to function. Anyway, I don't know why I put so much thought into what that person would want any more. She died."

Alexandr made no reply, but his face softened a little. He learned forward and topped off Sam's makeshift cup.

"She died," Sam repeated, "and I thought I wanted to die too. That's why I wasn't nervous about coming to the Antarctic. I knew it would be dangerous but I didn't really care. And now . . . I don't know what's changed, but I really don't fancy getting shot by those soldiers or freezing to death outside. Presumably I don't really want to die after all—but I'd definitely like to drink myself into oblivion for tonight, at least."

"Oblivion is more than this little flask has to offer, regretfully," Alexandr said. "But it can certainly take the edge off of your pain, I am sure. Here. Have another, and let us talk to something more cheerful. Perhaps I am wrong to be so pessimistic. And even if I am not, what would be the point of spending our remaining time in misery? You have finished your cigarette—let me show you how to roll one properly."

So Sam settled down to watch Alexandr's nimble fingers creating skinny cigarettes. The guide plucked a story out of the air, apparently at random, and began to tell Sam of an earlier adventure in which he had been stuck in a Siberian snowdrift trying to get an old-fashioned steam train to work years after being decommissioned. Sam did not follow the exact details of the repair, which seemed to have been conducted with little more than twigs, an oil can, and a Swiss army knife, but the Russian certainly spun a good yarn. Before Sam knew it he was smiling again, then laughing, then actually enjoying himself despite the danger and the constant underlying feeling that he was betraying Trish just by being alive.

The following morning Sam got up uncharacteristically early and sneaked down to the refectory before the others were up. His chat with Alexandr had given him a lot to think about, and he could not face another morning of bickering and tension. The taciturn PMCs at the end of the corridor let him pass without comment, but Sam saw that a few more had been posted on the other stories. In the kitchen he rooted through their supplies and found some tea, then picked as many berries as he could out of his porridge before adding the water. As he spooned the sloppy, over-sweetened mess into his mouth, he caught himself thinking longingly of Scottish Lorne sausages and steak bakes.

After breakfast he hit the showers. The water was gloriously hot and smelled faintly of sulfur, and the pressure was perfect. Heavy jets of steaming water thudded into the tense muscles of Sam's back and shoulders and thundered down on his head. After seasickness, tents, dehydrated food, and hard bunks, this was luxury. He peeled off a couple of sheets of compacted soap and scrubbed himself clean, then stood and let the water flow over him for far, far longer than necessary. He could not remember the last time he had actually enjoyed a sensation like that.

Sam had just finished lathering up his hair, ready at last to wash it and come out of the shower, when he heard a sudden banging and yelling from outside. He dived out of the cubicle and threw his towel around his waist, then ran into the corridor. At the far end two PMCs were rolling on the floor, one of them landing blow after blow on the other and screaming incoherently. A section of the corrugated iron hung loose where one of them had been slammed into the wall.

Without thinking Sam charged toward them and hurled his full weight at the one doing the punching, lifting him clear off of his opponent and sending him sprawling on the floor. Just as Sam realized that he had waded into a fight between two men who were considerably stronger than him, Alexandr appeared out of nowhere and leaped on the fallen soldier.

"His arm!" Alexandr yelled at Sam, who quickly got the message and pinned the PMC's right arm to the floor while Alexandr took the left. Then he noticed the ginger curls sticking out from under the soldier's helmet and the pale, freckled face contorted into an expression of rage. It was Private Hodges.

The other PMC had recovered from the surprise of Hodges' attack and was back on his feet, ready to restrain the young man. His face was a bloody mess, his thick nose certainly broken and his left eye beginning to puff up. With difficulty, he hauled Hodges up, yanked a length of cord from his belt and bound his wrists while Sam and Alexandr held the private in place. Even though Hodges was a soldier, Sam would not have believed that he could be so strong. He was thin and wiry, but he was putting up quite a fight against this three captors. Soon a handful of PMCs arrived to respond to their comrade's call for help. It took six of them in total to drag Private Hodges away, and by the time they did the rest of the expedition party had appeared at their doors.

"Well, that was an unexpected excitement." Alexandr retrieved Sam's towel from the floor and handed it back to him.

"Thanks." Sam hastily replaced the towel and cursed himself for not noticing that it has fallen. Now he would never be able to look Alexandr, anyone else in the group or either of the PMCs in the eye again.

"However long they have been here, "Alexandr wondered aloud as Sam skulked back toward his own room, "it is clearly too long. I've seen this kind of aggression before, but usually only in people who are overwintering. I wonder when they arrived—and whether they intend to leave before winter sets in?"

A couple of hours later, when Sam heard the others coming back from breakfast, he was sprawled on his bunk and staring into space, still only half-dressed. He had got as far as pulling on his last fresh long johns and clean trousers, then out of nowhere, a deluge of memories had hit him, knocking him off his feet.

It was the moment with the towel that had triggered them. At first he had not been aware of anything more than his usual reserve, the standard feelings of foolishness and embarrassment at being naked in front of people. Sam had no particular hang-ups about his body—he knew that it was a little on the skinny side, not especially offensive to the eye— but he had been brought up to keep it to himself around strangers and acquaintances. The last time he had scuttled naked along a brightly lit corridor in front of a host of mildly concerned near-strangers, he had been in the hospital, shortly after Trish's death.

He was surprised that he remembered it all so clearly, considering how thoroughly he had repressed the memory until now. The hospital had been busy and noisy, an overflowing medical behemoth in East London, close to the warehouse where the shoot-out had taken place. Even in the seclusion of his private room, Sam had been unable to escape the screams of the terrified young man awaiting psychiatric assessment down the corridor, sounding for all the world like Private Hodges as he was dragged away.

Sam had drifted in and out of consciousness thanks to a

combination of concussion and medication, desperately asking every nurse or doctor who came into his room whether Patricia was all right. He knew it was a lost cause. He was well aware that Trish's injuries were extensive. Every time he closed his eyes he could see the remaining half of her lovely face, bewildered and destroyed. But he could not let go of the hope that somehow she would have survived.

In the middle of his first night in the hospital, Sam had woken up in a morphine-fueled frenzy. He was convinced that Patricia was somewhere in the hospital, still alive, and that the arms ring would send more of their goons to kill her unless Sam could find her and protect her.

One by one, Sam had ripped the cannulas from his hands and feet and dragged himself out of bed. The sheets were twisted around his legs and caught up with his hospital gown so he threw them all off, feeling the tabs fastening the gown snap. Then, step by painful step, he hauled himself along the corridor toward the double doors. Somewhere beyond them, he would find Patricia. As he blundered toward the main stairwell he yelled her name over and over.

The touch of the first nurse's hand was like being woken from a fever dream. Sam never had any idea how many there had been. All he knew was that there had been hands everywhere, calming him, shushing him, turning him around and guiding him back toward his room. He was suddenly aware of the eyes of patients and staff staring at him from the other rooms, and when he felt the soft weight of the blanket falling around his shoulders he realized that he had been wandering naked.

They had sent a psychiatrist in then. As Sam was hooked back up to the saline and morphine drips, a gentle-voiced young woman spoke soothingly to him. She reminded him as sensitively as she could that Patricia was dead and that Sam needed to rest and recover from his injuries, but that she would be there to help him work through his trauma when he was ready. A nurse discharged a syringe of sedative into Sam's vein and he drifted back into unconsciousness, feeling more powerless than he ever had in his life before.

"Sam?"

A cautious tap on the door recalled Sam to the present. He glanced up to see Purdue's head sticking around the door, peering over the top of his glasses with a concerned expression on his face. "May I come in?"

"Yeah, sure." Sam hauled himself into a sitting position as Purdue entered and seated himself at the other end of the bunk. "What can I do for you?"

"Amuse me, first and foremost," Purdue said. "It would seem that I'm still confined to barracks. The others are planning to go and continue their explorations, but the soldiers have informed me that I am to remain here."

"What?" Sam was surprised. "Just because you asked if you could go back into the missile room yesterday? Seems a bit harsh."

"It's not just that," Purdue admitted. "It may also have something to do with them catching me out in an attempt to sneak back in during the night . . ."

"Ah." Sam tried not to laugh. Despite Purdue's knack for dragging the group into dangerous situations, he could not help but admire the billionaire's devil-may-care attitude. He could just picture the scene—Purdue on the point of getting into the room, caught in the soldiers' torch beams, a hint of frustration visible beneath his customary calm as he raised his hands and allowed them to escort him away. "Does that mean you want to work on the profile now? Shall I get my voice recorder set up?"

Purdue shook his head. "So boring. I would prefer that we talk off the record. I'm interested in you, Sam."

"Me? Why?"

"Because I know what you did. I know how you got your Pulitzer. An incredible feat—Interpol had been trying to find a way into that arms ring for over a year, and it was you who led them straight to their door. The things you did, the risks you took . . . Your courage was tremendous."

"I didn't do it alone."

"I know. What was her name . . . Patricia Highclere, wasn't

it?"

"Yes."

"I've read some of her work. She was a truly excellent writer."

"Yes."

"And brave, by the sounds of it. I'm only sorry I never met her." He looked straight at Sam, outright curiosity on his face. "You were engaged to her?"

Sam went pale. "How do you know that?" No one knew that. No one could. Sam had only asked Patricia to marry him hours before that fateful tip-off. There had been no time to announce it or celebrate. It had been a spur of the moment thing, a sudden outpouring of how he truly felt. He hadn't even bought a ring yet. There was no way for Purdue to have that information, surely.

"I have some contacts within Interpol, Sam," said Purdue, unfazed. "When I want to find out about someone, I do it thoroughly. Did you not realize that you were under close observation? You and Ms Highclere both? As soon as it became clear that you were getting somewhere with your investigation, you were both kept under scrutiny so that in the event of anything happening to either of you, the leads you had obtained could still be followed."

Sam's eyes narrowed. He had always assumed that his investigations would have led to a certain amount of surveillance, but he had not realized that it would be so invasive. A tiny spark of irritation flickered in the pit of his stomach, then began to grow into anger. Those moments were private, he thought. In his mind's eye he could see Patricia lying in bed, her chin resting on her folded arms and the early morning light playing over the smooth, golden skin of her naked back, her green eyes wide and incredulous as she realized that Sam had just proposed. That was just for her and me, not for any fucking spy who happened to be listening in.

"What else do you know, Purdue?" Sam demanded. "Since you seem to know everything about everyone? Did you have every single one of us investigated?"

"Of course." Purdue looked puzzled by the questions. "I like to know who I'm traveling with."

"So you know about Charles Whitsun?" The angry flame inside of Sam was growing now, fueled by Purdue's implacability. "You know, the man who was running the arms ring that killed my . . . that killed her. The man whose best friend is Nina's ex-lover who almost certainly had her flat broken into, and whose father, whose fucking father is on this wee trip with us? You know about all that? What the fuck, Purdue? What kind of sick bastard are you? What is it that you're trying to engineer?"

CHAPTER 21

YES, BUT IF the base was in use right up until the Cold War, that would explain why there are so many—"

"Nina, you have to let go of this ridiculous fantasy! There cannot have been anyone using this base by the time of the Cold War. Try to start from the least dramatic option, not the one taken straight from Hollywood."

Nina threw up her hands and turned away. She could not stand the sight of Professor Matlock's arrogant face for a moment longer. Yet another simple discussion about how to translate a particular word had degenerated into a slinging match. Privately she believed that Matlock was either so overwhelmed by their surroundings that he was refusing to acknowledge the reality of the situation, or he was trying to withhold his theories from her. She strongly suspected the latter.

"Come on, Frank," Jefferson Daniels clapped Matlock on the shoulder. "Let's take a break. Things are getting a little tense in here. Again."

"Jefferson's right," sighed Fatima, rubbing her temples. "Listening to you guys fight is giving me a migraine. Could you maybe just clear out for a little while and let me work in peace? I know the soldiers want us all to stay together, but maybe you could take the books back to your rooms or something?"

Nina mumbled an apology to her friend and began to collect the notebooks she was working on without waiting for Matlock's response. He could do as he pleased, she decided. She was going to take these books and work on a few theories of her own. Based on what they had read, she believed that the ice station had been operational all the way into the 1950s, when they had attempted to build an ICBM tipped with some kind of biological weapon.

In every notebook she examined, the notes came to an abrupt end. She couldn't determine the exact date since all dates were written in a code that she had yet to crack, but whenever it had happened, it seemed that the ice station had been abandoned in a hurry due to an experiment that had gone wrong. It looked as if there had been a plan to resume work there at some point, which had never come to fruition. Matlock was determined that they could not take these things at face value, that the notes must be code for something else, but Nina could find no evidence of it.

"Dr. al-Fayed?" Major Alfsson appeared at the door to the lab, a hint of worry on his face. "Dr. al-Fayed, we need your help. Some of our men are sick. One is in a critical condition, another is unconscious but stable. Unfortunately the unconscious man is our medic."

Fatima leapt up from her seat. "Just a second," she said. "I just need to wash my hands and I'll be right with you."

"Can I be any help?" Daniels asked. "I haven't practiced for a while but I'm still a member of the American Surgical Association."

"Yes," said Major Alfsson. "Thank you, Dr. Daniels, your help would also be appreciated. Come with me."

As soon as the two medics were ready, Alfsson lead them away. Nina found herself alone in the lab with Professor Matlock and the pile of notebooks. She could tell from his white-knuckle grip on his pen that he was not entirely happy with the situation either.

"We should probably take that break, then," Nina said brightly, gathering up a few
books and heading toward the door.

"Nina."

She turned, her hand on the handle. Matlock was still sitting at the lab bench, gripping his pan tightly and tapping it against his chin.

"I wonder if you and I might have a word." He patted the bench awkwardly, indicating that she should join him. Tentatively Nina approached and perched on the stool opposite. Matlock steepled his fingers and took a deep breath before he spoke again.

"I believe I owe you an apology, Nina," he said. "I hope that you will understand. I realize that I have been nothing but obstructive toward you during our time here. You are young, and it is the duty of older, more experienced academics, like me, to ensure that your enthusiasm does not overtake your rigor. However, sometimes this can manifest as being a killjoy or worse, simply seeming to shoot down every idea you put forward. Finding myself here, in a place that I hardly believed could really exist . . . it is immense.

"I feel it is my duty to ensure that whatever we find here, we understand it thoroughly. Everything must be interpreted correctly. And rigor is my defense against the enormity of the implications of this place's existence. I am sure that you must be experiencing a certain amount of awe as well. If I am being too hard on you, please . . . forgive me. And I must also ask you to forgive me for doubting you when you brought me your evidence in the first place."

Nina was gobsmacked. She sat in silence, her jaw dropping slightly with amazement. Dr. Frank Matlock, one of the most notoriously arrogant academics in the entire department, had just freely offered an apology—and judging by his stooped shoulders and hangdog expression, it was a genuinely humble one.

"It's fine," she said, holding out her hand for him to shake. "I know I'm not always the easiest person to work with either, and I hope you understand that it's just because I really, really care about what I'm doing. Let's both try to go a bit easier on each other, shall we?"

Their unexpected truce agreed, Nina and Professor Matlock reopened the books and prepared to try again.

Neither Jefferson nor Fatima turned up in the refectory for lunch. Nina, Matlock, Alexandr, and Admiral Whitsun sat together, an odd little group making stilted conversation. They had agreed not to talk shop during meals in order to prevent arguments and intervention by the PMCs, who would step in to put a stop to any discussion or speculation regarding the missile room. Any mention of the ICBM would result in a polite but firm reminder that no such room existed, that the group had never been in it, and that such a development at this base was impossible.

At the end of their lunch break the little group split in two.

Alexandr and Admiral Whitsun set off back in the direction of their quarters, while Nina and Professor Matlock prepared to return to the laboratory. As they approached the door one of the PMCs on duty was muttering into his radio headset. He stepped into their path.

"I'm sorry," the PMC said, "but you have to return to your quarters."

"Sorry?" Nina was taken aback.

"Major Alfsson's orders. All of you have to go back to your quarters and remain there until further notice."

"But why? Has something happened? Is everything ok?"

The PMC stared into the middle distance, refusing to make eye contact. "I'm sorry, ma'am, I can't discuss that with you. Please return to your quarters."

Nina gave a sigh of frustration. "Can't we just go and get the notebooks we were working on first? Please?"

"Nina . . ." Professor Matlock touched Nina lightly on the arm and shook his head. "Come along. We can resume our work later. We might be best not to argue."

Annoyed, unwilling, and full of questions, Nina let herself be led out of the refectory and back up the stairs. Each door they went through fell heavily, permanently shut.

Nina sat on her bunk, kicking her heels. The thought of

those notebooks, full of information that she needed, sitting on the workbench doing nobody any good, was driving her mad. She had gone alone to Sam's room earlier and tapped on the door to see if he fancied a smoke, but there had been no reply. Probably still sleeping off the effects of an evening with Alexandr, she thought. She considered the possibility of seeking out the Russian's company, but she was more in the mood for Sam's down-to-earth cynicism than Alexandr's unpredictable flights of fancy and sudden plunges into melancholy.

Approaching Admiral Whitsun for a chat was tempting— she was eager to know more about his father's connections to the ice station, but considering her link to Charles Whitsun it seemed more tactful to leave Matlock to acquire that information. All of which left Nina with no option but her own company. She rummaged in her backpack, pulled out a dog-eared copy of The Turn of the Screw and did her best to settle down and read. She had no idea how long had passed before she heard the tapping on her door. She opened it to find Fatima looking red-eyed and shaky.

"Fatima! What's the matter? Come here." Nina pulled Fatima into the room and into a tight hug. She felt her friend's shoulders shake as she buried her face in Nina's shoulder and sobbed silently. "Sssssh. It's ok. Sssssh now. Come on, tell me what's wrong. I wish I had some tea to offer you."

She led Fatima over to the bunk and made her sit down, then crouched beside her and held her hand while she cried it out. Nina had never seen Fatima in a state like this, not even during the most stressful moments of their finals year.

"Oh god, Nina, it was horrible," Fatima choked the words out through her tears. "That poor kid . . ."

"What kid?" Nina asked gently. "Do you mean the soldier? Private Hodges? What happened to him?"

"He's sick," Fatima whispered. "Really bad. He's the reason why they needed our help . . . but Nina, there was nothing we could do. I've never seen anything like it! They've got him in this little room up in the PMC quarters, it's like a padded cell but there's a window, floor to ceiling, completely transparent and . . . unbreakable, seemingly. Private Hodges kept beating his fists against it, again and again, his hands were a mess of bruises and I think his fingers were broken, they looked like they'd been snapped like twigs. He kept throwing himself against the glass every time we went near it and I could hear the noises, oh god . . . his bones. They were cracking. I think he fractured his skull, Nina. But he didn't stop.

"His face was covered in blood and he didn't stop! And every time we backed away from the glass he would stop lunging at us and instead he would start noticing the damage and trying to move his fingers or touch his head and he'd scream in pain and then I'd go closer and try to communicate with him and then he'd throw himself at the glass again and . . . oh, god. Oh god! It's just . . . he was in so much pain, Nina. I could see it. His face . . . rage and pain and hate. He's losing so much blood, but we couldn't get near him to help. I couldn't even tell what was him hemorrhaging and what was him bleeding from his injuries." She sobbed again.

"Here," Nina grabbed a bottle of water and handed it to Fatima. "Sip this. Do you know what's wrong with him?"

"Kind of," she said, swallowing a mouthful of the water. "They had taken some blood from him before he got this bad. We took a look at it. It's not really my field, viruses that occur in humans, but I still remember enough. It's definitely some kind of virus, like a mutation of Ebola. I guess it's the thing they were trying to develop here to put on that missile."

A cold thrill of fear shot through Nina's spine. "Does that mean it's going to spread? Ebola's pretty virulent, isn't it?"

Fatima closed her eyes and pressed the heels of her palms into them. "Yes," she said, her voice quiet with despair. "I think it's spreading already. The two soldiers who took the blood sample . . . they were in the room next door. Same set-up. They're both unconscious, or at least they were when we left. Major Alfsson said that's what happened to Hodges too. He had a violent outburst, then he was out cold for a little while, then when he came to he was . . . like that."

"Is there a vaccine? Can we do anything about it?"

Fatima's face collapsed into a look of devastation, answering Nina's question. For a long moment neither of them spoke. They clung tightly to each other's hands. "I asked them to let me see if I could find an antidote," Fatima said. "It was a long shot, I know . . . but I didn't want to just do nothing. He's just a boy! I don't want to leave him to die . . . But they wouldn't let me back into the labs. They just brought us back up here and said we have to stay here until further notice." She gulped. "Sorry. I'm not dealing with this very well. But if you think this is bad, you should see Jefferson—he's really taking it hard. He went really pale and just kept saying he's got a son about Hodges' age and there had to be something he could do. Alfsson had to physically drag him out of the medical bay in the end."

"Oh, Fatima . . ." Nina sighed. "This is such a mess. How the hell did we get here?"

"It gets worse," said Fatima, unconsciously twisting her engagement ring around in circles on her finger. "Aren't you wondering why I'm not in quarantine? Because I sure as hell was, until I realized the answer."

Puzzled, Nina waited for Fatima to explain what she meant. Fatima remained silent, angry tears welling up in her eyes. After a long, long silence, she finally spoke. "They think it's airborne." Her voice was flat, all traces of her anger and frustration carefully suppressed. "If they're letting me and Jefferson walk around after being exposed to Private Hodges' blood, it's because they already think it's in the ventilation system. They think that we're already dead."

Nina felt her stomach drop. She had always known that this expedition might be dangerous. While she was preparing she had considered all sorts of possible ways in which it might result in her death. Most had involved plane crashes or freezing to death. She had never considered the possibility of dying trapped underground, having fallen victim to a failed attempt at biological warfare. She pictured life in Edinburgh, strangely normal yet extremely weird without her.

She pictured some other group finding the ice station decades later, stumbling across their skeletons. Has this happened before? she wondered. Those bone fragments that Alexandr found . . . I thought there must have been an accident. What if there was an outbreak before and they burned the bodies? Then what? The survivors left? They must have, or we'd have found them too . . . I wonder how far they got. I wonder if they knew. What do you do when you're waiting to die? How does that work? Do we just sit around and wait to see if we're infected? Is it definitely fatal? I'm not just going to take this.

"Then why bother keeping us here?" Nina asked. "If we're already doomed, there can't be any harm in us moving around freely. Unless . . . is this the plan? They're locking this place down so that we can't spread the virus, aren't they?" She pushed her hands through her hair, dragging her fingertips across her scalp. "No. Fuck that. Fatima, we can't just sit around and see how this plays out! We've got to at least try to . . . I don't know, to get out of here or find a cure or something. I refuse to die quietly."

"We can't just leave without trying to help those men," Fatima was adamant. "We've got to try to help if we can. If I could just get into the labs I could at least try to find an antidote . . . But they're not going to let us anywhere near the labs now. There are soldiers everywhere. Every door. I just don't know how we can do anything."

Nina got to her feet. "You wait here," she said. "I'm going to get Alexandr"

CHAPTER 22

S AM, SAM . . ." Purdue chuckled. "What do you take me for? Some kind of evil genius? I'm afraid the truth is less well-organized than that. I'm just interested, that's all. In everything. And everyone. Tell me the truth, if you had the resources to have all of these very interesting people thoroughly investigated, then throw them together in a remote place and see how they interacted—wouldn't you? Wouldn't anyone? I am sorry if it's a little insensitive."

"A little?" Sam stared at Purdue, incredulous. "That's one way of putting it. Using my life as a soap opera would be another."

"Then I apologize. Sincerely. Understanding how other people will react to things has never been a strong point of mine. If truth be told, that's why I find these little experiments so interesting."

Sam scrutinized Purdue's face, searching for any hint of

insincerity, anything that would tell him if he was still being toyed with. What is he up to? Sam wondered. He had no idea what to do with the anger that was knotting his stomach. Part of him wanted to lash out, to knock Purdue to the ground and punch him over and over until his face was a bloody pulp for dragging everyone here and putting them in danger, as well as for treating Sam's private life as some kind of entertainment or experiment. Yet at the same time, he couldn't help but see Purdue's point. Perhaps I've just been a journalist too long, he thought, but if I had access to all that information, then . . . yeah. I probably would use it.

"I've been wondering about a few things," Sam said. "There's a lot about this expedition that doesn't make sense."

"Then ask questions, Sam," Purdue admonished him. "Surely you know that that's how you find things out. Or have you been getting sucked into the vortex of unnecessary mystery?"

Sam let the gibe pass, knowing that he had. "Ok. How did you know about this ice station in the first place? You've never explained that."

"Professional rivalry led me to this place," said Purdue. "I was working on a design for a new type of solar cell that could be used to replace jet and rocket fuel and redefine the way we think about air and space travel. I am still working on it, if truth be told, and when I am done with it you will see space travel become as common as commercial air flights."

"Really?" Sam tried to hide the note of skepticism in his voice but failed.

"Yes," Purdue chose to ignore the disbelieving tone. "My research led me to consider the work of Wernher von Braun. It would have been immensely useful for me to have conferred with him, but since he was already dead I decided to track down those who had worked with him instead. This led me to Dr. Lehmann, who first mentioned the existence of this place quite by accident. He tried to pass it off as the ramblings of a senile old man, but I knew I was onto something interesting and that if this was a place where Wernher von Braun continued his work, it was a place I wanted to find. I knew about his work in America, of course, but so little of his truly interesting work is ever discussed! I had some investigations carried out, which led me to Harald Kruger and brought those notebooks into my possession."

"And you genuinely didn't have them stolen from Nina's flat?"

Purdue looked wounded. "If I had known that it was Nina who had them, I would simply have asked her to show them to me. She would probably have refused, and I would have found a way to bribe her. She is ambitious. I would have found something she wanted."

"And if they'd still been with me?"

"Oh, in that case they would have been spirited out of your home, copied and returned before you were aware that they had gone. My people are very good. Messy break-ins are simply distasteful. That's how I had planned to get copies of the notebooks from Mr. Kruger, until someone with a much less delicate touch got there first. No, Sam, I did not have the notebooks stolen. They were offered to me as a particularly shady private purchase."

"Who by?"

"An anonymous individual who approached me via the shadow web. The entire transaction was carried out via intermediaries, and the notebooks were part of a package of materials concerning this place."

Sam let out a long, low whistle. "The shadow web? Wow."

Purdue shook his head. "It sounds good, but it is less impressive than you think." He reached into his inside pocket. "Perhaps I should have been more open with you," he said. "Not with the rest of the group—one has to preserve some sense of drama, after all—but with you, and possibly with Nina. Keeping things entirely to myself, usually in order to play games with people, is a failing of mine. So, in the interests of correcting that . . ." He pulled out a small leather document wallet and dropped it in front of Sam. "Here. Perhaps this will be of interest to you. Show it to Nina—if I gave it to her she would assume I had ulterior motives, and she would be correct. Don't show it to Matlock, though. Let this be Nina's to catalogue, write about, or ignore as she pleases."

With that, Purdue stood up and strolled out of the room, leaving Sam with a head full of questions and an overwhelming sense that he had had all the answers he was going to get. He fumbled with the document wallet until the cords tying it shut were undone. Inside were two items; a letter and a slightly tattered old photograph of a woman in a floral sundress, laughing and holding her hat in place as the wind tried to take it from her head. She was holding the hand of a smiling toddler. On the back of the photograph someone had written "Sabine," which Sam assumed to be the woman's name, and beneath that, "Friedrich." Sam turned his attention to the letter.

My darling Sabine,

How many times must I remind you, my love? You must write to me only in English now. We can no longer be German. We must put our old lives, our old identities behind us. Karl and Sabine Witzinger will soon be no more, and we must get used to being Charles and Sally Whitsun. I hope you are being strict about speaking to Frederic only in English. It will be easier for him never to think of himself as German at all.

I long to be with you, to build a new home for ourselves. With you, my darling, I am certain I can forget the horrors I have seen and the things I have done to spare our family from unwanted attention. I am grateful to have your forgiveness and pray that I shall have God's, since God knows I shall never have my own.

I pray that I shall be home soon. It should not be much longer. I have done all that has been asked of me, and there is no longer any need for me to be here. My contribution is made. Other men can continue the work from here.

The letter seemed to end abruptly there. Beneath those paragraphs, it looked as though a new, separate letter began. The handwriting was the same but the color of the ink had changed and the writing was wilder, shakier, as if the letter had been dashed off in a great hurry.

Darling Sabine,

If you receive this, rejoice—it means that I have escaped that terrible place and am on my way home to you!

I am about to embark on a desperate voyage. There are others who are working here against their will, brilliant men whose families were threatened should they refuse to comply. Tonight we shall steal a submarine and strike out for South America, where I shall attempt to post this letter. We may not succeed. We may be shot, we may end up at the bottom of the ocean, we may be arrested the moment we set foot on Argentinean soil—but by God, we will have tried. We cannot do the things that they are asking us to do. I believe that I was put in this world to cure diseases, not create them. Other men may have their price for such things, but I do not.

If you receive this but I never make it home, know that I died with your image in my mind, your name on my lips and joy in my heart because you were mine. I hope that when you tell Frederic of me, you will speak of a man who finally found the courage to oppose that which he knew to be wrong. Guide him, my love, and teach him to be a man of honor and bravery.

I must go now. My hands shake, but not with fear. If I tremble now, it is at the prospect of finally coming home. May God hold you in his keeping and see me safely back to you.

Your own forever,

K

When he had finished reading the letters, Sam stared at them for some time without blinking or seeing. In his mind's eye he pictured Karl Witzinger, perhaps occupying this very room, lying on the bunk and wishing for nothing more than to be home with the woman he loved.

They had a life planned, Karl and Sabine, he thought. They were building something together, and then . . . I know the end of the story, for him at least. He didn't make it home. She got a letter saying he was dead. I wonder how he died. How she coped. Fuck, I wonder what they were asking him to do here that was so bad he needed to escape. What did he think was worse than working in a concentration camp—was he working on biological weapons? God . . . I wonder what they were trying to do in this place. Will we ever even begin to figure it out?

CHAPTER 23

ALEXANDR TURNED AROUND, or at least turned as far as he could in the tight space, to look at Nina and Fatima. He raised a finger to his lips, but it was hardly necessary. Both women were well aware of the need for silence, especially at this point in their journey. Nina in particular wished that he would skip the dramatic gesture and just get on with leading them through the vents. It was dark and cramped and she was fighting the urge to have a proper claustrophobic meltdown.

When Alexandr had suggested that they use the air vents to get back into the labs, Nina had laughed. Despite the gravity of their situation, she found the idea of the three of them scrambling through the ventilation system like action heroes irresistibly funny—especially considering her fear of enclosed spaces. It was only when Alexandr dragged the chest of drawers over to the back wall, climbed on top of them and began unscrewing the vent cover that she realized that he was entirely serious.

She had protested then, saying that he must be mad and that there was no way it would work outside of a movie. But Alexandr had insisted that there was no other way of getting past the soldiers—unless Nina and Fatima were prepared to entertain the idea of killing them, which they were not. Nina did not even want to think about how Alexandr would have attempted to kill the PMCs. If there was anything worse than being trapped in an enclosed space with a crazy guide, it was being trapped in an enclosed space with a homicidal one.

Inch by inch they crawled right over the top of the PMCs at the end of the corridor. The first problem they ran into was the vent dropping away steeply, plunging downward to serve the other levels. Alexandr peered down into the darkness, muttering something to himself. Then he wriggled a hand down to his pocket and pulled out a tiny obsidian pebble. Carefully he released it and cocked his head to listen as it fell. Just on the edge of hearing, there was a tiny scraping sound wherever the stone touched the metal.

At the back of the line, Nina heard Fatima gasp then try to stifle it. Nina raised her head just far enough to see Alexandr's feet tipping up and disappearing into the black hole. Neither woman breathed. Then seconds later, they heard the soft, barely audible sound of Alexandr's laugh floating back to them. A sharp intake of breath from Fatima, then she also vanished into the darkness.

Nina dragged herself forward on her forearms and stared down the shaft. She felt her breathing becoming ragged and short. Adrenaline surged through her veins. All she wanted was to claw at the sheet metal and rip her way out into the cool open air of the corridors. She would take her chances with the soldiers, she would fight her way out if she had to, she would—

Then the vision of the silent ice station peopled only by skeletons flashed through her mind, and she realized that she had no choice. I feel like I'm going to die in here, she thought. I have no idea how I could plunge head-first down this pipe and not die. But if I don't do this, none of us are making it out of here . . . Forcing herself to take a few deep breaths, she inched toward the edge. She reached down and felt the drop, and suddenly she realized that it was not completely vertical. It fell away at just enough of an incline that she would have some control over the descent. Nina gritted her teeth and hauled herself into the chute.

"It's a long drop," Alexandr whispered, staring down through the gap left by the ceiling tile he had just removed.

"If I can get to the other side I can lower you down part of the way. Wait there."

Jamming his limbs precariously against the walls of the metal tunnel, he clambered over to the other side of the hole and maneuvered himself around so that he was face to face with Fatima. "Here," he said, holding out his hands to her. "Take my wrists. Bend your knees when you hit the floor."

Fatima did as she was told, wriggling herself into position over the hole then letting Alexandr lower her as far as he could before she dropped. As soon as Fatima was out of sight, Nina charged forward as best she could in an army crawl, spurred on by the prospect of being in a room rather than a tunnel. She grabbed his wrists and let gravity take her, collapsing gratefully onto the floor as her shaking knees refused to hold her up. A moment later she heard Alexandr drop down behind her.

"I'll get the lights," Fatima whispered. "They're right over here."

"No lights!" Alexandr hissed. "They're bound to be patrolling. We need to work as far back within the room as we can, and with just the flashlights. Come with me—and stay down."

Crouched low, they scurried over to the workbench and sheltered behind it, letting its solid mass conceal them from the eyes of any PMC who might pass the glass door.

"This is going to be impossible," Fatima sighed. "How am I supposed to do anything if I can't access the bench?"

"It's only temporary," Alexandr reassured her. "I will figure out something to do with the window."

"Ok, we'll get to work in the meantime," said Nina, grabbing the pile of notebooks. "Are we in the right lab for the blood samples?"

"No, they're across the hall."

"Oh, they bloody would be . . ." Nina rolled her eyes. "Right, I'll be back in a moment."

"Nina, you should let me—"

"No, Alexandr, it's fine," she held up a hand. "You sort out the window. Let Fatima get set up. I can do this."

By the time Nina got back, Fatima was setting up her test tubes on the floor and had a box of samples retrieved from the freezers beside her. Alexandr had found a thick black liquid and was spattering the window with it. Nina handed the vials of blood over to Fatima.

"So, what's the plan?"

"I have an idea," said Fatima. "My original plan, before the expedition got hijacked, was to spend some time investigating the antiviral properties of a particular kind of blue algae indigenous to Antarctica. Evidently I'm not the first person to have been interested in it, since we found those samples in the freezers, but whoever was investigating it previously never got to complete their research. I'm going to try to create a vaccine using the algae and Private Hodges' blood samples. It'll be a killed vaccine, so I don't know whether it will save him, but . . . at least we'll have tried. And at least it might protect everyone else. Though I'm not sure that these algae samples are going to be any use after being frozen for so long. What we really need is a live vaccine and fresh algae. Oh, and a few years of peer review and clinical trials would be good, too."

"I have faith," Nina said, patting her friend on the shoulder. "If anyone can do this, you can. And if not . . . well, like you say, at least we'll know that we didn't go down without a fight, right? And I'll be right here holding the torch."

Pulling a pair of latex gloves from her pocket and slipping them on, Fatima gritted her teeth and prepared to get to work.

"Freeze! Hands in the air!"

The beams of light from the PMCs' helmets crisscrossed in the dark. As Nina slowly got to her feet and put her hands up, her heart began to pound beneath the red dots picking out targets on her chest. Fatima's hands shot up so fast that she did not even remember to put the pipette she was holding down.

"What's that in your hand?" Major Alfsson barked. "Drop it, now!"

"Please," Fatima's voice was rapid, urgent. "Please, let me put it down gently. It's a vaccine."

Alfsson strode over to her and snatched the pipette from her hand. "A vaccine? What for?"

"For the virus that Private Hodges and those other two men have. I think—"

"Two." Under his breath, Alfsson gave a bitter laugh. "You still only know about two."

"There are more?"

"That is classified," Alfsson replied. "You must all return to your quarters. Now. Or we will have no choice but to open fire." He took hold of Fatima's arm and began guiding her toward the door.

"PLEASE!" Fatima cried out in desperation, digging her heels into the floor. "Please! I have something here that might save those men—that might save everybody! Can you at least let me test it?"

"She has a point," Alexandr chimed in, briefly attracting extra red dots on his abdomen. "Why not let her try?"

"Surely it has to be better than just letting everyone die without even trying," Nina added.

Major Alfsson paused, irresolute for just a few seconds.

Then with one quick gesture he called off the alert. The red dots disappeared. "You can try," he said, and Nina could hear the resignation in his voice. "Is it ready now?"

"I think so."

"Then let's go."

Fatima gathered up the test tubes and pipettes, arranged them neatly in a freezer box, and let the soldiers escort her, Nina, and Alexandr through the maze of corridors toward the padded room and, she hoped, the proof that they were all saved.

Fatima's hands were rock steady as she inserted the needle into Private Hodges' vein and pushed the plunger. He was securely strapped to his bed, completely exhausted after his self-destructive exertions, and his face was crusted with his own dried blood. He snarled and snapped at Fatima with as much energy as he could muster, but the attempts were weak.

Only when Fatima had withdrawn the needle and returned the syringe to its box did her hands start to shake. Not just her hands. Nina could see Fatima's legs trembling.

"Now what happens?" Alfsson asked. "What signs do we look for?"

"Now I inject the others," Fatima said. "And then we wait

and see if they return to being themselves."

Nina and Alexandr were escorted back to quarters after that. Only Fatima was permitted to stay and observe the condition of Hodges and the other infected soldiers. To Nina's alarm, Fatima had also insisted on injecting herself with a dose of the vaccine. Nina had protested that she should see how it affected the infected men first, but Fatima had pointed out that by that time, it could be too late for her and that if it didn't work they were all doomed anyway. Reluctantly, Nina had agreed and returned to her room to wait out the night.

She wanted to go and see Sam, to tell him all about the turn that the day had taken, but when they arrived at the officers' quarters the number of PMCs in the corridor had increased. There was now a soldier outside every occupied room.

"What's all this about?" she demanded, addressing the soldier stationed at her door.

"Major Alfsson's orders," he replied. "In light of your escape attempt, all members of your expedition are to be kept apart except at mealtimes. We have also checked your rooms for possible escape routes and sealed them up. Now, please step inside."

Battling the urge to argue, Nina walked into her room and heard the door click shut behind her. Once safely inside, she grabbed her empty backpack and dropkicked it across the room.

The next morning the soldiers came around and knocked on everyone's doors to summon them to breakfast. Nina had planned to update Sam while they were in the refectory, but as the group marched down the stairs and sat around the long table, the PMCs barked orders at them not to speak. Purdue tried to negotiate with them, of course—but Major Alfsson himself pointed his gun at Purdue's head.

"No need for that, major," Admiral Whitsun stepped in and diverted the barrel of major Alfsson's gun before Blomstein could intervene to protect his employer. "I'm sure everyone will be happy to accede to your request." He turned to the rest of the group. "Won't we?" A flurry of emphatic nods was the response. As much as the expedition members might want to argue, it was increasingly clear that Major Alfsson genuinely would shoot if provoked.

Fatima appeared when they were nearly finished with their tense, silent breakfast. The look on her face told Nina everything she needed to know. Private Hodges was dead or dying, and if Fatima's tears were anything to go by it had not been pretty. She refused all offers of food but accepted a cup of coffee, which she could not bring herself to drink. She sat with her eyes pressed shut, one hand tightly clamped over her mouth, rocking gently back and forth. Nina took her free hand and squeezed it.

As they sat in silence the group heard the crackle of a voice speaking to Major Alfsson over his radio headset. It was too faint for them to make out the words, but the expression on Alfsson's face was grim. He said little, merely making affirmative noises, until the voice fell silent and he addressed the group.

"I have just had confirmation from my second-in-command," he said. "Dr. al-Fayed's attempt at curing the infected men has not worked. The virus continues to spread."

"In that case, Alexandr and I should strike out for Neumayer at once," Jefferson Daniels spoke up. "As the two most experienced trekkers, we have the best chance of making it there on foot. Then they can send medical assistance."

Major Alfsson shook his head. "No. Given the unknown nature of this virus, we cannot risk exposing the rest of the world to it. Our only possible course of action is to remain here, in quarantine, and let the disease run its course. We have ample supplies. Once we have gone fourteen days without a new case, then we will attempt contact with Neumayer again."

"We'll all be dead," Fatima said softly, half to herself.

"We've done a thorough sweep of the station," Major Alfsson continued, "and you'll find men posted at every possible exit. Please refrain from any further escape attempts —if you are caught trying to leave the station you will be shot on sight. However, now that we have covered all the exits, you can move freely about this part of the station again." He rose and signaled his men. "I am sorry that it came to this." They departed in the direction of the far section of the station, leaving the expedition party alone together.

For a while, no one spoke. Out of habit, Sam went to heat more water for tea. Nina put a comforting arm around Fatima and tried to encourage her to drink her coffee.

"I owe you all an apology." Admiral Whitsun sat bolt upright, his hands neatly folded on the table. He looked around the group, meeting each pair of eyes with a clear, forthright gaze. "This is my fault," he said. "I insisted on joining this expedition knowing that I am, in point of fact, too old and infirm to be here. Were it not for my infirmity, that set of vials would never have been knocked over and this virus would never have been released. I am terribly sorry."

Sam, standing by the door to the galley kitchen, watched

everyone avoiding one another's eyes. They all knew that it was true that the admiral had put them at risk, and whatever their opinions were on his culpability in spreading the virus, no one wanted to share them. It was Sam who spoke first. "Look, don't worry about it," he said, silently marveling at the ridiculousness of his words. He's released a deadly virus, he thought, not spilled my pint. Yet he continued. "You fell over. It could have been any one of us."

"Yes," Admiral Whitsun said, "but the fact remains that it was me. I brought this terrible thing on us."

Sam shrugged. "Nothing anyone can do about it now."

"I disagree, Mr. Cleave. I can at least try to put things right. Mr. Purdue, I wonder whether I might borrow Mr. Blomstein from you for a little while."

At once, Purdue and Blomstein moved to join Admiral Whitsun, who led them off into the corridor. Whatever the admiral's plan, the rest of the group was clearly not to be included.

"I wonder what that was about," Sam said. "So what's our plan? Major Alfsson said something about an antidote. Are we looking for one?"

"We can't," said Nina. "The labs are over on the PMCs' side of the station, and from what Alfsson said I think that's out of bounds."

"Shit. Ok. Anyone got any other ideas?"

"We should make some kind of record of our time here," Professor Matlock spoke up. "We may have been the first to find this place since it was abandoned, but I doubt that we shall be the last. Let us put together a report on our time here, something that will explain how we came to be here and what we found. Perhaps then we can spare our successors the same fate—or, if we get out of here alive, it can become the basis for an account of our exploits."

Sam pounced on the idea at once, delighted to have something productive to do. "Sounds great," he said. "Someone take over making the tea and I'll run up and get my notepad."

CHAPTER 24

AFTER SO MUCH excitement combined with so much time spent cooped up, Sam had excess energy to burn. He bounded up the metal stairs two at a time, at least until he got a stitch and had to slacken his pace. He badly wanted to run. His whole body ached with longing for some kind of physical release.

He reached the door to the officers' quarters and turned the handle. The door did not budge. He pushed harder. It gave a little, but it felt as if there was something blocking it from the other side. He backed up a couple of steps and rammed his shoulder against the door, shoving it hard enough to push it partway open. He squeezed through the gap into the corridor and stepped straight into a puddle of blood.

Sam stared down at his foot in disbelief. Why is there blood? He looked at the puddle, then followed the line of the blood flow back to its source—the torso of the PMC who had been guarding that door. The man was definitely dead. He had been shot in the chest and also in the head. At the sight of the dark hole of the entry wound and the traces of white bone around the edge of it, Sam felt the memories trying to flood back in and his mind slamming its defenses into place. It's completely different, he told himself. This man hasn't lost half his . . . Well, put it this way, his is just a small wound by comparison. Not that that's done him much good.

At the opposite end of the corridor lay the other PMC, having met a similar fate. But how? Sam wanted to know. These guys are highly trained, aren't they? You can't just walk up and shoot them. Something is badly wrong here.

Without stopping to collect the notepad he had come for, Sam turned and fled back to the refectory to tell the others what he had found.

"Sam, calm down!" Jefferson Daniels commanded, pushing Sam into a seat. "Slow down, buddy. You're saying the soldiers upstairs are dead?"

"Shot. Chest and head." Sam nodded, staring blankly at the table.

"But how is that even possible? These are elite soldiers. Are you sure, Sam?"

"If that's what Sam says he saw, then I believe him," Nina said. "But I agree that no one should have been able to walk up to these soldiers and shoot them. That sounds to me like one of their own has gone rogue. We know that this virus causes violent mania, and it's only a matter of time before that symptom shows up in someone holding a gun."

Fear rippled around the group. Suddenly they found themselves yelling at one another, having heated arguments across the long table about whether they should go in search of the gunman, look for weapons, find a safe place within the station to hole up and wait out the virus, or take advantage of the death of the guards to make a break for Neumayer.

"Where's Purdue?"

Alexandr lobbed the question in gently, almost as if it were a social inquiry. Everyone stopped talking.

"Purdue," Alexandr repeated, speaking slowly and carefully, ". . . and Ziv Blomstein? You remember? Tall, silent, ex-Mossad? Or to be more precise, ex-Kidon."

Fatima stifled a gasp. "You know that for sure?"

"You know it's impossible to be certain," said Alexandr, "but let us say that, judging by the brief conversations we had . . . it would not surprise me."

Nina looked from Fatima to Alexandr and back again, confused. She glanced at Sam, who was clearly in a traumatized world of his own and not listening to a word anyone was saying, and at Matlock and Daniels, who both looked as nonplussed as she was. "If no one else is going to admit their ignorance, I will," she said. "Fatima, Alexandr— what does Kidon mean? I know about Mossad, but that's a new one on me."

"It's a branch of Mossad," Fatima said, a haunted look in her eyes. "No one knows much about it, though. It's really covert. But the Kidon are believed to carry out political assassinations—"

"Among other things . . ." Alexandr added in a half-whisper.

"Right. Among other things. They're some of the most dangerous men in the world if you get on the wrong side of them."

"Ok . . ." Nina fought to keep the nerves out of her voice and the roiling sensation in her stomach under control. "So we know there's someone here who might have been capable of killing those two soldiers upstairs. But what we don't know is why he—"

Her words were cut off. Suddenly the air filled with the sound of machine gun fire. Fatima and Alexandr dived under the table. Daniels, Matlock, and Nina followed, but Sam did not. Nina looked up and saw him sitting still, staring in the direction of the gunfire. Under his breath she heard him utter the word "Trish." Then she reached up, grabbed him by the front of his jacket and dragged him down into their makeshift shelter. She wrapped an arm around him as they crouched there, and told herself that it was solely to comfort him.

How long they waited there, none of them knew. The noise of the guns did not last long, but none of them dared move or speak. All they could do was wait, tense and terrified, to learn whether it would be their turn next.

When Sam heard the door handle click he turned to face it, anticipating the hail of bullets that would follow. He was ready. This is what should have happened last time, he thought. He stood up unsteadily, arms slightly extended to welcome the conclusion to his story, and waited for the PMCs to flood in and open fire.

Instead he saw Admiral Whitsun enter with a submachine gun clutched in his hands and a look of devastation on his face. Sam thought he was hallucinating. What would Admiral Whitsun be doing with a gun? Then behind the admiral came Ziv Blomstein, also holding a gun, and an unarmed Purdue.

"Admiral?" Professor Matlock scrambled out from beneath the table and dusted himself off before helping the old man into a chair. "Admiral Whitsun, what happened?"

The admiral did not make eye contact, not with Matlock nor with any of the others. His gaze was fixed on the middle distance. Sam recognized that look. It was the same one he himself had worn as he had been led out of that warehouse.

"I could not leave them to suffer," Whitsun said, his voice flat. "It was my duty. God forgive me . . . it was my duty."

Fatima came over to the admiral's side and knelt by him. "You killed them?"

"All of them. It was easy—surprisingly easy. Most of them were unconscious when Mr. Blomstein and I arrived. The disease had already begun to claim them."

There was silence in the room. Fatima took Admiral Whitsun's hand and patted it gently. Then she looked up and saw the shocked expressions of her companions. "Don't be so quick to judge," she chided. "You didn't see what kind of a state those men were in—well, except you, Jefferson. But everyone else—believe me, if the soldiers were infected, a quick death was the most merciful option."

"And what about us, Admiral Whitsun?" Professor Matlock was stark white and shaking with fury. "Do you believe us to be infected too? Shall we line up against the wall, would that be more convenient for you?"

"Leave him alone!" Fatima sobbed. "You might not agree with what he did, but look at him—it wasn't an easy thing for him to do!"

"It was also the most sensible way to increase our own chances of survival," Purdue said, as strangely calm as ever. "I understand that you have attempted to create a vaccine, Dr. al-Fayed—but that we only have a limited supply?"

"Yes, that's right," Fatima said. "There's enough for all of us, but there definitely wouldn't have been enough for all the PMCs as well. But Mr. Purdue, I don't even know for sure that it works. The only people I've tried it on were the first men to die, and I don't know whether that's because they weren't treated in time or if my vaccine just doesn't work at all."

"Or whether the vaccine itself is likely to kill us," Professor Matlock chipped in.

"Well, it might not be a proper clinical trial," said Fatima, deep pink spots of anger beginning to show in her cheeks, "but I used it on myself yesterday when I was treating the soldiers. So far I've had no adverse effects. That's not to say that it'll be the same for all of you, but if you want to take the chance there's a tiny bit of evidence that you won't die, ok?"

"It's ok, Fatima." Nina stepped between Fatima and Professor Matlock, soothing her friend with calm tones and a hand on her back. "We're all adults. We can each choose for ourselves. But look, first things first—I'll go and get the vials, shall I? I can bring them here, save everyone traipsing over to the labs. You stay here and look after Admiral Whitsun, ok?"

As Nina headed for the door she called out to Alexandr and Sam to come and help her. There was no reason why it should take three of them to bring back a small box of vials, but she just hoped that no one would challenge her on it. They walked in silence along the corridor, down the stairs, through the U-boat dock. Not a word was exchanged until they were safely in the far section of the ice station.

At the bottom of the ladder into the new section, Nina dug her fingers into her scalp and let out an anxious snarl. "He's insane! They both are—Whitsun and Purdue both! That's their solution to the problem? Shooting everyone? We have got to get out of here before one of them decides to turn the gun on us."

Sam and Alexander both agreed. Admiral Whitsun was clearly in a disturbed, traumatized state of mind, and it seemed that Purdue was on his side and lending Blomstein's muscle to back him up.

"The trouble is, how?" Sam wondered as they entered the lab corridor. "If Jefferson and Alexandr trek to Neumayer, isn't that going to take ages? We could all have bullets through our heads before they got back with the hovercrafts."

"You're right," Alexandr said. "Besides, we have no news about the weather conditions outside. Even I would hesitate to set off into the unknown like that. What we need is transport, and we can only assume that there is nothing for us here."

"Except the U-boats . . ." Nina suggested.

Alexandr stopped in his tracks. A slow, wolfish grin spread across his face. Then, suddenly, he lunged forward, grabbed Nina's face in both hands and planted a joyful, forceful kiss on her lips. "Of course! The U-boats!" He turned tail and ran back along the corridor.

"What . . . Alexandr!" Nina, wide-eyed with shock after the surprise kiss, yelled after him. "Where are you going?"

"Back to the boats!" he shouted over his shoulder. "I will see you soon!"

When Sam and Nina passed back through the U-boat dock with the box of vials, Alexandr was busy examining the remaining sub. He was on his back, stretched out and examining the hinges on the entry trap, swearing softly to himself in Russian. They decided not to disturb him. He looked too happy and serene to interfere.

The atmosphere back in the refectory was somber. In the short time that Nina and Sam had been out of the room, it seemed that Jefferson and Purdue had had an argument and Matlock had continued to fume silently. Blomstein was sitting at the far end of the table, away from everyone else, and the sense of fear that he inspired had become palpable. There was no need for Nina and Sam to concoct an explanation for Alexandr's absence—no one else had even noticed that the Russian was missing.

"I appreciate your words, Dr. al-Fayed," Admiral Whitsun was saying. "You are a sweet young woman, and your future husband is a lucky man. But you must understand, this is how men like me do things. It is the only honorable course left to me." He reached down and wiped the tears from Fatima's cheeks. "No need for that," he said. "I have done what I came here to do. There is nothing to be sad about. Chin up, eh?" He smiled at her, waiting for her to smile back. Weakly, she fought back her tears and complied.

The old man rose stiffly from his chair and stepped into the kitchen, emerging a moment later with a glass bottle in his hand. Sam recognized it at once. God only knew where the admiral had concealed it, because Sam would certainly have spotted it if it had been out in the open in the kitchen. It was a very old bottle of Dewar's White Label—eight years old at the time of bottling, sometime in the 1930s. That was probably a fairly cheap whisky when it was brought here, Sam realized.

It was not until Admiral Whitsun's fingers closed around the gun on the table that Sam realized what he was planning to do. Instinctively he reached forward to protest, but halfway through the gesture he checked himself. Beside him, Nina did the same. Admiral Whitsun's mind was clearly made up. It's his choice, Sam thought. He's a grown man, and if that's how he wants to deal with his grief and guilt, it's not for us to stop him. Let him make his exit with dignity.

The last they saw of Admiral Whitsun was the old man framed by the door lintel, a gun in one hand and a bottle in the other, retiring to his private quarters.

"Hand me the wrench!" Alexandr yelled. Nina obliged, while Sam busied himself trying to help Jefferson Daniels appease Professor Matlock.

"This is lunacy," Matlock was ranting. "Look at it!" He gesticulated wildly at the U-boat. "Look! It's been sitting here since who knows when, 1945 at least, and you people think we're just going to get it working and sail out of here!"

Jefferson followed him as he strode up and down the dock, making all the right noises about how they had to try. But Sam could see that Matlock was afraid, and he was sure that this anger was his way of attempting to cope with it. He could also see that it was starting to wear Jefferson down and was upsetting Fatima. Unfortunately, Sam had spent too much of the expedition winding Matlock up to be much help when it came to calming him down. In reality, all he was doing was trying to convince himself that he was being helpful and useful. Anything to prevent himself from thinking about the gunshots, and the blood, and anything that connected the day's events to that day in his past.

"These vessels are intended for a forty-five-man crew!" Matlock was blustering. "A crew which, I might add, would have been properly trained! You can't sail a U-boat on a wing and a prayer, it's preposterous."

"We don't have to get far." Purdue was leaning against a wall, watching Alexandr's comings and goings with interest. "Or navigate, really. No one is proposing that we sail home in this. All we need to do is get as far as the surface. I have a charter boat stationed at Deception Island that was to take us back to Ushuaia when we were ready, but once we reach the surface I should be able to summon it."

"Oh?" Professor Matlock's tones were icier than the water lapping in the empty pens. "How?"

"You wouldn't ask a magician to reveal his techniques." In any other person's voice it might have been a question, but in Purdue's flat monotone it was a simple statement of fact.

"Oh, well that settles everything, doesn't it?" Matlock rounded on Purdue, his mouth open for a barrage of sarcastic insults, when suddenly Jefferson's fist connected with Matlock's jaw. The academic reeled and fell to his knees.

"Shut up, will you?" Jefferson yelled. "Just shut the fuck up! I can't listen to you for a second longer!" He lurched forward. His foot swung back. Sam, never usually the physical type, threw his arms around Jefferson and tackled him to the ground. Jefferson recovered in an instant and rolled, coming up on top of Sam. His hand balled into a fist. Sam screwed his eyes shut in anticipation of the blow.

It never came. Instead he felt Jefferson's weight being lifted off of him as Ziv Blomstein stepped in. As they scrambled to their feet Sam, Matlock, and Daniels glared at one another, then silently scattered to different parts of the room. Only Purdue was unperturbed—at least, until he heard the sound of the U-boat's diesel engine sputtering to life.

"Alexandr! You genius!" Purdue shouted above the engine's roar. Moments later Alexandr's head appeared through the trapdoor, beaming triumphantly. "All aboard!" Purdue cried.

"Aren't you forgetting something?" Matlock called. He pointed at the sluice gates that kept the pen dry. "What is the point if you can't get it out of here?"

For the briefest of moments, Alexandr looked thrown. Then he climbed swiftly down from the deck and jumped lightly onto the dock. The lever that controlled the pen was located at the far end of the dock, so it took him only a few steps to reach it. Theatrically, he threw it.

Nothing happened. Alexandr tried the lever again, listening carefully to it. Nothing happened. "Its gears are damaged," he muttered, then strode out of the room, back toward their quarters, leaving everyone to stare in silence. Within seconds there were angry yells from Jefferson, from Matlock, and a stifled sob from Fatima, but all the frightened noises were abruptly cut off by Alexandr's sudden return.

He rushed to the end of the dock, down by the sluice gates, and glanced around wildly. "I need a box," he said, pulling a small black carton from his pocket and tapping it impatiently. "Nina, I believe you had a pack of these as well? Give it to me, please. Sam! Where is the box that contained the vials? Is it still in the refectory? Go and get it, at once!"

Sam asked no questions but set off immediately, running up the stairs to grab the box, then dashing back down as quickly as he could. By the time he got back, Alexandr was cross-legged on the ground, whittling away at something with his knife. As Sam put the box down beside him he saw what it was.

"He's lost his mind," said Matlock. "Completely. We need to get through that gate and all he can think of to do is carve up some playing cards."

"Ssssh," Purdue raised a finger to his lips. "I think I know what Mr. Arichenkov is doing. I want to know whether I am right."

One by one, Alexandr flipped over the cards. If the card was black he discarded it, tossing it to one side. If it was red, he would carefully slice off the pips and place them in the box. His hands moved at frantic speed. Finally, when he had reached the last card and removed its three diamond-shaped pips, he got to his feet. "Stand back," he instructed the group.

Purdue clapped his hands. "Ah, it is what I thought! Excellent! I have always wanted to try this."

"What is it?" Sam whispered, watching intently as Alexandr crouched by the vacated pen and scooped freezing water with his hands, dumping it into the wooden box.

"Nitrocellulose," Purdue replied. "This is how William Kogut nearly escaped from his cell in San Quentin in the 1930s—a most remarkable man."

"Nearly escaped?"

"Well, he may have overdone things a little. He inadvertently blew himself up as he tried to blast his way out, but the theory was flawless." Purdue reached into his pocket and pulled out a lighter. "Alexandr! You'll need heat! Try this." He dashed forward as Alexandr was closing the box and shaking it up. He held the flame underneath. As the box caught fire, Alexandr threw it toward the sluice gate and the two men turned and ran.

"Everybody down!" yelled Alexandr They barely had time

to cooperate before the explosion happened.

When Sam looked up there was a gaping hole where the sluice gate had once been, and water was flooding in from the icy ocean. The group scrambled up the ladder and down through the trapdoor into the U-boat, closing the hatch just as the ocean water began to swell and carry the submarine out of its moorings. Alexandr seized the wheel that controlled the rudder, and their desperate journey began.

Chapter 25

AT THE TOP of the stairs, Admiral Whitsun took a left turn along the dark corridor that led to the surface. Slowly but steadily, he made his way up the slope until he reached the door by which they had initially entered. It took all the strength he had to turn the wheel that opened it, but after a certain amount of groaning and wheezing he managed it.

He stepped outside, into the frozen landscape, and looked up at the clear white sky. From his coat pocket he pulled the small satellite phone that he had discreetly taken from the corpse of Major Alfsson, flipped it open and dialed.

"I'm ready," he said. "Send the transport."

"You're kidding, right? Tell me you are kidding."

"I'm not, Jefferson," Fatima was scrutinizing the sonar. "We're really deep down, and there's a solid mass above us. There's nowhere we can surface around here."

"And nobody thought to check this before we set off?" Daniels' face was turning livid pink beneath the tan.

"It's not like there was a map!" Fatima snapped. "Nobody was exactly planning this!"

"Ok, ok," Sam took Jefferson by the shoulders and steered him away. "Come on. Let's try to keep our cool. We've been making steady progress for a while now, we'll find somewhere soon."

"We're not looking for a motorway service station, Mr. Cleave," Professor Matlock joined in. "We have been sailing for around forty minutes. Unless we find a place to surface within the next fifteen minutes or so, we will run out of oxygen. You do know what happens in that eventuality, don't you?"

"Stop talking!" Fatima snarled, her gaze never wandering from the sonar. "The more you talk, the more air you use up."

Jefferson and Professor Matlock clearly wanted to argue, but they knew that she was right. They fell into a surly silence. Sam picked his way along the U-boat toward the navigation area, where Purdue and Blomstein were waiting for any new information from Fatima to tell them where to go. The division of tasks had happened swiftly and naturally.

Alexandr had taken responsibility for the engine room. Fatima, who had done a few dives before, knew how to read sonar. Blomstein had served aboard a submarine previously, although he did not divulge the circumstances. Sam and Nina were acting as runners, transferring communication from one part of the boat to the others. In theory they were sharing this task with Jefferson and Professor Matlock, but they could not be torn away from the sonar, where they waited desperately for any signs of open water. Sam shot Nina a smile as they crossed paths. He was not feeling particularly brave, but he knew that she was struggling to keep her claustrophobia under control and wanted to be supportive.

"Anything?" Purdue asked as Sam entered. Sam shook his head. "I see," said Purdue. "I will start looking for any oxygen tanks, then."

Sam nodded and slumped against the door. Is this really going to be it? he wondered. I never thought I'd suffocate in a cramped metal tube beneath the Antarctic Ocean . . .

"We've got one!" Fatima yelled. "Prepare to take her up!"

The hatch creaked open. Purdue was first to climb out. They found themselves in a vast grotto, hewn from the ice by the hot springs, with dripping stalactites reaching down from the high ceiling. Nina had never felt as small as she did in that space, nor so glad to be in a cavernous chamber.

When they were done with gulping down lungfuls of the fresh, salty air, they made their way down the ladder. By great good fortune, the grotto contained a small outcropping of rocks that was within jumping distance and made a decent makeshift dock. Once on the rocks they had to clamber over a little mound to reach the plateau on the other side.

"Oh!" Purdue stopped as he reached the top of the mound. He looked around at the others. "You might want to prepare yourselves," he said. "We are evidently not the only travelers ever to have found our way into this cave, and some of you might find the presence of our predecessors a little distressing."

This stopped some of the others in their tracks, but Sam's curiosity got the better of him and he could see that the same was true for Nina. Sam was secretly pleased to see that the bodies that lay scattered across the plateau had long since decomposed and were now just skeletons. After his encounter with the murdered soldiers, he was in no hurry to see any more fresh corpses.

Much more disturbing than the dead bodies was the rusted, partly-submerged U-boat. Evidently there was more than one point of access to the grotto, but this party had never made it out again. Perhaps it was because their own means of exit was by no means certain, but Sam found the sight of the abandoned boat quite chilling.

Alexandr and Nina, on the other hand, were exhilarated. They scrambled straight onto the plateau and rushed toward the objects of their fascination—in Nina's case the corpses, which she wanted to examine, and in Alexandr's case the defunct submarine, which he wanted to plunder for fuel.

"Stop!" Fatima's voice rang out urgently, amplified and echoed back by the cavern's acoustics. "Nina, Alexandr, wait!"

But it was too late. Nina was already on her knees next to the nearest skeleton, her fingers in the pocket of its duffel coat, and Alexandr had reached the U-boat and laid a hand on its rusty surface.

"Oh, shit . . ." said Fatima, "What have you done?"

"What?" Nina asked. "What's the matter?"

"Where do you think that U-boat came from?" Fatima demanded. "Because I'll bet it came from one of those empty spaces in the dock at Wolfenstein. What if these guys were trying to escape from exactly the same thing that we were? We don't know what they died of. We don't know whether it's something that's still alive—and we may just have exposed ourselves to it, again."

Sam felt a prickling, uneasy sensation creeping up the back of his neck. "But we've been vaccinated now, right? So we should be ok?"

"Some of us were vaccinated," Fatima said darkly. "And for all I know, it could have mutated over time. If we're looking at a different strain, my vaccine won't be worth a damn— assuming that it ever was in the first place."

"Shit," said Sam. He waited for the feelings of doom and hopelessness to take hold, but all he felt was a certain resignation. "Look, does anyone mind if I smoke?"

An argument broke out after that, of course. Accusations flew as everyone blamed one another for the danger they were now in. There were recriminations about whether they should have taken the U-boat, whether they should have opened the locked doors in Wolfenstein, whether they should have set out for Antarctica in the first place. None of it brought them to any kind of conclusion except that if they were infected it was too late to do anything about it, and they were not going to be rescued down here.

"The device needs a satellite connection to work," Purdue lamented, prodding idly at the tiny, paper-thin device in his hand. "That will have to be my next challenge, I think. Building a device that satisfactorily avoids the normal constraints placed on communications."

"So we must reach the surface," Alexandr said. "There is

likely to be a little fuel left onboard the other boat. Give me long enough to transfer it to our own tanks and we will try again."

While Alexandr busied himself with siphoning fuel from the defunct U-boat, Sam joined Nina by the skeletons. She was carefully searching through their pockets, trying not to disturb them more than was strictly necessary.

"I just want to find something that tells me who they are," she said, placing the contents of their pockets a little pile at each skeleton's feet. "Presumably they either came from the ice station or were on their way to it. Their uniforms aren't from the 1940s, and this one has an appointment diary from 1953."

1953! Sam suddenly remembered Karl Witzinger's letter. His hands flew to his pockets, feeling for the leather wallet, but he found nothing but a filled-up memory card and a lighter. He checked his inside pocket. Nothing. It's in my backpack, isn't it? He thought. Along with my camera. And my tobacco pouch. All sitting neatly next to my bunk . . . Shit.

"What's up?" Nina asked, seeing him searching for something. "What have you lost?"

Sam opened his mouth to tell her about Witzinger's letter and how these skeletons were probably the scientists who had attempted to escape from the ice station, but at that moment

Alexandr called out to them.

"We have all the fuel we are likely to get," he cried. "So let's get out of here!"

Nina stuffed the skeletons' possessions into her pockets. "Sorry lads," she said, "but you're not going to need them, and I might. Come on, Sam."

Admiral Whitsun alighted from the hovercraft in a remote bay. He crossed the beach, marching smartly past a small cohort of PMCs, and made his way to a small speedboat, which was waiting to transport him to the destroyer anchored nearby.

"Welcome back, sir!" His second-in-command, Captain Belvedere, saluted as Admiral Whitsun stepped onto the boat. "Did things go well?"

"Exceptionally well, Captain Belvedere," Whitsun replied as they sped across the water. "The virus is definitely still live and highly communicable. Our friends in the East will pay a great deal for it. However, there was one slight hitch—I believe that the rest of the expedition party might attempt to make an escape, and if they do we need to be ready for them. Either they will come by land, in which case the platoons surrounding Neumayer will deal with them, or they will find a way to get that old submarine working. Oh, it seems unlikely, I know. But I may have underestimated both Mr. Purdue and the guide. In retrospect I should simply have killed them all. Mr. Blomstein might have posed me a problem there, but perhaps he could have been paid off and recruited. The others . . . I should have contented myself with seeing Mr. Cleave dead, rather than succumbing to the temptation to leave him and his friends to die slowly. But forgive me, I am allowing myself to be distracted. If they succeed in making it to the surface, they will emerge somewhere to the southwest of Deception Island. While our colleagues recover the biological material from Wolfenstein and prepare it for transport, we shall wait near Deception Island. If that submarine appears, we shall destroy it."

"Oh god . . . I don't know if I can. I'm sorry." Nina physically recoiled from the black hole on the top of the submarine. "I just can't. I'm sorry, I'm so sorry."

"Come on, Nina," Alexandr cajoled. "It is only a submarine. If you do not get in we have to leave you here with the skeletons."

She stood by the hatch, staring down into it, her head full of images of the tiny submarine surrounded by the vastness of the ocean. She could see the U-boat collapsing under the pressure of the water, or losing power and sinking like a stone, or running out of oxygen as they had so nearly done before.

"I can't," she moaned, digging her fingers into her scalp. Her breathing was harsh and ragged, and tears were beginning to stream down her face. "Please don't . . ."

Purdue was watching Nina from the bottom of the ladder. "She's not going to come down of her own free will." He turned to Blomstein. "We need her to get aboard. Take care of it."

Without a word, Blomstein climbed up to the hatch. Nina had sunk to her knees on the little platform and was clinging to the rails with one hand. The other covered her face. There was blood under her fingernails where she had anxiously dug them into her skin. Blomstein bent down to lift her up, intending to carry her bodily into the sub.

"Get the fuck off me!" Nina screamed. She lashed out at Blomstein with both hands, clawing at his face and kicking out wildly as he lifted her up. For a moment he struggled to keep his grip on her, but only for a moment. Nina's small frame was easy enough for him to subdue. She continued to scream and writhe as he pinned her arms to her sides and threw her over his shoulder. She landed several kicks on his abdomen, but Blomstein was indifferent to both her kicks and her shrieks as he began to climb down the ladder.

When they reached the bottom, Blomstein dropped Nina unceremoniously, knocking the wind out of her. "She is mad," he said, pressing the back of his hand against his bleeding cheek.

"No, she's not," said Purdue, helping her up. "She's just claustrophobic. Let's not rush to any conclusions, Ziv. Let's all get back to our stations. I'll take Nina through to Sam, he's helping Alexandr in the engine room. He can keep an eye on her."

"Oh, great idea," Jefferson sneered. "Get her boyfriend to watch her. Because he's going to be the first one to report it if she starts freaking out."

"He's not my boyfriend . . ." Nina whispered, still winded.

"If she's got the virus, we're all dead," Jefferson said. "We'd be doing her a favor by just putting a bullet in her head right now."

Purdue's face went a shade paler than usual. "Mr. Daniels," he said, gathering Nina close to him, "if I hear any further suggestions along those lines, it will not be her who gets a bullet in the head. She is perfectly well. Now go and ask Dr. al-Fayed if she is ready to set off. With Sam taking care of Nina, we will need you and Professor Matlock to run messages between stations this time."

With difficulty, Purdue helped Nina through the small

hatches that led from one section of the submarine to another. Jefferson and Blomstein watched them go, then shared a silent moment of agreement before going about their assigned tasks.

"Open water!" Fatima's voice rang out through the submarine. "We're coming up for open water, dead ahead!"

Alexandr gave a jubilant whoop and waved the oil can in his hand. He was performing a complicated dance with the neglected machinery, racing back and forth as the legs of the motor whirred and thumped. Every time one of them stuck due to long inactivity, Alexandr would hear the missed step in the dance and rush over to oil it and manually operate it until it was back in rhythm.

"Not much longer now!" he called to Sam and Nina over the clatter of the motor. "Soon we will have fresh air and wide open skies, Nina! Think of it!"

Curled up in the corner of the engine room, Nina could not reply. She could hardly believe what she was hearing. All she could think about was the metal tube she was in, the crushing weight of the water that lay between it and the surface, and the walls closing in around her. She tightened her grip on Sam's hand and tried as hard as she could not to whimper.

By the time the U-boat broke the surface of the water, Nina was standing at the bottom of the exit ladder and Sam was at the top of it, his hands on the wheel that opened the hatch, just waiting for the all clear to open it.

"We're up!" Purdue dived through the little doorway, shouting the news at the top of his voice. "We are officially above ground for the first time in days! Let's see some daylight, Sam!"

The trapdoor swung open, sending an icy shower of salt water splashing down over Sam, Nina, and Purdue. Sam laughed aloud as the cold liquid crashed over his face. They were out of the ice station, they were alive, and he was elated. He pulled himself up through the hatch and onto the observation platform, making room for Nina and Purdue to climb up behind him.

Slate blue water stretched out ahead of them, dotted with ice floes as far as the eye could see. Behind them lay the ice field that they had just sailed under, and above them the sky was white and streaked with dark-grey clouds. It was the most welcome sight that any of the trio had ever seen.

Sam laid his hand over Nina's on the rail and gave it a squeeze. "There we go," he said. "You've made it."

"I've never seen anything so beautiful," Nina said, managing a faint smile.

"You'll be all right now," Sam reassured her. "We'll be able to stay up here until Purdue's boat arrives to pick us up. No more tin tubes for—oh!" Without warning, Nina flung her arms around Sam's waist and hugged him tightly.

"I thought we were never going to get out of there," she sighed. "I can't believe I lost it like that. I'm so sorry."

"Well, this is odd," Purdue muttered distractedly. He had his tiny communications device in the palm of his hand and was tapping it, staring at it, then tapping it again.

"What's wrong?"

"The boat is not receiving my communications." He frowned and looked up at the sky. "Extreme weather conditions would explain it, but there should be nothing interfering on such a clear day. The device is functioning perfectly." Frustrated, he sighed through gritted teeth. "I told them that only the captain was authorized to use that equipment! If I find out that someone else touched it and damaged it, I will make sure that not a single member of the crew ever sails again. Excuse me." He climbed back down the ladder, and as he descended Sam and Nina heard him calling to Alexandr, telling him that they needed to find the flares.

Captain Belvedere strode across the observation deck, halted beside Admiral Whitsun and saluted. The admiral was glaring out across the waters, watching the distress flares shoot into the air and flicker out as they fell.

"We have their position, sir," Belvedere reported.

"You do surprise me," Admiral Whitsun replied dryly. "Are they in the vicinity of those signal flares, perhaps?"

"Yes, sir . . ."

"Well then. Intercept course. And as soon as we have them in range—open fire."

Nina bounced up and down and waved her arms, nearly hitting both Sam and Purdue in the face. "We're here!" she called to the distant ship.

"They know, Nina," Sam laughed. "Look—they're heading straight for us, they'll be here in no time."

Purdue caught hold of Nina's arm, stopping her in mid-wave. His face was ashen. "That is not the boat I chartered," he said. "That's a destroyer. Luzhou class. Of Chinese origin. And it's—get down!"

He grabbed Sam and Nina and dragged them down just as the first missile crashed into the water nearby. It sent up a wave that drenched all three of them.

"Dive! Dive!" Purdue shouted as he pushed Nina onto the ladder. "Arichenkov! Blomstein! Dive, now!"

Sam was last down the ladder. With all the strength of terror he hauled the trapdoor into place and spun the wheel to seal it shut, then slipped and fell from the ladder as the submarine went into a steep nosedive. He picked himself up from the floor, only to be sent flying again as the U-boat was rocked by the impact from another missile narrowly missing them.

Blomstein dragged Sam to his feet. "You need to take the rudder," he said. "Just keep us pointing in the direction we're going." The bodyguard dropped his large frame low to swing through the hatch.

"Ziv!" Purdue called after him. "Where are you going?"

"Torpedoes!" Blomstein's voice echoed back, then he was too far gone to communicate.

Sam rushed through to the navigation room and grabbed the wheel to prevent it from turning of its own accord. Purdue was hot on his heels and ready to read the displays, while Nina took up a position between navigation and the sonar, ready to relay information between the two.

The first torpedo did not fire. The mechanism was simply too old and rusty to discharge.

The second torpedo made it out of the submarine, but the motor propelling it was barely functioning. The expedition party listened for the sound of impact, of detonation, but nothing came. They could only assume that it had lost its momentum and sunk.

Before Blomstein could activate the third, the U-boat was rocked by a depth charge. Even Alexandr gave a cry of alarm. It was close, and the boat groaned and strained under the impact.

"They're almost on top of us! Ten thousand meters and closing!" Fatima screamed. "Now, Ziv!"

Blomstein grabbed the lever that controlled the last torpedo release with both hands and wrenched it to one side. The machinery screeched and complained, but the motor snarled into life. The tank flooded, the charge fired and the torpedo shot out into the water.

For an agonizing ten seconds, they counted. No one dared breathe. Sam stole a glance at the rudder wheel, hoping that he had not accidentally nudged them a degree of course. This has to work, he thought. It has to.

Then the air was thick with the heavy sound of an underwater explosion and the scream of a metal hull being ripped apart, and amid the sounds of wreckage was Ziv

Blomstein's primal shriek of triumph.

"Captain Belvedere, damage report!"

Admiral Whitsun strode along the deck toward the prow of the ship. In truth, the damage report was superfluous. He could see the thick black smoke billowing from the lower decks, and he could tell by the slight list of the ship that the damage was not negligible. However, he also knew that the destroyer could sustain a lot more injury than that and continue to sail. His temper had taken more of a battering. He was furious that they had not yet scored a direct hit on the U-boat.

"Admiral Whitsun, they're surfacing!"

"What?" Whitsun spluttered. "Why the devil would they —"

He leaned over the railing and squinted in the direction of the submarine. Sure enough, it was breaking through the waves. Snatching a pair of binoculars from Captain Belvedere, he watched as the trapdoor opened and Nina emerged onto the platform, a piece of white cloth clutched in her hands. She held it above her head, letting the wind blow it out like a flag, and waved it slowly back and forth.

"They're surrendering, sir!" Belvedere said. "Shall I send a craft to pick them up?"

Admiral Whitsun handed back the binoculars. "No," he said. "We shall get as close as we can, then we shall destroy them. See to it, captain."

Chapter 26

"SURRENDER?" Blomstein looked stunned.

"I think we must," said Purdue. "If it looks like that hit was sufficient to cripple the destroyer, then we needn't wave the flag. We can wait for rescue to arrive for them and be picked up at the same time. If they are not crippled, then they will be coming for us and surrender is our only chance of survival. No, don't snort at me, Ziv. What other option do we have? We have little fuel and can stay underwater for less than an hour at a time. Their sonar equipment is much more sophisticated than ours, and they can move a lot faster. We have no chance of outrunning them or hiding underwater. We have to surface. Which means we must be prepared to surrender."

The dark glare on Blomstein's face made it clear that he would never agree, but he was outnumbered. Nina volunteered to be the one to offer the surrender. While the others prepared to surface, she sped off to the bunks in search of a white sheet.

She got back just as Fatima called out to her to get ready. Sam was at the bottom of the ladder, preparing to open the hatch for her. He saw her twisting the sheet between her hands. Her dark hair was a matted mess, she had dark circles under her eyes and her clothes were disheveled. It was a far cry from the stylish, polished academic Sam had met back in Edinburgh.

"If this doesn't work they're going to shoot me," she said.

Sam opened his mouth to reassure her, but before he could say a word her arms were around his neck, her body pressed against him and her lips locked onto his. For a few precious seconds Sam was lost in the soft comfort of her kiss. He held her tight, barely able to remember the last time he had experienced these sensations. Then she pulled back, looked into his eyes and nodded.

"I'm ready," she said.

Standing on the observation platform, a white sheet held aloft, Nina could hardly believe that she was really experiencing all of this. She gazed at the destroyer. I've seen so many pictures of these ships, she thought. I've seen U-boats in museums and in films. Now I'm standing on a working—or barely working U-boat, signaling a destroyer. There's no way that this is my real life. Is this anyone's real life? Is that ship meant to be moving so fast?

The destroyer was moving toward them, which she had expected, but it seemed to be approaching at great speed. Nina was no expert, but deep in her gut she felt the absolute conviction that something was wrong. I'll ask Fatima to check it on the sonar, she decided, and leaned over the hatch.

"Sam?" Nina was taken aback to see Sam climbing the ladder, closely followed by Purdue, Fatima, Matlock, Jefferson, and Alexandr "What's happening?"

One by one the others squeezed onto the deck, which could comfortably hold two or three people but not seven. Purdue was yelling Blomstein's name over and over, along with demands to know what he was doing, but he got no response. As soon as they were all off the ladder, the hatch slammed shut and they heard the squeak of the wheel being turned to seal it.

"He's gone mad!" Purdue cried. "Is it the virus? He just ordered us all off the boat!"

With a sickening lurch, the nose of the U-boat began to tip downwards.

"He's diving!" Nina yelled. "Alexandr—with me!" She half-climbed, half-vaulted over the platform's railing onto the slippery surface of the submarine. Without question Alexandr followed, and together they heaved open the life raft container attached to the hull. The water lapped about their ankles as they unrolled the rubber raft, and as Nina popped the CO2 canister it was up to their knees. "Get in!" she shouted, pulling herself up over the side. "And hang on!"

They clung to the sides of the raft as the U-boat submerged, each one hoping that the flimsy vessel would not be capsized by the wave created in the submarine's wake. Purdue gazed at the water closing over the submarine, a look of perplexity on his face as Blomstein dived alone.

Admiral Whitsun permitted himself a slight smile as he lowered the binoculars. He had seen the expedition party abandon ship and watched as the U-boat sank beneath the waves. The binoculars were not powerful enough for him to make out facial expressions, but he could tell from everyone's body language that there was panic among the group. He allowed himself to imagine the look of terror on Sam Cleave's face as he realized that his only possible fate was a freezing watery grave. The sale of the biological weapons from Wolfenstein would go ahead, and the memory of the admiral's son would be avenged. All in all, risking a trip to the Antarctic at his age had turned out to be worthwhile.

"One has to admire their spirit," he mused. "Getting that thing working in the first place was quite a feat. However, it has let them down at the last." Once the U-boat was well and truly out of sight he turned to Captain Belvedere. "Change of plans. Shoot down their raft. I shall be in my quarters, arranging the rendezvous."

"Admiral Whitsun!" The voice of the navigation officer crackled over the radio. "Incoming! The submarine is approaching from the southeast, sir! It looks like it's on a collision course, aiming straight—"

The young man's voice cut off as the U-boat crashed headlong into the fuel tanks.

"He's hit the fuel tanks!" Purdue laughed and punched the air. "Well done, Ziv! That will sort them out!"

Sam and the others watched in horrified amazement as the ship's fuel tanks exploded. Dirty orange flames licked up the side of the destroyer and twisted the metal hull into filigree. Tiny dark figures besmirched with streaks of fire leaped from the decks into the deadly water below, early casualties who could not wait for the lifeboats. The white sky darkened to a lowering black as the columns of thick smoke dissipated and spread out.

Eventually, after what felt like an age, they saw the lifeboats being lowered and men from the destroyer piling in. Their own little raft bobbed and rocked as the destroyer fell to pieces, sending aftershocks surging across the distance between them. In the constant diffuse daylight of the Antarctic, it was impossible to tell how long they sat silently watching the demise of the ship.

"Listen," Alexandr whispered. His head was cocked and he was trying to pick out a new sound, something that was not the scream of a dying ship. Suddenly he pointed upward.

"A helicopter!" Professor Matlock cried. "At last!" He stretched his arms as far as they would go and began to wave them frantically. It only took a split second for the others to join in, yelling and signaling until they nearly overturned the raft.

It did no good, though. The helicopter flew on, disappearing into the dark billows of smoke. Just as the expedition party was about to lapse into dejection, Fatima spotted another vessel on the horizon.

"Do we hail it?" she asked. "Or is this one coming to finish us off?"

"No," Purdue sat bolt upright and smiled. "We hail this one. That's my boat!"

Nina had never been so grateful to feel a blanket around her shoulders or a mug of hot tea in her hands. Feeling the solid deck beneath her feet, sitting in a comparatively spacious crew room—it all felt luxurious after the events of the past few days. Best of all, the crew was incredibly lax about antismoking laws and generous with cigarettes. As she sucked the smoke down into her lungs she felt it warm her, comfort her, calm her down, and console her when she put her hand in her pocket and realized that the letters and diaries she had taken from the skeleton were now just mush. The waves that had soaked her as she stood waving the white flag had ruined the artifacts. She took another puff and tried to put it from her mind. Much to her surprise, Sam was sitting beside her with a cigarette in his hand, not smoking it. She checked that it was lit and saw that it was.

"Sam? Are you ok?"

Sam did not reply. He just sat staring at the floor, not moving. The blanket hung loosely from his shoulders. Now that she thought about it, Sam had not said a word since the U-boat had hit the destroyer. She wondered whether to push him further, but she had never seen him looking so far gone into his own private world. Best leave him alone, she decided.

Purdue was busy haranguing the captain of the charter

boat, demanding to know why they had not responded to any of his transmissions. The captain, an American by the name of Lassiter, insisted that they had received two signals from Purdue and had responded to both before losing his position. Unable to locate the group by GPS, they had waited at Deception Island until the destroyer had broadcast a Mayday call asking any vessels in the area to respond. The charter boat, being close by, had set out on a rescue mission—and found the expedition party by accident, mistaking them for survivors of the destroyer wreck.

"Well, be that as it may," Purdue waved a dismissive hand at Captain Lassiter. "The important thing is that you're here now, and we are more than ready to return to Ushuaia. Let's get on our way, shall we?"

"Um, Mr. Purdue?" Captain Lassiter looked uneasy. "We'd better go pick up the remaining survivors first."

The look Purdue gave him could have shattered glass. "I did not charter this boat as a rescue vessel, Captain Lassiter. Set a course for Ushuaia, if you would be so good."

"Maybe I should get our doctor to come and look you all over, Mr. Purdue," Captain Lassiter suggested. "You're obviously under a whole lot of strain right now, and I completely understand that, but—"

"Captain Lassiter," Purdue hissed, two pink spots appearing in his pale cheeks, "I am ordering you to ignore the destroyer. Leave it to its fate. Take us to Ushuaia. Now."

The young captain looked Purdue up and down, and Nina could see his jaw tense. "Mr. Purdue," he said calmly and carefully, "I am going to turn this boat around and pick up any survivors I can find. We will then take them to Deception Island. Then, and only then, will we proceed to Ushuaia. I can see that you have been under a lot of pressure and are not thinking straight. I suggest that you go to your quarters and recover. If you refuse, I will have you escorted from the deck and placed in quarantine for your own safety for the rest of the journey. Is that clear?"

Purdue stared furiously at the captain. He looked like he was about to speak, but then thought better of it. Instead he turned on his heel and stormed off in the direction of the cabins, without saying a word more to Captain Lassiter.

"For what it's worth," Nina said, "you did the right thing. If you'd agreed with him I'd have decked the pair of you. Is there anything I can do to help with—"

She cut off abruptly as Sam slumped forward in the seat beside her and passed out into unconsciousness.

Chapter 27

S O, WAIT, YOU got a snog off of Nina? Lucky bastard."

Sam scowled at Patrick Smith. "Everything I've just told you and that's what you choose to remember? Not the private army or the deadly virus or the bit where I found out that it was actually Admiral Whitsun and not his son who was running the arms ring? None of that?"

Patrick pretended to give it some thought for a moment. "Nah. Another pint?"

Sam handed over his empty glass, then sat back and stretched out his legs. It felt very strange to be back in Dagda after the Antarctic. On the one hand he felt as if the whole thing had never happened, as if it was just some mad dream. On the other hand, he couldn't shake the feeling that it had been more intense than life in Edinburgh had ever been and that perhaps it was all the more real for that.

Still, there was comfort in the familiarity of the pub. Nothing had changed there. It was still full of academics trying to avoid their undergrads and postgrads trying to cozy up to the academics. There still weren't enough seats. Sam caught a dirty look from a group of vertical drinkers and gave them a cheery smile in return. Outside the Meadows was lined with spring flowers and populated by twenty-somethings practicing tightrope walking or strumming ukuleles. They all seemed utterly incompatible with a world where men could buy and sell deadly viruses or use submarines to blow up destroyers.

Across the floor from Sam, a lone drinker was reading a newspaper. The political scandal surrounding Admiral Whitsun had broken while Sam was still in quarantine in Ushuaia, and Sam had earned a near-permanent place in the heart of his editor, Mitchell, for handing him the story. Now, a few months later, the tabloids were still speculating as to the Admiral's whereabouts. The headline the man was reading was hopeful:

WHITSUN SPOTTED IN CHILE: POLICE CLOSING IN

This was in stark contrast to the previous day's front page of the Times, which had declared:

WHITSUN: THE BODY IS FOUND

Sam had been asked again and again whether he thought that Admiral Whitsun had survived the wreck of the destroyer. He had no idea. It had been a shock to realize that the old man had not killed himself, let alone finding out that he had been playing them all along and that he had, in fact, been the brains behind the arms ring that had killed Patricia. If he is dead, perhaps that's some kind of justice for her, Sam thought. Not to mention for all those PMCs, and for the men on the destroyer. Then again, Trish always hated people thinking that way. He realized that it had been a few days since he had heard Trish's voice in his head. Her presence in his mind was not constant the way it had been.

"So," Patrick said, returning with their drinks, "you were going to tell me about you and Nina . . ."

"Paddy, leave it," Sam groaned. "Honestly. Nina's great, but it's too soon. I already feel guilty enough. But you know what? I'm working on it . . ." Sam paused for dramatic effect. " . . . with my therapist."

Patrick's eyebrows shot up. "You've got a therapist? How did that happen?"

"They made us all talk to one while we were in quarantine. Then when I got back I had to go for a follow-up at the doctor, and he said I could talk to someone about bereavement, so . . . it's free, so I thought I might as well." He picked up his pint and took a deep swig. "But you know what? I got off lightly. You know Jefferson Daniels, the explorer? He's so stressed out by the whole thing that he's refusing to do any more polar exploring. He's gone to Arizona to do a vision quest."

"Christ."

"I know. I'm not even sure what a vision quest is. If it's something that calms you down, Nina could probably do with it."

"I heard," said Patrick. "She got in touch to ask whether she could go after Matlock for stealing the notebooks, but she doesn't have a leg to stand on. They were just addressed to the department, not to her personally, and she's got no way of proving that they were ever hers to start with. Which they weren't, really. They were yours. I take it she still doesn't know who sent them?"

Sam shrugged. "Purdue, probably. He likes doing that kind of thing and he's the only one I know who would have the resources to track them down. I don't know how he did it. I'd ask him, if he hadn't vanished off the face of the earth when we got back. Of course, if he hadn't vanished I could have told him where to find the letter he gave me from Karl Witzinger. I'm still kicking myself for leaving it in my room when we escaped. I could have told him to get my camera too, then we'd have the pictures of the ICBM."

"You reckon he went back to the ice station, then?"

"Maybe. Either that or he bribed whoever was sent out to destroy it."

"Destroy it?" Patrick nearly choked on his beer, sputtering foam across the table. "Wait, hang on a minute—who destroyed it? Why?"

"Because there were biological weapons, you numpty!" Sam rolled his eyes. "No idea who, though. I heard it from Fatima. She was trying to sort out permission to go back and do a proper expedition, but she was told it's gone now. Wolfenstein is no more. So she's back at Neumayer doing things with algae. Very clever, that one. You'd like her. Doubt she'd like you, though."

"I don't know," Patrick pulled a face. "Nina likes me well enough."

"Nina's got no taste." Sam drained his pint and set the glass carefully on the beer mat. "Speaking of Nina, I have an appointment at the university. Some very important questions to be asking."

"Are you going to ask her out?"

Sam stood up and adopted an attitude of haughty disdain, looking down his nose at his friend. "You, Patrick Smith, are an old fishwife. No, I am not going to ask anyone out." He dropped back into his customary slouch and pulled on his jacket. "I wish it was anything that interesting. No, I'm off to interview Dr. Frank Matlock about his forthcoming and extremely hastily written book. Here's the title, get this— Wolfenstein: Secrets of the Lost Nazi Ice Station. He's obviously going for a very subtle, literary kind of slant."

"I'd read it," Patrick said.

"You would not. He's already talking to the BBC about turning it into a series, so you'd just watch it on TV. He's an old bastard, though, not letting Nina have any of the credit. But it's his retirement plan, so she's down to a wee quick mention in an early chapter. He didn't even want to credit me, but I said he wasn't getting to use my pictures if he didn't. Not that he got any of the really good ones. The only memory card that survived the journey home was the one with all the boring stuff on it. Dormitories and the like. Still . . ." He raised his voice just loud enough to be audible to the others in the pub. "Academics, eh? Bunch of egomaniacs, the lot of them!"

Patrick shushed Sam frantically, then finished his drink and bundled Sam out of the pub and into the street.

"I'll be around to collect Bruich tomorrow!" Sam called as he and Patrick went their separate ways.

You know what, Sam thought as he strolled along to the Braxfield Tower, maybe I will ask Nina out after all. Everyone seems to think there's something going on anyway, and we get on, so . . . it's probably time I give it a try. He did not admit it to himself, but the thought of seeing Nina put a spring in his step.

He arrived at the Braxfield Tower and walked past the little sheltered area where he and Nina had shared their first cigarette. Cutting through the lobby, he got in the lift and emerged on the fifth floor, where Matlock now had his office. Matlock was yet to arrive, so Sam took a seat in the office and settled in to wait.

When he heard the door open and close behind him he turned around expecting to see Matlock. Instead, it was Nina. She was back to her glossy, stylish self in a smart black trouser suit, an acid green scarf at her neck and elegant high heels on her feet. Sam looked her over for just a moment too long. He had almost forgotten that she could look like that. She rushed toward him and gave him a hug. Sam tried very hard not to remember the last time her soft, warm body had been pressed against his.

"How did you know I started back today?" Nina asked. "Ugh, it's been strange being back—not to mention frustrating! Everyone keeps asking me about Matlock's new fucking book. Did I help him write it, or did I even go in the first place? God, it's exhausting having to keep giving out polite answers! Look, I've got a class to teach in about ten minutes, but do you want to go and get some dinner after that? "

Sam opened his mouth, then shut it again. Then opened it. Then shut it. How did she know? he wondered. That thought was swiftly joined by another. She thinks I'm here to see her. And I'm not. At least not entirely. Not even primarily. Oh, god . . .

"Dinner would be great!" Sam decided to concentrate on the positive stuff first. "I can hang around here until you're done with teaching. There's a really nice wee Mexican place around on the Canongate, if our time in Argentina hasn't put you off that whole continent's food for life."

"Sounds great!" Sam could have sworn he heard Nina giggle. "I'd better go. You can wait in here if you like, but I should warn you—this is actually Matlock's office. I know the receptionist just directs people in here if they ask about German history, just so you know. In case you don't fancy rehashing old times. Or having to wax lyrical about his fucking book."

In a fist of excruciating honesty, Sam thought it best just to come clean. "That's . . . actually what I'm here about. Oh, don't get me wrong, I wanted to see you too! But my editor sent me here, because they want an editorial feature on his book ahead of its publication . . . Nina, don't. Don't look at me like that!"

Her hands had balled into tight fists, her fingernails digging into the palms. "Like what?" she asked with acid sweetness. "Like you're a money-grubbing bastard who would sell me out for the sake of a story? Like you're a fucking traitor who would work with someone who stole all my best material and even the idea in the first place and would fuck me over and not care? Oh, well guess what, Sam Cleave, I'm looking at you that way because that's exactly what you are! No, don't touch me. Don't talk to me. We should have left you behind in Antarctica. I said don't talk to me!" She stormed over to the door and flung it wide, then stepped through it and fired her parting shot back over her shoulder. "And you can forget about dinner tonight—or any night!" The door slammed. She was gone.

Ah well, Sam thought with a deep sigh. That's the end of that. He sat down in the chair opposite the desk, then swiftly began to wonder where Matlock's secret stash of alcohol would be. Every academic had one, he was certain. Matlock's, it emerged, was relatively easy to find—a bottle of Highland Park in the top right drawer. Sam poured himself a tumbler of whisky. Matlock won't mind, he told himself. And if he does, well . . . that's the price of publicity.

Sam settled into Professor Matlock's leather armchair,

sipped the whisky and looked idly out of the window at the rugged beauty of Salisbury Crags. He raised the glass in a silent toast, as he usually did when drinking alone—but for the first time in a long time, his toast was not to Trish and the hope that he would soon be with her. It was to life, to the prospect of adventures yet to be had, and to Samuel Fergusson Cleave being very much alive.

~ THE END ~

Sam and Nina return in

OPERATION FIRESTORM
ORDER OF THE BLACK SUN - BOOK 2

Made in the USA
Middletown, DE
05 October 2014